Loneliness is a Monster

J. Boote

Copyright © 2024 by J. Boote
All rights reserved.

No part of this book may be reproduced in any form or by any electronic or mechanical means, including information storage and retrieval systems, without written permission from the author, except for the use of brief quotations in a book review.

This is a work of fiction based on a real-life incident. Names and locations have been changed.

Formatted by Red Cape Publishing.
Cover by Grim Poppy Designs.
Edited by Ali Sweet.

Chapter 1

She could do nothing but stare, powerless to stop what was happening to her. She had never seen an exposed bone before, and it was something both alien and horrific. Even more so to see the maggots squirming inside the now gaping hole, slowly eating away the rotting, stinking flesh of her thigh. There were many ways to die, but she had never considered that she might be eaten alive by maggots—and to watch them do so. And as the hole grew larger, so did the swarm of flies, greedily accepting this unexpected gift like a group of followers accepting a new reward from their cult leader for their allegiance.

They weren't the only ones to feast on such delicacies, either. Her captor, curious, sat beside her picking off bits of drying flesh and nibbling at them like a chef sampling a new dish.

Chapter 2

Jeremy Chan stood at the table, ravenous. He hadn't eaten much at lunch time because one of the bigger kids had stolen his lunch. Again. The waft of freshly cooked steak and vegetables drifted towards him as though tormenting him as well—even the food, it seemed, was in league with all his enemies. His younger sister, Kelly, was also glaring at the food spread out across the table unable to take her eyes off it. He guessed the same thoughts were going through her mind, too. But whether she was starving or not, he couldn't care less. Stupid little girl, with her wailing and whining every five minutes.

His mother, Katherine, was humming as she, too, waited to sit, a fake smile on her face as though it was perfectly normal to stand starving in front of a mountain of food yet unable to touch it. Jeremy thought it was sadistic, like a starving prisoner being tortured for information. But he would never again make the mistake of saying or doing anything. Once, he had been so hungry, he had dared to grab a potato from the steaming bowl while waiting, and the consequences had seen him starve like never before. No supper that night and for the rest of the week, his food had been rationed and him forced to sit at the table while the rest of the family tucked in. He cried himself to sleep every night that week while also dreaming of punching his stupid sister, who had been secretly casting him sly looks with a mouth full of food knowing full well how desperate he was. He vowed she'd pay for that one day.

Finally, when Jeremy thought he might start drooling if he had to wait any longer, the sound of footsteps on the stairs brought a sigh of relief from him and Kelly.

Even Katherine visibly relaxed. Jeremy's father, Reginald, was coming down.

"Mmm, smells good," he said in his booming voice as he sat down. Immediately, the other three family members did the same. Reginald's voice sounded like Jeremy's stomach right now—a rumble like thunder.

"Thank you, dear," said Katherine.

Then the next process in the ritual had to be carried out. All four closed their eyes while Katherine prayed and thanked God for His blessings, and for good health.

"Amen," they all said in unison.

As soon as Reginald was served, Katherine served the kids, then herself. Jeremy was so hungry, he would have grabbed his steak and vegetables with his hands and greedily scoffed it all down, but this would have been very foolish on his behalf. Scoffing his food was not tolerated. Lots of things were not tolerated. Should anyone dare incur the wrath of Reginald, the consequences would be dire. He was the man of the house, and the rules were made by him. Not even his wife would question him.

As they ate, usual conversation was made; how did the kids do at school; what did Katherine do during the day, but more importantly how was Reginald's day at the office. Jeremy wasn't entirely sure what his father's job entailed—something to do with numbers—but everything in this household revolved around him. He was both terrified of him yet in awe at the same time. Reginald was like God at home, and many times he had sat Jeremy down for a father to son chat. Reginald Chan had been brought up by strict, religious parents that had emigrated to England from China before he was born and brought their culture with them. A culture where women were there to serve while the man of the house put bread on the table. It was the way of the world. How it had always been, and someday it would be Jeremy's turn to follow in his father's footsteps. Jeremy relished the moment when it would finally come. Right now, he was just thirteen years old and prayed he didn't have to wait forever.

He only wished he could exercise such self-control at school.

Part not wanting to disappoint his father, and part because he early on discovered it came easy to him, Jeremy excelled when it came to classwork. Straight As in every subject which meant that at least the teachers weren't on his back. Unfortunately, being the class nerd gave the bullies more ammunition. As if they needed it.

The next day, he was in class, sat far at the back so as to go unnoticed, when his math's teacher asked a particularly complicated question. Only Jeremy raised his hand. Snickering came from Pete and Tommy, the biggest bullies in school. Feeling his face flush, he answered the question and then quickly buried his head in his book when congratulated by his teacher—who subsequently reprimanded the two boys for taunting him. Jeremy groaned inwardly. He knew what was coming.

And he was right.

When the bell rang for morning break, Jeremy rushed outside and tried to find somewhere to hide. He had few friends in Bradwell High School because the majority feared that if they became part of his inner circle, they would become victims themselves to the pranks and jokes. Anyone who was friends with Jeremy Chan was obviously a freak, too, they surmised. Skinny to the point of emaciation, with a mop of black hair—that might have been fashionable a hundred years ago—coupled with a similar sense of style; Jeremy was an easy target.

He found a suitable spot around the back of the school

Loneliness is a Monster

and sat down with his book, and sandwich, trying to eat it as quickly as possible before the bullies found him.

"Well look who it is. Mr Fucking Know-It-All. Whatcha reading, clever boy?"

Pete and Tommy had found him. He groaned and took the biggest bite out of his sandwich as he could, so big it almost lodged in his throat.

"What's up, Dickface? Cat got yer tongue? Too fuckin' clever to speak with us?"

Before he could come up with a suitable response, what was left of the sandwich was kicked out of his hand, almost breaking his fingers at the same time. The two bullies chuckled.

"Leave me alone," he finally managed.

"Leave me alone," replied Tommy in a taunting voice. "You made us look stupid in maths earlier, right, Pete?"

"Yeah. Did it on fuckin' purpose, I reckon. Tryin' to be all smart. Thinks he knows everythin'. Prick."

"No, I wasn't. I just answered the question, that's all. Wasn't my fault."

"Bullshit. Teacher's fuckin' pet. You fuckin' her yet?"

Jeremy stood up and tried to make his way to the corner so he could run, if necessary. The other two were bigger but fatter than he was, and he was faster. It was his only option, but before he could make a mad sprint back to the doors, an explosion of agony erupted in his stomach, causing him to crumple to the ground. Barely able to breathe, he gasped, clutching his stomach where he'd been punched.

"Fuckin' goin' somewhere, was yer?" taunted Pete. "You know what happens to fuckers like you that make us look stupid in class? Huh? Want us to show yer?"

"Please, just leave me alone," he wheezed.

But they did no such thing. Tommy snatched what was left of Jeremy's sandwich from the ground and looked around then he smiled and headed off a short distance before squatting, his back to Jeremy. When he returned, all Jeremy's thoughts of his stomach being on fire evaporated. Replaced by a desperate need to get the hell out of there.

"Guess what, Pete? He looks like he's starvin'. And what do little shits eat? More shit."

Before Jeremy could get up, Tommy was kneeling on his chest. With one hand, he punched Jeremy in the mouth causing him to yell, but by opening his mouth he inadvertently allowed Tommy to do what he had been planning all along. What was left of the sandwich was covered in a slimy, brown substance. The potent stench it gave off told him exactly what it was. Dog shit. As if a dog had walked past just seconds before, with a nasty case of diarrhoea after eating some rotting, dead thing. Small lumps from a now soggy sandwich dropped onto his face as the sandwich was rammed into his mouth.

"Eat it!" demanded Tommy as Pete roared with laughter.

Warm vomit rose to Jeremy's throat, blending with the suffocating, pungent taste of fresh dog shit. He spluttered, trying to shake his head free from the hand that was clamped over his mouth but was utterly incapable. He felt the sandwich disintegrating in his mouth, pieces dribbling down the back of his throat. He was going to die from suffocation unless he did something quick, his lungs already burned with the need to inhale oxygen. But Tommy was never going to let him free before he complied with his demands. So, sobbing, Jeremy swallowed the slimy mess in his mouth, lumps he couldn't swallow sticking to the back of his throat. As soon as he did so, Tommy and Pete yelled in delight, then burst into hysterical laughter. The second Tommy removed his hand, everything that had collected in Jeremy's throat and stomach shot out, covering his face and shirt in a mixture of wet dog shit, vomit, and bread.

"See, told yer!" exclaimed Tommy. "Shit's gotta eat shit. That taste good, Shitty?"

His throat burned, the combined fumes of shit and vomit shoot up his nostrils, Jeremy threw up again, this time while sitting up. He cried harder while wiping the gooey mess off his face, the sheer humiliation of what he'd been forced to do too much for him. If his dad saw this, he would be ashamed his son hadn't stood up for himself, tried to at least fight back. As the two bullies wandered back to class, still chuckling,

Jeremy vowed that one day, he would get his revenge on them. But for now, the humiliation and stench of the shit he'd been forced to eat—and from having soiled his own pants—would follow him until he got home later that day.

Chapter 3

It was bath night. Since Jeremy had been born, his mother would take a bath several times a week in the evenings and Jeremy was expected to share the water with her. The opposing nights would be Kelly's turn. Katherine said it was to save money as water was so expensive which made him wonder why she didn't just take a quick shower instead, but it had become such a routine he never questioned it anymore. Routine was important, his father would often say, and that tradition was vital to any household. They went to church every Sunday in the same attire they kept for such occasions, bedtime was the same every night, no exceptions except at weekends when they could stay up an hour later. Discipline was key, his father also said. Maintain a healthy routine, keep to the family traditions and life will be so much easier. Change was unwelcome. Change was dangerous; a temptation to be avoided.

"If you stray from the path God set out for you, only evil and temptation will come your way," was his favourite saying. "Look at women now, all wanting to have careers and be treated equal. No good will ever come from it, son. You mark my word. A place for everyone and everyone in their place."

Reginald's parents had lived by strict rules and, according to him, so should they. The number one rule above all others was that the decisions made by the man of the house were never questioned. His mother seemed to accept her role as subservient housewife, and, as far as Jeremy could tell, she was happy. He wished she would treat him like the teenager he was fast becoming, though. Having to share a bath with her at this age, made him feel awkward.

Loneliness is a Monster

"You are growing into a big lad, Jeremy," she said as he got undressed. "You still need fattening up though. Maybe I should take you to the doctors. It's not natural, all skin and bones. Your father is getting worried too. Are you eating your lunch properly at school?"

"Yes."

"The other boys don't bully you, do they? You'd tell me if they did, wouldn't you?"

"Yes, Mum," he said as he climbed in.

"The teachers don't pick on you, do they?"

"No, Mum."

Another routine, his mother constantly bombarding him with questions about how things were at school. Yet how could he tell her the truth? That almost every day the bullies stole his lunch, that the girls laughed and made fun of him? He imagined his father storming into class and causing a huge ruckus which would do nothing more than embarrass him immensely and give the kids even more ammunition to use against him. Even so, he was twelve, nearly thirteen, yet she treated him as though he was still eight, Kelly's age.

He watched as she poured soapy water over her chest, feeling as though he shouldn't really be watching. She massaged soap onto his chest, as she continued to pry into his life at school.

"Have any of the other boys and girls started talking about…adult things yet? Like what boyfriends and girlfriends do? Has anyone tried to make you do something you don't want to?"

Yes, the other day I ate a sandwich covered in dog shit. How do you feel about that?

"No, Mum. I don't have many friends anyway. They think I'm weird because of how I dress."

"Well, you don't listen to them. They're jealous, that's why. You think your father listens to or cares what others say?"

"No."

"Exactly. You just ignore them. Now lean over, let's wash that gorgeous hair of yours."

He did so, looking down into the water, seeing her thick bush of pubic hair. He suddenly had the urge to part it to see what was hidden behind it, but the thought shocked and embarrassed him. He closed his eyes tightly as warm water ran down his face. Never once had he been the slightest bit interested in what women's parts looked like before and couldn't understand why he was now. If his father knew what he'd just been thinking…

He shuddered.

"You okay? The water too hot? Cold?"

"It's fine," he mumbled.

He'd lied to his mother about what the other kids talked about in school. For many of them, it was pretty much the only thing they talked about. Using words and phrases he didn't understand. A girl he didn't like, Sammy, asked him if he'd started jerking off yet, then burst out laughing at the look of confusion on his face. He wasn't allowed access to the internet at home and didn't have a mobile phone like most of the others, but he had wanted to find out what it meant. After hearing that phrase so many times, he finally built up the courage to ask a teacher. For a few seconds she stared at him, seeming to struggle not to burst out laughing which made him feel horrified he'd said something terrible. He was about to mumble an excuse and make a hasty disappearance when she told him it was something he should ask his mother about. But he didn't, and it was overhearing another conversation between kids later, that he finally understood. Jeremy avoided looking into his teacher's eyes for the rest of the week.

His hair washed and his mother's too, she stood to get

Loneliness is a Monster

out. Again, he couldn't resist the urge to take a quick peek at what was between her legs, feeling as though he was carrying a dirty secret. He blushed and looked away quickly. When she had covered herself in a towel, he pulled out the plug and stood up himself.

"You dry yourself off quickly, young man, or you'll catch yourself a cold and we can't have that, can we?" she tutted as she examined his body—barely any muscle tissue on him. "We're going to have to start giving you some vitamins or something, Jeremy. Fatten you up. Make you into a big, strong man like your father."

Jeremy was about to reply when there came a long scream from downstairs. They both jumped, startled, terror in his mother's wide eyes. They ran downstairs wrapped in towels to find Kelly screaming and sobbing, yelling their father's name again and again. On the living room floor, sprawled on his back was their father, clutching his chest, grimacing and struggling to breathe.

"Oh my God! Oh my God!" exclaimed Katherine. "What is it? What happened?"

"Call an ambulance," he wheezed. "My heart."

When Reginald Chan walked into a room, people got out of his way or politely stepped aside. Anyone who wasn't an acquaintance of his would go silent, perhaps glance into his eyes then hastily look away, as if by doing so he might not notice their presence and guaranteeing their safety. At six feet, with a firm, muscular body, he might have been a nightclub bouncer in another life or a security guard. He was big and burly, with a perfect military-style haircut, a strong, square jaw, and dark eyes. His only concession was the big, thick beard that covered his face like an abandoned bird's nest. He liked to stroke it when pondering some minor nuisance. When Reginald Chan walked into a room it was as if God himself had just entered, and no one dared say anything for fear of incurring His legendary anger.

But the frail-looking man lying in the hospital bed was nothing like the man Jeremy revered and feared. His skin was deathly white, and he wheezed instead of breathed. His eyes were sinking into their craters as if trying to hide from the onslaught to come. Jeremy's father was dying, and he knew it.

"Sit down, boy. Close," he muttered.

It was just the two of them now, Jeremy's tearful mother and sister were told to wait outside. Terrified of what he might be about to hear and for the future, he grabbed a chair and sat beside his father, wanting to touch him for one last time yet almost repulsed to do so. As though some ghoul lay in the bed instead of his father.

"You listen to me good, boy, and heed what I say. I've always tried to be a good father to you. Stern but fair. One day you'll come to understand and, I hope, appreciate it. But my time has come. God has called to me and very soon I will have to go."

Tears began to well in Jeremy's eyes. He wanted everything that had happened in the last few hours to have been a horrible nightmare, but this was confirmation of the complete opposite.

"Don't cry. Crying is for the weak. Like your mother. God knows I've tried to stop her pampering you and your sister, but she's a woman, a mother, and I guess it's built into her system. But she's a good woman, Jeremy. You would do well to find someone like her one day.

"Now listen, soon, very soon, you will be the man of the house. It will be your responsibility to ensure our standards are maintained. Your mother and sister will expect a lot from you. Don't let them down. Don't let me down. Now, call your mother and sister back. We'll spend my last remaining time together."

The surge of adrenaline that rushed up Jeremy's body like a rocket had been lit inside his chest. Despite the horror of knowing he was about to lose his father, the knowledge of what had just been passed onto him was like a gift from God. And the one thing he knew, right there and then, was that he would fulfil his dying father's wish.

Chapter 4

The funeral followed a few days later. Despite his strict ways with his children, Kelly, cried throughout, unable to comprehend how her father had gone so suddenly and early. She had always been scared of him, like her brother, but she understood that she never lacked for anything, had never gone hungry unless being punished, and at Christmas and her birthday, all the gifts she asked for had been delivered. She knew of many girls at school who weren't so lucky.

Katherine wept too, more discreetly than Kelly, as though afraid to annoy her husband, even though he was buried deep beneath the ground. As if his spirit would get angry at a show of weakness and come back to haunt her. Lots of people Jeremy didn't recognise also turned up, stern-faced and sad, plus relatives, many of whom he hadn't seen in years. They cried too, hugging Katherine and the two children, all repeating the same cliché phrases throughout the day.

But Jeremy didn't cry.

At times he wanted to, especially when the coffin was lowered, and friends and family spoke about how much of a respected and honest man his father had been during his short life. He wanted to cry for the respect his father had commanded over all that knew him, the way he had evidently portrayed himself and his family judging from the words being said. It was as if Superman himself had died and everyone was in utter shock, a superhero who could never to be replaced. He wanted to cry for how he didn't live up to his father's expectations. How he surrendered his lunch to the bullies every day, how he was forced to eat dog shit while they laughed and mocked him. Jeremy felt he had let his father down, that

Loneliness is a Monster

his father had gone to heaven disappointed in him. And now it was too late to make it up to him.

Or was it?

He'd replayed his father's words in his head over and over since that fateful evening, as though trying to memorise the answers to an important exam. He recalled all the times both he and his sister had been caught doing things they shouldn't, and the subsequent punishments that accompanied such acts of misbehaviour. Yet afterwards, once the punishment was over, Reginald sat them both down and explained why discipline was so important in life, that one's sins must be atoned for. He'd told them about his time in the army, how discipline and respect were above everything else, about tradition and following the footsteps of one's peers. God was watching and missed nothing. It was embedded into their heads like a mantra, and now those words would be heard no more.

If Jeremy was to make up for his miserable failings in life, it was time to start. He would show everyone he was just as capable as his father in keeping the family tradition together. And that meant not showing weakness at his father's funeral.

Now, he was the head of the family.

And he wasted no time.

The next day, the house finally quiet and settled again, all relatives having gone back home, Jeremy sat up in bed, feeling refreshed. It was the beginning of a new life, a new start. Part of him wished it was a school day so he could let the stupid girls and the bullies know who he had become. A new man. An adult. He was now the head of his household and must be treated with the utmost respect. But that would have to wait.

He could hear noise downstairs. Probably his mother preparing breakfast. In the room next door, he could hear his sister, the occasional thud or sliding of a chair. Jeremy smiled and banged on the wall.

"Kelly, come here!" he yelled.

There was no reply. He banged again, louder. "Kelly! Come here now, I said!"

"Whadaya want? Leave me alone!"

"Get your stupid arse in here, now! If I have to get up and come after you, you're gonna regret it."

There was a loud sigh, more thuds, as she threw her door open and then Jeremy's. Kelly stood there in her pyjamas, hands on her hips.

"What?!"

"For starters, don't you ever talk to me like that again. You didn't speak to Dad like that, you don't speak to me like it, either."

"What? What are you talking about? Who do you think you are suddenly?"

"I'm the man of the house now, so you better get used to it and do as I say! For starters, I want a warm glass of milk and two slices of toast. And hurry up about it."

Kelly stared at him for a short time, perhaps expecting him to burst out laughing, trying to lighten the darkened mood currently residing in the household, but instead Jeremy barked at her again.

"The hell are you waiting for? If I have to get up and make you do it, you're gonna be in trouble. Go!"

"I'm telling Mum!" she bawled and ran downstairs.

Let her. Mum won't say anything. Dad had told her the same thing, too—Jeremy had been listening while they had a private chat just before it had been Jeremy's turn. Sure enough, a short while later, a sulky-looking Kelly entered the bedroom and practically threw the milk and toast onto his bedside table. He grunted, took a sip of milk then spat it out.

"What's this crap? It's too cold! You get back

Loneliness is a Monster

downstairs and warm it up. You've got two minutes."

Now sobbing and looking both shocked and horrified at this sudden change in his attitude, she grabbed the glass and hurried away. Jeremy smiled and took a bite of toast. This was going to be fun, and Kelly was going to have to learn a lesson about making sure she got things right when he demanded them. His dad would say that was slacking, getting things wrong the first time around was the work of a lazy individual. One who didn't care about standards. Well, he'd take care of that later.

Kelly returned shortly and without even looking him in the eyes, put the glass of milk on the table. He, in turn, never took his eyes off her as he tried it. Perfect, just how he liked it.

"That's better. When I'm ready to get up, I'll call you to bring my clothes. Now get out, but don't go far."

He thought of spending the day in bed, or at least the morning, perhaps watching movies. It wasn't as if he had a ton of friends to spend the weekend with, but his father wouldn't approve. Staying in bed all day was lazy, too, and he felt that as the new man of the house, he should assert a little authority. He finished breakfast and called his sister again. When after a few moments she didn't come, despite being in her bedroom, he bawled her name out, now furious. This was not how things were meant to be.

She came this time and stood at the door, her eyes bloodshot from crying.

"When I call you, you come immediately. I don't want to have to call you twice. You got it, you useless idiot?"

She nodded.

"What?"

"Yes," she mumbled.

"Good. Come here."

She hesitated, but did so, standing beside his bed. Jeremy sat up and slapped her across the face. "That's for bringing me a cold glass of milk."

She burst out crying and made to run off, but Jeremy quickly grabbed her tightly by the arm, jumped out of bed and dragged her to the toilet.

"You need to learn how things are gonna be around here. And quick. You're lazy and useless. Dad would be disgusted."

"But Dad's dead! Why are you being like this? You're hurting me! Mum!" she yelled.

Jeremy pulled down hard on one of her pigtails. She screamed and wriggled, trying to break free, inadvertently elbowing him in the ribs. He grunted. This accidental act infuriated him, that she would have the audacity to try and resist at all. Gripping her tightly around the neck, he lifted the toilet seat and thrust her head into the dirty yellow water that someone had forgotten to flush—probably himself.

"Drink it," he ordered. "Drink it all."

Bubbles rose from the water as she tried to breathe. He raised her head, let her get her breath back then dumped it back in. "Drink it and I'll let you go. That or you're going to drown."

Now panicking, Kelly did as she was told, the water visibly lowering in the bowl. He smiled. Then it occurred to him that he needed to urinate anyway. With his free hand, he lowered his pyjama bottoms and urinated on the back of his sister's head, filling the bowl once again as it ran down her hair and cheeks. Once he finished, he dragged Kelly's head out and she slumped on the floor, gasping for breath and stinking of fresh, acidic urine.

"Next time you disrespect me, I'll shit on your head."

He left her gasping and sobbing and headed downstairs to see what his mother was doing.

Chapter 5

It was Monday, Jeremy's first day at school after coming into his new role. He relished it. A new beginning. The teachers would look at him with utter respect, no longer smirking as they whispered about his lack of dress sense. He knew he was still powerless to physically beat off his bullies, but once he explained the situation, that he was head of the household, they too would look at him in a new light. They would be in awe of him, perhaps like those who looked up to authority with caution and inferiority.

As always, his mother had ironed his shirt for him, and laid his clothes neatly on the chair beside his writing desk. He'd given her orders on what he wanted for breakfast. Three slices of crispy bacon, two fried eggs—not too runny, not too overly done—and two pieces of toast. If she got any of it wrong, he would make her throw it away and do it again. She never said a word.

Jeremy dressed and headed downstairs to find his sister already eating her breakfast. He was shocked.

"What are you doing?" he asked her as he walked into the kitchen.

Suddenly pallid, Kelly looked up, still chewing a piece of toast. "Having breakfast," she said, a piece of toast flying from her mouth and landing on the table.

He could feel his cheeks warming, adrenaline burning his veins as it shot through his body. Jeremy glared at his mother, surely she should have known better, but the fear in her eyes suggested she had forgotten or didn't think the same rules applied with him.

"You eat when I say to eat. And not before I sit or are you fucking blind as well as deaf?"

His mother gasped, a hand rushing to her mouth.

Kelly's bottom lip quivered as she looked to Katherine for help. But she wasn't getting any. Slowly, Kelly rose and swallowed the toast in her mouth. Jeremy was tempted to punish both of them harshly for their incompetence, but he didn't want to be late for school. He sat down, while his mother brought over his breakfast. Just as Kelly was about to sit back down and continue her breakfast, he raised a hand.

"Uh-huh. You can go without for misbehaving. Go get ready for school."

Kelly stifled a sob and ran off.

"Is it okay, son? Just as you like it?" asked Katherine timidly.

He simply grunted and bit into his bacon. Only a couple of days had gone by, and both his mother and sister were already in fear of him, just as they had been of his father. He smiled.

"You know," she said slowly and carefully, "you shouldn't be so harsh on your sister. She's only little. Your father was stern but loved you both a lot. He wouldn't…he wouldn't want either of you to get hurt."

So, Kelly had told her what he had done in the toilet, then. He was going to have to set things straight with her at some point. Young or not.

"Don't tell me what to do. If she did as she was told the first time, I wouldn't have to punish her, would I? Dad taught us that one and he's not here anymore, is he, so it's up to me."

"Of course, just…"

But she stopped and went to clean the dishes. Jeremy thought he caught a sob coming from her but ignored it. He finished breakfast and headed upstairs to brush his teeth. Kelly rushed past him, and he soon heard the front door slam shut. He shook his head. She wasn't learning, was she?

Loneliness is a Monster

His grabbed his schoolbag, prepared for him by his mother, said goodbye and headed off to school, a bounce in his step for the first time ever. The first person he saw when he arrived was Sarah Forbes, one of the girls that mocked him the most. She was with a friend and nudged her when they saw him approach. Both giggled.

"Hi, Jeremy," they both said in unison, struggling to contain a smirk etching its way across their faces. "You're looking very smart again today. Is that your granddad's shirt? Was he buried in it?"

They both burst out laughing, almost hysterically. The shirt had belonged to his father. The first thing Jeremy did after the funeral was choose his favourite items and claim them for himself. He had also taken his father's braces for his trousers and his favourite tie. The blood rushed to his cheeks again. He stormed straight up to them, his face inches from theirs.

"Don't you dare talk to me like that again. I'm the man of the house at home now and I demand you show me some respect."

The girls stopped laughing and stared at him, looking dumbfounded.

"You're what?" said Sarah.

"You heard what I said. From now on you show me more respect. I'm far more important now than you'll ever be."

Their jaws dropped. They glanced at one another, then simultaneously burst out laughing again. Jeremy frowned. This was not how it was meant to go. His hands curled into fists, and he had to use all his willpower not to slap them.

"Well look at Mr High and Mighty Grandpa Chan! Gonna bend us over and smack our bums, are ya?"

Jeremy's cheeks were on fire, his tongue welded tight to the roof of his mouth. He had nothing to come back at them with and it was killing him. He glared at them and stormed off.

He could barely focus at first as he sat down to start his history lesson. Other kids in his class glanced his way, snickering, Sarah and her friend among them. Whispering to each other then stifling giggles, as the teacher walked in. Something hit him on the back of the head. He looked down to see a tiny ball of wet paper, shot from a hollowed-out Bic pen. Jeremy pretended to ignore them, but in his mind he was punishing them all. Thinking up ways he could torture his classmates, how he could make them sorry for humiliating him. When the bell went later for break, he rushed outside to find somewhere to hide and consider his next move.

They were girls. Stupid like his sister. They obviously didn't understand the consequences of their behaviour. Stupid, ignorant, little, baby idiots who probably still played with dolls. He imagined taking their dolls, pulling the heads off and ramming them down their throats until they choked to death. Let's see you laugh then. But he'd show them. They'd come to learn who and what he now was.

He opened his lunchbox and brought out his sandwich when he noticed that Tommie and Pete had spotted him and were heading his way. He stiffened and got to his feet, prepared to make it clear that the bullying was now going to stop.

"Well look who it is! Hey, Shithead, whatcha eatin'? Shit sandwich?" They both sniggered.

"You can't talk to me like that anymore or bully me. Now that my dad is dead, I'm the man of the house and you have to show me respect. He told me so."

Tommy and Pete bore the same look of disbelief the girls had. No one had ever spoken to them like he just did, telling them what to do. It was a few seconds before

Tommy spoke. "What did you just say, Shithead? Are you tryin' to be funny or somethin'?"

"No. In my house, I rule now and so you're not allowed to bully me anymore. And you're not to call me Shithead either. My name is Jeremy and that's how you must address me."

"That right? And if I don't, whatcha gonna do about it?"

Jeremy desperately tried to think what his father would say. But, of course, no one would ever have dared to question his father's words or threaten him. Why were things not working out the same for him?

Tommy gripped one of his braces, pulled it back and let go. It slapped onto Jeremy's chest, making him cry out in pain.

"You leave me alone! Don't you know who I am!"

Suddenly, without warning, the grin vanished from Tommy's face and before he could raise an arm to protect himself, Tommy's fist connected with his jaw and he found himself on the ground, head spinning.

"The fuck do you think you are, Shithead? Fuckin' talkin' to me like that. Think you're clever just 'cause ya fuckin' dad died and now you're the boss? Well, fuck you."

He kicked Jeremy in the stomach, the wind taken from him and he doubled over. Jeremy tried his utmost to resist crying in front of them, not wanting to give them the pleasure of seeing him act like a baby, like a girl. He imagined his father watching from above, shaking his head, incapable of understanding how he managed to create such a cowardly wimp. But he knew that for now there was no way he would win a physical fight against Tommy or Pete. They were just too big and strong for him. He told himself that he was going to change this too. Make himself stronger, go to the gym every day after school. Things had gone terribly wrong and no one at all seemed to appreciate or even care about his relevance in the world now. They were going to pay. Every single one of them.

"See, not so tough are ya, you prick. You're a fuckin' freak, Chan, and I'm sick of seein' ya around here."

Tommy squatted beside him and hawked back a huge amount of phlegm in his throat. He forced Jeremy's mouth open then spat down his throat, a massive greenish blob, then forced his mouth shut again. Jeremy had no choice but to swallow it. It was like swallowing vomit that seemed to slide down his throat slowly, getting stuck on the way, like when he had a cold or the flu and suffered a seemingly permanent bout of snot congested in his nostrils.

Chuckling to themselves, Tommy and Pete left him sobbing on the ground. They took his schoolbag with them, which they dumped over a high wall beside the school field. Jeremy lay there for some time, even after the bell rang to resume class. All he wanted to do right then was die. That or magically grow the biggest biceps the world had ever seen, and punch Tommy's head clean off.

He was still infuriated, humiliated, and feeling ashamed of himself when he arrived home from school. Jeremy had been so excited to tell the world who he was now, commanding respect and awe from everyone. He could not have imagined in his worst nightmares that the exact opposite would play out. He was the man of the house now, but he might as well have been beneath even his little sister. As such, when he opened the door and Kelly did not come rushing to attend to him, his fury increased by tenfold.

"Kelly!" he barked. He'd specifically told her that she was to be at the door waiting for him when he arrived

Loneliness is a Monster

home to receive orders. His mother had told him she had to visit her solicitor regarding his father's will, so it was just him and his sister at home. He called again and this time he heard Kelly's bedroom door open, and she poked her head over the banister. She looked terrified seeing him standing there and she slowly came downstairs.

"I didn't hear you come in," she mumbled.

He slapped her across the face. "Then clean your ears out or I'll do it for you. Take my jacket off and hang it up."

She did as she was told. Jeremy grabbed her wrist and dragged her upstairs to his bedroom where he threw her onto the floor. She started howling in terror.

"I'm sorry!" she yelled. "But why are you like this now? Dad never used to hurt me. Why are you hurting me all the time?!"

"Because you obviously don't understand how things are here yet. Just like them other idiots at school. They'll learn too, just as you will. First, you start breakfast without waiting for me, now you make me wait to take my coat off. You need to learn discipline and respect."

All the frustration and anger he had felt at school was oozing from his pores like toxic waste, Kelly's screaming and struggling only fuelling it further. His humiliation was going to be hers. Perhaps tomorrow she'd go to school, tell all her friends and it would subsequently pass on to older kids in Jeremy's classes. Then they would know exactly who they were dealing with.

"Get undressed," he demanded.

"What? No!"

He sighed. Such disobedience. "You say no again, you won't speak for a month. Do it."

She was about to say something, then closed her mouth and stood up and slowly pulled off her jeans and t-shirt. "I hate you, you know. I don't know what has happened, but you're mean and horrible."

"Underwear too."

"No! I won't! I'm gonna tell Mum. She'll phone the police and you'll go to prison forever!"

He slapped her again. "No, you won't, and besides the police won't do anything. As the man of the house, I can do what I like. Now take them off. I'm going to punish you for your constant misbehaviour. Perhaps then you'll learn."

When she still refused to do as he asked, he threw her onto the bed and pulled off her underwear himself. He grimaced when he saw she had peed herself slightly, the stain dark and wet.

"You're disgusting. I bet you still wet the bed." He dragged her to her feet again and spun her around. Jeremy bent her over but first put her underwear on her head, so she had to smell her own urine while being punished. Next, he took off one of the braces holding his trousers up, wrapped one end around his hand, took a step back and whipped Kelly's bare buttocks. She screamed, her legs buckling as she slid down to the floor. Jeremy picked her up again, pushed her onto the bed then delivered another five whips. Vicious red welts appeared, thin lines of blood running down the backs of her legs, more urine running down the front, pooling beneath her. He'd never heard his sister cry and scream as much as she was doing now. Nothing their father had ever done had caused her as much pain as he was causing her now.

And Jeremy loved every second of it.

He whipped her two more times for good measure then put his brace back on. He thought of getting her to make him a sandwich and a warm glass of milk but even though his mother wouldn't dare say anything to his face, she might do so to others, so he had a better idea. Jeremy gripped Kelly's arm and dragged her to her bedroom. He threw open the wardrobe doors and threw her inside as she begged to be let out. For good measure, he tied her wrists to the clothes hangar so she couldn't sit down, forced her soiled underwear into her mouth and tied them in place with one of her shirts.

"If you behave and don't make any noise, I'll let you out in the morning. Think about things while you're in there tonight," he said before closing the doors and pushing her heavy writing desk against them so she couldn't get out. Happier now than he had been earlier, he headed downstairs to make his own snack for once.

Chapter 6

Something strange was happening to Jeremy. A month after his father died, he was still having his regular baths with his mother. Despite his new position in the household, he still allowed shared baths and revelled in being pampered and washed by her, listening to her tell him how he was growing into a big, strong boy. That he was going to be the spitting image of his father, tall and strong.

He'd barely noticed any changes in himself even though he'd started using the school gym more and had taken to going jogging before supper, when it was dark so no one saw him. The last thing he needed was to give more ammunition to any kids who lived nearby. Not until he was strong enough to finally be able to fight back, at least.

There was one change, however, that he had noticed. And at first, he was shocked and disgusted. But only at first.

The water was filled with soap bubbles, thus making it impossible to see beneath, she was massaging his favourite gel across his chest when he started getting a tingling sensation in his groin, not unpleasant but the suddenness of it caused him to feel somewhat embarrassed. As she continued, Jeremy stared at her breasts—for reasons he didn't know and his penis started stiffening beneath the water.

He recoiled, as though his mother had scratched him.

"Oh, baby, are you okay? Did I hurt you?" she asked, taken aback.

But Jeremy was too embarrassed and confused to reply. He quickly put a hand down to stop his erect penis from poking up above the water, like a periscope. He wanted to get out of the tub and away from there, but if he stood up, his secret would be discovered.

"I think I'm done. You can get out first."

"You don't have to do that. Let's get out together so I can dry you off. You might catch a cold otherwise."

"No!" he replied more sharply than he had intended. "You get out. I'll...I'll get out after."

He still had his hand pushing his penis beneath the water, which was having an even more pleasurable effect. He had the urge to play with it, see what would happen. Finally, looking confused, his mother smiled and stood up. Jeremy couldn't help but fixate on the thick bush between her legs and when she stepped out and turned around showing her buttocks, something Jeremy had seen a million times, he had to suppress a gasp. Jeremy had just had his first orgasm.

He'd never felt so embarrassed in his life, despite the wonderful sensation. He prayed his mother didn't turn around and see the globules that were now floating to the surface.

"What would you like for supper, Jeremy?" she asked, as she did indeed turn around showing her naked body again while grabbing her underwear.

"Umm, anything. I don't care," he muttered. The last thing he cared about right now was what was for supper. All he wanted was for her to leave so he could get out and rush to his bedroom, analyse what just happened.

"Okay. Don't you be long now, or your skin will prune. And Jeremy."

"What?"

"Try not to be too hard on your sister. She does her best."

The last thing he cared about was her, too. His mother finished dressing and left. Jeremy exhaled in relief. He looked down at what had shot out from his penis. It reminded him of snot. Even so, he began to squeeze and stroke his penis again. He'd heard other kids joking and giggling about masturbating but having no real idea what they were talking about, he ignored them. Now though, as his penis stiffened again, he knew exactly what they had meant. And when he ejaculated for the second time, it was his mother's naked body he was thinking about.

Over the next few days, it was pretty much the only thing he could think about. His mother came to wake him in the mornings, wearing just her nightie, and after she left the room and he'd masturbate to the image. When he came home from school, he'd sit in the kitchen or living room and study her body while his sister attended to his every demand. Such was his infatuation with her, that sometimes even when Kelly brought him a glass of milk and it wasn't the exact temperature he wanted, he would forget about punishing her.

But when Katherine suggested it was their bath time, he refused, saying he had homework to do, he didn't want to accidentally ejaculate in front of her again. But really, the one thing Jeremy wanted more than anything else was to do just that. Stare at her beautiful body and furiously masturbate. Maybe even with her help.

While lying in bed at night, he started thinking about some of the other girls in his class. Specifically, the ones that had already developed breasts and in many cases were happy to flaunt them. Even though he was masturbating at least once a day, always with the image of his mother in his mind, something, a little voice at the back of his mind, suggested this probably wasn't normal. And Jeremy figured it was probably telling the truth.

She wasn't the slightest bit overweight, but Jeremy had taken note of the scars and wrinkles on her face and body, the way her breasts sagged when she took off her bra. There was also the fact that despite bathing together hundreds of times he'd never actually seen her vagina before in all its glory. Because his father, above all, considered the internet to be sinful and full of disgusting content, neither he nor his sister had computers or mobile phones. They refused to buy him either. His mother, with Reginald dead, still refused. It meant that he'd never seen a vagina before. And this was something he desperately wanted to change.

School had finished for the day but afterwards was netball practice for the school team. And that gave Jeremy an idea.

As the other kids all hurried out and home, Jeremy casually made his way to the changing rooms. Because he had no friends, nobody stopped to ask where he was going, and the teachers completely ignored him, too. Which was fine by him. He was hoping the girls had already changed and gone to the court for practice, and he tentatively opened the door and poked his head in. It was empty. He grinned, the adrenaline rushing through him. He had grown an erection in anticipation of seeing a vagina for the first time—without all the messy pubic hair hiding it. He dashed inside and headed straight to the toilets, locking himself in one of the cubicles that would give full view of the girls changing if he looked beneath the door.

Then he waited, stroking his erection in his trousers. An hour later he heard giggling and laughing growing louder as the girls returned. On his hands and knees, Jeremy watched, mesmerized, as the girls all got undressed. But something went terribly wrong. Instead of getting completely naked and showering as he had expected, they simply removed their kit and got back into their normal clothes again.

Jeremy was furious.

He had used all his will power not to start

masturbating and ejaculate before he got to see their naked bodies, and the failure for things to turn out as he'd expected was crushing. The girls were taunting him, and they weren't even aware of it. The idea that maybe he was condemned to never see a vagina in his life passed through his mind. As he returned home, utterly dejected, he briefly considered telling his mother to shave hers so he could see it.

But then he had another idea.

The next day, his desperation was like a cancer growing and spreading throughout his entire body. With five minutes left to go until morning break, he told his teacher he needed the toilet. Given permission, he rushed to the girls' toilets before any of them could appear. He'd brought a knife with him, hidden in his front pocket, and once inside a cubicle he made the tiniest of holes on each side so he could peer through. Not enough for a girl to hopefully notice, but enough for him to see, just at the height of the toilet seat. He waited.

It didn't take long.

The bell rang and within seconds the bathroom door burst open, and a girl came rushing in. She went to the toilet to his right. Squatting, Jeremy peered through the hole. It was Carla, one of the girls who taunted him the most about his lack of dress sense and old-fashioned hair style. He held his penis in his hand, barely breathing in expectation, as he watched her pull up her skirt and lower her underwear. There it was, barely a hair on it, exposed for him to see.

He ejaculated seconds later.

Carla left and Jeremy knew he was trapped here until the bell went again. Another girl came in but used a cubicle at the opposite end, leaving him disappointed. In the end though it didn't really matter; he achieved what he set out to do.

And he was obsessed.

For the next three days, he spent every morning break hiding in the cubicle with the holes he had cut into the walls, watching the girls as they urinated. On the fourth day he was caught coming out of the girls' toilets by a passing teacher. He told the teacher he had been thinking about something and was distracted, he hadn't realised his mistake. He got away with it but knew he couldn't risk it again.

But it didn't matter—Jeremy had other plans.

Chapter 7

No matter how many times Jeremy fantasised about the girls at school while masturbating, it never quite worked for him. He would imagine them begging to have sex with him or dragging him to the toilets for it, hearing their groans and cries as they begged for more, but he always had to return to thoughts of his mother to keep his erection.

Often, while lying in bed at night, he would think about what it was that made her so special to him. Some of the girls at school wore provocative clothes—short skirts, tight-fitting tops—or were heavy on the makeup. He realised it was because his mother was the complete opposite of all that. They were a conservative family and Katherine never wore makeup. The only piece of jewellery she wore was her wedding ring and she dressed in long skirts, sensible shoes, and tops that gave no hint of anything underneath. Her dark hair was always cropped short and she wore thick-rimmed glasses. He'd heard comments from neighbours when they thought they were out of earshot, giggling about how the whole family looked like they'd been born in the fifties and had gotten stuck there.

It was this conservativeness that turned Jeremy on more than anything. The girls and other women he saw around were sluts as far as he was concerned, asking for trouble, tempting men on purpose. They might as well be whores, he told himself. Not his mother though; she was pure like an angel. But he still wanted to see beneath the hair.

Jeremy lay in bed, trying not to fall asleep, waiting for his mother to head upstairs. To stop himself from drifting off, he'd start stroking his penis, not enough so

Loneliness is a Monster

that he ejaculated, just enough to keep his heart and adrenaline pumping. He finally heard her gently coming up the stairs. Now was the hard part—waiting for her to fall asleep. He knew that since his father had died, she had been taking sleeping pills among other things, so figured he wouldn't have to wait long. And he was right.

After fifteen minutes of standing outside her room, his ear pressed against the door, he heard her soft snoring. Jeremy quietly opened the door and poked his head in. She was lying on her back, in her pyjamas, fast asleep. Perfect. Jeremy crept into the room and slowly climbed in next to her. Instantly, his erection hardened. The warmth emanating from her, the flowery scent of her skin. But that wasn't what he had come for.

He peeled back the blanket, careful not to disturb her, and pulled himself further down the bed until his head was next to the top of her pyjama bottoms. Then with two fingers, as if he was about to pick up something nasty or dangerous, he pulled back her pyjama bottoms and pulled them down. There it was—inches from his face. He could smell it, wanted to kiss it. Among other things. Instead, he used his thumb and forefinger and gently parted her thick pubic hair until he could see the thing he had been obsessed with for so long.

Jeremy was aware he had been holding his breath and released it, then sniffed his mother's vagina. It had a mildly sharp tang to it but he was more focused on studying it. He wanted to see how big and wide the hole was. He fantasised every day about pushing his penis into it. Would it fit or would he need to use saliva or something? Jeremy had no idea if his penis was big or not. He'd heard kids talking about their own, bragging, but he figured they were all exaggerating. He overheard a girl one day saying how her boyfriend's penis had been too big, and they had had to use some kind of lubrication she found in the bathroom. Jeremy imagined carefully rubbing lotion into his mother's vagina then climbing on top of her, easing his penis in slowly so as not to hurt her. He would then...

"Jeremy, what are you doing?"

She spoke so suddenly and without warning he yelped, recoiling so hard he almost fell out of bed.

"Nothing. I, umm, I was cold and wanted to snuggle up a bit." "Jeremy, I think you need to return to your own bed. Put the heat on in there, you know how to do it."

Embarrassed, yet at the same time annoyed that he hadn't been able to carry through with his plan, he jumped up and ran back to his room. It was another twenty minutes before he fell asleep. He masturbated first, the image of his mother's vagina embedded deeply in his mind.

The next day neither of them mentioned the incident, acting as if nothing had happened but Jeremy couldn't get the image out of his mind. He was grumpy, having wanted to masturbate while inspecting and touching her vagina the night before but not having the opportunity to carry out his fantasy. He sat at the breakfast table and told Kelly to bring him a glass of warm milk.

Ever since the punishments he had given, Kelly did everything she could to keep out of his way. As soon as she attended to his needs, before and after school, she hid in her bedroom, refusing to come out unless absolutely necessary. He caught her staring at him on multiple occasions, a look of utter hatred etched onto her face, but he couldn't care less. He punished her regardless, though, making her go without supper or locking her in the wardrobe all night, naked, with the window wide open when it was freezing cold outside. The power and authority gave him an erection at times, and he rushed off to his bedroom to furiously masturbate.

Kelly got up and warmed his milk. She brought it to him, refusing to look him in the eyes. He tasted it and quickly spat it out. It was too hot, scolding his tongue. Kelly gasped, utter terror written on her delicate features.

"You stupid, useless little girl! Look what you did. It's too hot. You burnt me!"

Kelly started apologising then gasped loudly herself, bursting into hysterics when he threw the contents of the glass in her face. Katherine jumped up, saying nothing to Jeremy, but rushing to her daughter's aid. Even more annoyed, Jeremy left them to it and headed off to school, disgusted with his sister. He spent the day in class thinking about the morning's events. The glass of milk had been so hot it must have burnt Kelly's face, but his mother had said absolutely nothing about it. Then he realised why.

His mother was secretly in love with him just as he was with her! The reason she hadn't mentioned a single word about him being in bed with her last night was because she wanted him sexually as much as he did her. He almost slapped himself across the face for being so stupid. For not seeing the signs. This was why she never said anything about the harsh punishments he handed out to Kelly. Such was her love for him, it prevented her from saying anything, and the only reason she hadn't told Jeremy how much she wanted him was because she was embarrassed by it. And surely, as man of the house, it was his duty to make the first move.

Maybe she was worried that Kelly would be jealous or would disapprove and say something about their relationship. He would have to do something about that. Maybe he could lock her in the wardrobe forever so she could never escape and open her big mouth, ruining everything. Yes, that was what he would do. But he had to make his desires known to his mother first, consecrate their love for each other.

"Are you okay, Jeremy? How was your day?" asked his mother when he arrived home from school. "I haven't seen you look so happy in a long time."

"I am happy. Very happy. Aren't you?"

"Of course! Seeing you happy makes me happy. Would you like me to make you a sandwich or something? Your sister isn't too well. I took her to the hospital. Her shoulder was badly blistered. You really should control that temper of yours. She's so young."

"Yes, I'd like a cheese sandwich. The bread cut into triangles then warmed slightly. Kelly needs to learn how to act properly. She will in time."

Not the slightest rebuke for what he did to Kelly, as if it was nothing, which it evidently had been. It was nothing and his mother was smitten with him. She was able to overlook everything, so blinded was she by her love for him. He looked at the gap between her legs. She was wearing a long, grey dress, her usual conservative style, but he was sure it was a little tighter than normal. Maybe she was teasing him. There was a sparkle in her eyes too, a suspicious, mischievous gleam. If it wasn't for Kelly being here, albeit upstairs in her room, Jeremy felt that his mother wanted to throw herself at him there and then, ridding him of his virginity.

And he would let her.

For now though, it had to wait. And it was going to kill him.

The time for him to make his move, finally arrived.

He was too nervous to be in his mother's presence while he waited for his chance, so he stayed in his room, listening to Kelly sob and groan, no doubt for the pain she was in. He smiled; that was nothing compared to what he had planned for her, later, when his and his mother's love was consecrated.

Loneliness is a Monster

He heard his mother head upstairs to bed and then impatiently waited for fifteen more minutes. Jeremy grabbed a couple of things then went to her room. As before, he climbed in next to her, not wanting to wake her so he could explore again first. Everything needed to be right for when they made love together. He climbed under the blanket until his head was level with her waist, then he turned on his torch so he could see what he was doing. Very carefully, he lay the torch down then used his scissors to cut a small hole in her pyjamas exactly where her vagina was. He knew that if they made love, the chances were very high he would ejaculate almost immediately, so he wanted to familiarise himself with her first. He leaned in closer and smelled her, gently parting her pubic hair so he could see the lips of her vagina. Then he kissed them, all the time his penis throbbed, desperate for him to relieve himself. But he had to learn to be patient.

He slowly inserted his middle finger into her, needing to know the sensations his penis would soon feel. He heard his mother groan softly. She was enjoying it, too, then! Jeremy was surprised to feel his finger enter so easily, despite the inside of her vagina being dry. Maybe sex was going to be easier than he imagined. He pulled out his finger and sniffed it, enjoyed the smell, then leaned in closer to lick her vagina.

"Jeremy! What on earth do you think you're doing?"

He yelped, almost falling from the bed in his surprise. His mother pulled her legs up and saw where he'd cut a hole in her pyjamas. Her look of utter disbelief and disgust was all too clear but Jeremy couldn't understand why. Instead of answering her, he was gobsmacked, too shocked to speak.

"Jeremy, you need to get out of here and not get in my bed ever again. I don't know what you think you are doing but it has to stop. Do you understand me?"

The way she said it, her voice so stern and commanding, was unlike anything he had ever heard from her before. This was not how it was supposed to go. She was supposed to be opening herself for him, allowing him in, not brushing him off. She was in love with him, just as he was with her, and she should be welcoming him into her room, yet she was doing the exact opposite. Totally defeated, humiliated, and enraged, Jeremy stormed from her room, slamming the door behind him. The one and only person in the whole world he was deeply in love with, had hoped to lose his virginity to, had just discarded him like a piece of rubbish. Someone was going to pay for this.

Chapter 8

When Jeremy awoke the next morning, the recollection of being discarded by his mother came to him, and the rage that had barely allowed him to fall asleep the night before, returned. He'd never felt so humiliated in his life. Not even when he was forced to eat the dog shit sandwich. This was his mother, the person who was supposed to be in love with him in more ways than one, and who he now had to share his home with after being rejected. How was he going to look her in the eyes?

It seemed as though everyone in the whole world hated him. There wasn't a single person he knew that he considered a friend or ally, no one who respected or admired him. The girls still mocked him, the bullies still taunted and beat him. No one came to his rescue. Even the teachers seemed reluctant to break up the fights or bullying. And now this.

He was crushed.

His father would be ashamed and devastated if he was still alive. Jeremy was a pathetic successor to his legacy, a king incapable of living up to the task. But all this was secondary. The thing his mind focused on was being rejected by the one person in the whole world he had loved with all his heart, who he had fantasised endlessly about sharing body and bed with and it had all been for nothing. Not even his own mother loved him. He was a failure.

Stop feeling sorry for yourself. Prove to them there's a real man in there somewhere. Show your mother the mistake she's made and when she realises, it'll be too late.

It was his father's voice he heard in his head, but

Jeremy was so devastated not even this could force him to get out of bed and confront the day ahead. When he opened his eyes further, he wasn't entirely surprised to feel the sharp sting in them, they were puffy from having cried all night, even while he slept. He knew this because he had dreamed about marrying his mother. He had carried her in his arms to their bed and she had seduced him. He'd ejaculated at some point during the night because when he looked under the blanket, there was a suspicious stain there. She haunted and tormented him, even in his dreams.

It was the rage that overruled any hurt and despair he might be feeling, though. If Kelly happened to walk in on him right now, he thought he might take it all out on her, whip her with his braces until her flesh began to peel off like old wallpaper. If Tommy or his friend Pete entered, he would go into a violent frenzy and beat them with his fists until their faces were unrecognisable, blood pooling beneath them. Then make them eat their own shit. If his mother were to enter right now to tell him breakfast was ready, he might drag her downstairs and push her face into the boiling oil she used to fry his eggs with. He would watch as her skin and flesh melted like candlewax, then he would pour it down her throat until it exploded.

But none of those things happened.

He knew Kelly avoided him at all costs and he figured his mother was doing the same too, not wanting to discuss her reasons for rejecting him. Maybe she needed to pay for this in some way. Maybe they both did.

Maybe they all did.

His father's voice had just told him he needed to man up, get a grip on things. Lying about, whining and feeling sorry for himself was what a weak man would do. And Jeremy might be a lot of things, but he was not

Loneliness is a Monster

that. His father would say he was being weak, though, that he needed to show them this humiliation was not going to get in the way of who he truly was. His mother needed to learn who did the rejecting around here.

As though given a completely new personality and body to fit, Jeremy suddenly found the strength to get out of bed and brush away the tears. He wasn't going to hide from his mother, as had been his plan, but show her that she had not hurt him at all. He felt stronger, now, than ever before. If he couldn't have his mother, he didn't want any one and he would be just fine with that.

"I'll have two slices of toast and a warm glass of milk," he told his mother the moment he stepped into the kitchen. He looked her straight in the eyes, unflinching, as if last night's events had never happened.

"Of course, son. Sit down, I'll make it straight away."

Not a word about it from her, either. Just as well. Kelly walked in, avoiding making eye contact with him. There was still a red rash on her face from the boiling milk.

"Hi, Mum," she said as she sat down. "Can I help with anything?"

"No, I'm fine. I'm making toast for you and your brother now."

"Okay, great."

"And who told you that you could sit down?" spat Jeremy. Part of him still wanted to lash out at someone, relieve himself of all the emotions that had drained him last night. Any excuse right now would be perfect.

"I, umm, sorry. I just thought…"

"Stand up."

She did so, terror already etched onto her features.

"Now get outta here. You can go without breakfast for your disobedience."

Kelly's face scrunched up then she ran off. He

glanced at his mother. She had her back to him, but he thought he caught a momentary stiffening of her body before she continued preparing breakfast. He watched her as she hummed some senseless tune, wishing he could go up behind her and wrap his hands around her breasts, let a hand slowly slide down to her vagina. Remembering the image of it caused an erection to form and he squeezed it, putting a hand inside his pyjamas to stroke it, daring her in his mind to turn around and catch him.

Even though he told himself he hated his mother for what she had done, he couldn't avoid thinking about that brief moment they shared. Before leaving for school, he was going to have to take care of his erection, or it would be a constant source of irritation all day.

She turned around just as he removed his hand from his pyjamas. She must have noticed the sudden movement but acted as if nothing had happened. She gave him only the slightest of glances, as well. So, she was embarrassed then. Good.

He finished his breakfast in the unusual silence between them. It was as if she was afraid of saying the wrong thing. Jeremy left his plate at the table and headed upstairs to get ready for school, but first he had the erection problem to take care of. Once he was done, he dressed and left to go to school, just as his sister stepped out of her bedroom. She froze, clearly not wanting to bump into him. Kelly made to walk past him when he grabbed her.

"I bet you and mother talk about me all the time, don't you?"

"What? No, never!"

"I could pull those stupid little pigtails right off your head, you know. You'd be screaming for weeks. Maybe I should. I'm sick of all of you, especially you girls.

Loneliness is a Monster

Think you're all so clever and smart, don't you?"

"No! You're hurting me! Please let me go!"

She started sobbing, her delicate frame shaking in terror. Jeremy reckoned he could snap her in half if he wanted to, so small and frail was she. He wondered in that moment if she'd grow up to be a slut like the girls his age. Probably walk around with no knickers on, just to tease the boys. It made him sick. For a second he considered throwing her down the stairs, a lesson to all women that should cross his path but he decided against it. Instead, he gripped both sides of her cheeks, forcing her mouth open, then with one finger pressed against one nostril, his own mouth closed, he exhaled heavily, blowing a thick wad of snot down her throat, then closed her mouth until she swallowed. He let her go and chuckled as she rushed to the toilet to vomit.

Jeremy had been in a foul mood all morning at school, unable to shake off the idea he might spend the rest of his life a virgin. Having to go through the torment of seeing his mother every single day, unable to carry out his greatest wish. Even though he had semi-convinced himself he now hated her, the warmth of her body against his, the smell and touch of her vagina, the sight of her naked body in the bathtub with him, was too strong to shake off, much as he wanted to. It was a perverted memory that wouldn't go away.

The girls snickered both behind his back and to his face whenever he walked past them and all he wanted to do was wipe the stupid grins from their faces. Preferably with a knife. Ram it as far down their throats as possible until the blade came out the other side. That would stop them.

For some reason, even though Tommy and Pete had seen him several times today, they refrained from stealing his lunch or punching him. They seemed to be interested in something else, and it was only as he hid in his usual spot at lunch that he overheard what had their attention.

"Sarah. Sarah Greenwood. She finally got arrested, man. Don't you remember her?" said Tommy.

"Er, yeah, that bitch that killed all them people, right?"

"Fuckin' right! Got kidnapped as a kid, killed all four kids that kidnapped her, then escaped. Turned into some kinda hitman. Or hitwoman, whatever it's called. Killed about seven people. One guy she electrocuted shovin' a fuckin' dildo attached to live wires up his arse. Another one, she used a power drill. Drilled into his fuckin' ears until his ear drums burst. Then she glued his mouth and nose shut until he suffocated. That was after she poured gasoline onto his balls and set 'em alight! Woman's a fuckin' nutter, but they caught her and now she's in Nuttergate Hospital. Fuckin' hero in my books. Most prolific female serial killer in Norfolk's history and lived like twenty minutes away from my house!"

"Wow. That's fucked up!"

The conversation continued but Jeremy was no longer listening. Instead, his mind was reeling. Because they had always lived such a sheltered life and their father prohibited them from watching the news or having access to the internet and mobile phones, Jeremy had very little idea what occurred in the world unless he overheard people talking about it. He had a vague idea of some woman who had tortured and killed a few men in the area, but what he had just been listening to sounded exactly like the kind of things he had been fantasising about only this morning. Jeremy didn't know what a dildo was but it sounded nasty. And serial killer? What did that mean? He decided in that moment he

Loneliness is a Monster

needed to know.

During IT lessons that afternoon, he typed the word 'serial killer' into Google after quickly finishing his assignment and was astonished when tons of names and faces appeared. John Gacy, Jeffrey Dahmer, Harold Saggerbob, Clive Watson, Ted Bundy… Even more so when he read about their crimes. The horrific tortures they carried out.

He was hooked.

"I need money to buy some books and things," he told his mother the minute he got home. Since his father's death, his mother said they would have to go careful financial wise until the insurance money came through. When he told her it was for books and other things, she was usually happy to give him what he needed. She was a part-time author herself, writing romance novels—of which Jeremy had zero interest. Jeremy rushed to the High Street where all the main shops were and didn't return home until he'd bought everything he wanted.

On his walls went five posters. Charles Manson with his icy stare, Jeffrey Dahmer, Ed Gein, who looked old and frail, plus Ed Kemper and Ted Bundy. He tacked the other posters to his walls then threw himself onto his bed to read about Ed Gein. By the time his mother called him down for supper, he had almost finished the book and was both shocked and enthralled. The way Ed had skinned his victims, used it to make furniture and ornaments. He imagined bringing Tommy and Pete into his house under some false pretence, tying them down, then skinning them alive while they screamed in agony. He would use the skin from Tommy's face to make a mask and wear it to terrify Kelly. Stand over her bed as she slept then wake her, the first thing she would see would be the hideous mask which might make her piss and shit herself, scare her so badly she might die from

J. Boote

shock. That would be funny.

He would stand over his mother as she slept too, imagining getting in bed beside her, running his tongue over her hairy vagina before mounting her and having sex with her. She would open her eyes and think she was being raped by some terrible monster. But she was the monster—it would be her punishment for rejecting him.

And the girls at school too, he would cut out their vaginas and their breasts to make ornaments with, along with their eyeballs, tongues and lips. He would decorate the mantle. No more mocking and laughing at him then. Their bones he would carve and shave until they became sharp-pointed swords, and he would stab every single woman he ever met that rejected him with them. So lost was Jeremy in his fantasies, his mother had to come upstairs to get him. But he wasn't hungry anymore. Not for food, anyway.

Jeremy was hungry for revenge.

Three nights later, he had finished the other three books he'd bought. One about Jeffrey Dahmer, which had Jeremy fantasising about how Tommy's flesh would taste. And his sister's—so young and tender. His mother's vagina. Another was about a serial, sexual torturer called David Parker Ray, who would kidnap his victims for months, and torture and rape them daily. Just reading about the things David did caused Jeremy to get an erection and he would masturbate while fantasising about ramming the biggest items he could find up his mother's vagina. His fist, various implements from the kitchen, the sharpened thigh bone of one of the girls from school—Sarah, perhaps. Then she might say she was sorry, agree that she really was in love with him and beg for forgiveness. But it would be too late. Her vagina would be a massive, bloodied, torn hole.

Jeremy knew that Kelly had told other kids at school

what he did to her because he'd overheard her whispering, one day, as she walked home from school with a friend. Jeremy followed them close behind, eavesdropping. Kelly's friend said she should go to the police or tell a teacher but Kelly said she was too scared in case her brother found out. Well he had, and she needed to be severely punished.

The last book he read was about a local killer, Harold Saggerbob. In his basement he kept what he called his Pumpkin Club—the decapitated heads of all the boys that he tricked into coming inside after they had knocked on his door each Halloween. This was the last thing Jeremy needed. He saw himself bringing home all those that had taunted or abused him in some way, keeping them captive while sexually torturing them, then, when bored, he would skin them alive, eat them, then cut off their heads, proudly decorating the house. Just thinking about it was enough to make Jeremy ejaculate. It also made him want to carry out his fantasies and Kelly was the first one he had in mind.

Kelly struggled to fall asleep as she did so often these days. She was either too scared or too hungry. Every creak on the stairs or outside her room was Jeremy coming for her. Wanting to hurt and insult her, most of the time for no reason at all, just to remind her he was the man of the house, he said. He always came to her when their mother was fast asleep and Kelly knew she very rarely awoke during the night. Something about some kind of pills to help her sleep. Occasionally, Jeremy came bursting into the room, shouting and screaming at her about what a stupid little girl she was. All girls were sluts and whores who deserved to die, he said. Kelly, terrified, would scream and beg to be left alone, but it only seemed to spur her brother on. He'd drag her by her hair out of bed and slap her, use his braces and whip her buttocks until she couldn't feel it anymore. The next day, she couldn't even sit at the breakfast table, if he let her eat, and would make excuses. Jeremy said that if she ever told anyone she'd never sit down again and she believed him.

The only time Kelly brought it up to their mother, she explained there was nothing she could do. In their family, as was tradition, the man of the house could and would not be questioned. All they could do was try and keep him happy.

But it was so hard.

Jeremy would throw fits of anger at the slightest trigger, and sometimes, it seemed for no reason at all. If he was angry when he came home from school, Kelly knew it was because the other boys and girls bullied him—because of the way he dressed, because he was different to the rest of them. At first, she had found it hilarious. He was getting what he deserved. Until he started taking it out on her. When she told her friend what he did to her, Amanda was horrified and said she needed to speak to the police or a teacher, but there was no way she was going to do that. Who would they believe? A little girl or the man of the house? So she tried to fall asleep each night fantasising that he would get hit by a car, die from some horrible disease or just simply go away. Sometimes she felt guilty about thinking that, given he was her brother and he used to be nice to her. But then she would rub the scars on her buttocks and those thoughts soon disappeared.

She was just drifting off, confident Jeremy would leave her in peace tonight, when her heart dropped. The bedroom door opened.

Oh, no. Please. Please don't be him. Please be Mum just checking in on me.

"Get up," came his gruff voice.

Tears stung her eyes, utter terror scourging her body. She tried to pretend she was asleep so he might leave her alone, but instead, she yelped when her hair was tugged sharply, enough to drag her half out of bed.

"I said, get the fuck up."

"No. Jeremy. Please. I haven't done anything. Please don't hurt me."

"You haven't done anything? That's exactly the problem. You're slacking. And besides, I heard you telling that slut friend of yours I beat you. Opening your big, stupid mouth. You need to learn what happens when people open their big, fat mouths."

She yelped again when he dragged her across the bedroom floor. Kelly tried calling for her mother's help, but a powerful slap across the face stunned her. As she was dragged, she saw the trail of urine being left behind by her.

"You're a piece of shit, like all women, and so you should be treated as one."

He dragged her to her feet by her hair and took her to the spare bedroom, used mainly when a guest of their father's had occasionally stayed over. When he dragged her inside and locked the door behind them, Kelly knew she was in serious trouble. She should never have confided in her friend.

He threw her onto the bed and she started struggling even though she knew she was powerless against him. He ripped off her pyjamas. It was freezing cold outside, being mid-November, and no one had bothered to turn on the heating in this room. But she was too terrified to worry about the cold. That would come later.

"Jeremy, please. I promise I'll be good from now on. I'll do whatever you want, I won't say anything to anyone, just please don't hurt me! I'll make your favourite foods and learn how to cook better, I swear!"

But he wasn't listening. There was a gleam in his eyes she didn't like. He seemed a completely different person—a monster with a twisted grin carved onto his face like an old battle scar. She tried to resist, but Jeremy pulled her to her feet, then with the other hand, opened the large, empty wardrobe.

"No! No, Jeremy, no! Please don't put me in there. Anywhere but there! I'm scared of the dark and it's so cold, please!"

But again, it was as though Jeremy wasn't even listening, as though he had been replaced by something else entirely, something that completely lacked emotion. He gripped her around the neck and pushed her towards the wardrobe.

"You're gonna grow up to be a whore and a dog, just like the rest of them, so it's time you start acting like one. Get used to the idea."

Jeremy pushed her inside. She opened her mouth to scream as loud as she possibly could, but he clamped one hand over her mouth, and with the other he pulled out a length of rope that was fixed to one of the wardrobe doors. It had been tied into a

loop, which he pushed over her wrists and pulled tight, then he kicked her legs apart so she was almost bent over double.

"This is what happens to dogs and sluts. It's what they enjoy. You're gonna spend all night in here like this to get used to how things will be when you're older. Begging for it like the other bitches."

Unable to move her hands, she was horrified when he pushed her down until she felt something stiff and rough against her buttocks. When she turned around to see what it was, she saw a broom handle. She resisted and struggled as much as possible but inevitably she could

Loneliness is a Monster

do nothing as she was slowly pushed down. The broom handle entered her anus.

"Oww, it hurts! Stop, Jeremy, please!"

But Jeremy didn't listen. He continued pushing her down, then squatted and tightly tied both ankles to two other lengths of rope. Lastly, he clamped a piece of duct tape over her mouth so she couldn't scream.

"There, how's that? I guess in a few years, or even less, you'll be doing this quite often, but it won't be a broom handle up your arse, will it? Oh, no, of course it won't."

Kelly couldn't move. If she tried to stand, the restraints around her wrists and ankles tightened, rendering her powerless. She felt a warm liquid running down the backs of her legs and when she turned her head slightly, saw it was blood trickling down. He was going to force her to remain in this position all night, semi-squatting. Already her back was aching, her anus throbbed in agony. Her insides were on fire with the alien artifact inside of her. Jeremy gave her one last look, then hopped out of the wardrobe and closed the door, leaving her in pitch black darkness.

Utter panic enveloped her. Despite the pain to her anus, she writhed and struggled to stand, trying to get the broom handle to slide back out, but it was impossible. The more she struggled, the further in it went. It occurred to her that if she continued, the broom handle might go all the way up her body to her throat. But right now, she didn't care. To be left here all night, imprisoned and immobile, freezing cold already, right then, Kelly preferred to die.

But instead, she was left to suffer. Even when exhaustion caused her puffy eyes to close, any involuntary movement she made sent another jolt of agony up inside her. When Jeremy came and opened the door the next morning and released her, she crumpled to a heap on the floor, too worn out to even cry.

"Tell anyone, I'll do it again and leave you there a week."

Kelly barely even registered he was there.

Chapter 9

"There, how's that? Too hot or is it okay?" asked Mandy Cogsworth, as she took away the spoon from her daughter, Jane's, mouth.

"No, it's fine, thanks! Taste's wonderful!"

"Good, glad you like it! Nothing like some soup on a freezing day, right, to warm the bones!"

"Yes! Gimme more!"

Mandy did so, careful not to let any drops drip onto Jane and scald her. She smiled as she saw the colour return to Jane's face, so pallid lately that it made her worry. She would have to keep an eye on her weight too, being disabled brought too many complications and issues that Mandy had never even thought about before. If only the drunk driver had swerved left instead of right on that fateful night.

Jane, now twelve, just three years ago had her whole life ahead of her, a bright student, loved by all, with more friends than Mandy could count. It had all come to a tragic end when after a night out, she had been hit. Paralysed from the waist down, condemned to spend the rest of her life in bed or wheelchair. And, despite the horrific news from surgeons when Jane finally awoke after four days in a coma, she seemed to take the news with relative acceptance. Mandy had expected the worst, her daughter not wanting to live anymore, demanding euthanasia, becoming a pale shell of herself, losing any interest in living and becoming severely depressed. She worried her daughter would constantly be angry at the person who had done this to her—he was never caught—and that she would take it all out on her parents and friends. But none of these things happened.

It took a few weeks, but after the initial shock, and

with the help of child psychologists, Mandy, and Jane's father, Adrian, Jane took on a startingly positive attitude—something Mandy wasn't so sure she could even have herself. Mandy and Adrian had been just as devastated as their daughter.

"You remember I start a new job tomorrow, right? Your caretaker, Nicky, will be here first thing in the morning and will stay with you until I come home. I'm pretty nervous, but the cost of living is getting more and more expensive, and your dad's pay is barely covering expenses."

"I know, Mum! I said, don't worry. I'll be fine. Nicky seems really nice and she said she'll help me with my studies."

Mandy smiled, despite the knot in her stomach. It would be the first day she'd left Jane alone since the accident, but she wasn't lying when she said their financial situation was precarious at best. Adrian worked as a foreman on a construction site which often meant late hours and constant meetings. It also meant he earned good money. But after four years of her staying at home to look after Jane, their savings were starting to run out, despite selling their house and buying a smaller bungalow to help with Jane's needs. The government, it seemed, didn't appreciate the costs of raising a disabled child when it came to handing out benefits.

"Still want to be a teacher, huh, like me?"

"Yes. An English teacher, just like you. Nicky said there are grants for people like me which means I could buy software so I can teach online. Like, to foreign people wanting to learn English. It's expensive, but if I pass my exams and get the grant, that will cover the cost of everything."

"Well, let's hope so! I'm proud of you, you know. We both are, even if your father doesn't say so as often as I

Loneliness is a Monster

do!"

"Dad's busy, I know. Men never show their emotions anyway, do they? They think it's too girlish. Men are stupid."

Mandy burst out laughing. "Yes, they are, but don't you dare tell him I said that! Now, shall we get you bathed? Early night for me, I'm afraid. Did I mention I'm nervous? I haven't taught in years! I don't know if I have the knack anymore."

"You'll do fine, Mum. I've told you a million times, you're a natural. And if any of them kids give you trouble, you just tell them I'll come and kick some backsides!"

They both chuckled, as Mandy led Jane in her wheelchair to the bathroom specially equipped to make life as easy as possible. That knot in her stomach refused to abate though, as if she could sense some terrible, impending doom about to hit them at any moment. She knew it was just nerves about being in a room filled with kids again, but she'd never had problems before and was cautiously optimistic it would remain that way. Mandy could be stern, if necessary, but preferred a happy, likeable demeanour when teaching—the kids would be less likely to cause any problems if they liked rather than feared her.

Her bath over, Mandy helped Jane into her pyjamas then wheeled her to bed. During the nights, her and Adrian took turns getting up to move Jane for fear of bed sores. Even though they tried their hardest to keep Jane on a balanced diet, her increasing weight gain, due to lack of movement, was becoming a serious issue. Soon, Mandy wouldn't be able to move her at all. They needed to get her on a strict, healthy diet. Yet another thing that caused her anxiety, making her unable to focus properly on the new job. The school Jane had attended before the accident wasn't equipped for wheelchairs, so they figured it was best to home-school her. That way, Mandy could see to all her needs without having to worry about anything. Until now.

Mandy was determined to make this new job work. If she somehow screwed up, she wouldn't just be letting herself down; she'd be letting down her husband and more importantly, her daughter. If Jane could enjoy life in her current position and not let it get to her, Mandy was damn sure she could do the same.

Due to her nerves, she had a fitful sleep that night. She had a nightmare where one of the girls in her class was refusing to listen or do anything that was asked of her. When Mandy insisted that she pay attention and stop annoying the others, the girl would cackle and laugh at her, then throw things in Mandy's direction. When Mandy had finally had enough and told her to get out, the girl rose from her chair, headed over to Mandy and spat in her face. Mandy lost her temper, wrapping her hands around the girl's throat and squeezing and squeezing, until she suddenly bolted upright in bed. A cold sheen of sweat covered her body, causing her to shiver. She prayed this wasn't a bad omen of what was to come. When the alarm bell rang the next morning, she woke up with a knot of tension still in her stomach, like a tumour that refused to go away. Doing her best to ignore it, she rose and went to wake her daughter.

When Jane opened her eyes and smiled at her mother, Mandy felt guilty for all the nerves accumulating inside her. She had no right to be worried about teaching a bunch of kids when Jane faced much bigger issues on a daily basis. Mandy leaned over and kissed her daughter.

"Ready for the big day?" her daughter asked.

"Yes. I am!" she said after a moment's hesitation. "I'll go make breakfast; Nicky should be here any

Loneliness is a Monster

moment."

After she finished making breakfast and helped Jane get dressed, Nicky appeared and it was time for Jane to go. She once more went through everything with Nicky, ensuring the young woman had her telephone number in case anything went wrong, but, in the end, she was told to get out by her joking daughter. Mandy kissed Jane once more and headed off to Bradwell High School, that knot in her stomach now the size of a football.

It vanished, though, within minutes of beginning her class. She soon found herself getting back into the rhythm of teaching and more importantly the kids all seemed to warm to her straight away. When she mentioned she had a daughter that had been involved in a hit-and-run and was bound to a wheelchair, they appeared to grow fonder of her. The only thing she found slightly unusual about the whole day was the quiet boy sitting at the back of the class who hadn't said a single word to her since she arrived. The Chinese boy, whose strange, old-fashioned attire made him look different from all the others. But it was the way he looked at her that she found most unsettling. Every time she looked up from her desk, he was staring at her, but then immediately looked away and blushed when she caught him. As far as she was concerned, she was totally unassuming. She never wore makeup and dressed conservatively. She'd never had an instance where a boy in her class had a crush on her, but the strange gleam in this boy's eyes suggested that might be the case now. If she mentioned it to her daughter, Jane would find it amusing and would probably never let it drop. So, Mandy decided, that for now, she'd keep it to herself.

Chapter 10

She never said anything to her husband that night either. He'd make fun of her, too, and would more than likely tell Jane. Together, they would make her life hell. The teen kid with the crush on Mrs Cogsworth. Rather than amusing or cute, Mandy thought it was creepy and rather disgusting. This was the worst age to teach, when the majority of the kids were at a stage where they were more interested in discovering each other's bodies, and their own, rather than learning and studying. Perfectly natural, of course, but Mandy had been raised by conservative, religious parents who thought the word 'sex' was taboo, and never to be mentioned for fear of going to hell. She was taught to show as little skin as possible or the boys and men would turn into rampant savages. And God forbid if she wore make-up, which would only encourage them. Her husband, Adrian, had been her first and only boyfriend and she had insisted on waiting until they were married before consummating their relationship. Adrian had been slightly disappointed, but he, too, came from a strict, semi-religious family and fully understood and accepted her beliefs. When Jane was born nine months after they were married, their sex life had become almost non-existent, reduced to once or perhaps twice a month sessions and as far as Mandy was concerned that was fine with her. She had no reason to believe Adrian thought otherwise, and their marriage had never seen any rifts develop between them. If anything, it had only grown stronger, especially after Jane's tragic accident, years later. To think a boy in her class—a boy with a very strange dress sense and appearance—might be harbouring dirty, carnal thoughts towards her was not something she found particularly amusing. She made a mental note not to indirectly fuel his thoughts even further.

The next day, she got dressed, making sure she wore nothing that might provoke the kid, who's name she learned was Jeremy. She wore loose beige coloured trousers and a baggy, grey jumper. Mandy didn't have very large breasts but didn't want to encourage this kid's fantasises in any way, just in case. And as usual, she wore no makeup or jewellery. With any luck, Jeremy would find her boring and unattractive and look to girls his own age instead.

When she entered the classroom and greeted everyone, she looked around the room, trying her best to avoid meeting Jeremy's eyes. But she did, regardless. Only the slightest glance, but he sat there, eyes wide, as though meeting a famous actor for the first time, and he had one hand between his legs. He didn't look away and blush like yesterday either; instead, he kept his gaze firmly on her. Mandy involuntarily shivered.

When the bell rang for morning break, she started gathering her things to go and have a coffee, when a gentle nudge to her arm made her jump. She looked up to see Jeremy standing there, practically glaring at her but with a creepy grin on his face. Mandy waited for him to say something, see what he wanted, but he just stood there, hands by his sides, as though frozen. She could almost see the cogs spinning in his head, though, as if trying to think what to say.

"Anything wrong, Jeremy? Can I help you with something?"

"N-No. Nothing. I just…I just wanted to say I think you're a good teacher. I like you." Then he did blush, but still didn't take his eyes off her.

"Well, thank you. That's nice of you to say so. You seem like a good student, judging from your grades.

Keep it up."

She collected her things and made to leave quickly, so she wouldn't have to continue the conversation, but he gently tugged on her jumper, forcing her to stop.

"You think so? You like me, too?"

"Of course. I like all my students, now I really have to go. Go outside and enjoy yourself."

And before he could reply, she left. When she reached the bottom of the hall that led to the staff room, she turned around. Jeremy stood there watching her while kids jostled and pushed past him. He seemed completely oblivious of anyone else's presence except her own. And as before, he appeared to be scratching himself at his groin area.

Please, this is all I need, she groaned to herself. *Find yourself a girlfriend, boy, and leave me alone.*

"How'd it go today? Getting into the rhythm of things, yet?" asked Adrian, that night, as they lay in bed.

"Yes! As though I'd never stopped teaching. The kids are all well-behaved, which is unusual at that age and there's barely any banter between them. I'm lucky, I guess. Except…"

She let the word hang there, unsure whether she should mention the creepy kid from class, but she'd heard horror stories before, some first-hand, others in newspapers, about kids who developed crushes on certain teachers and things sometimes got seriously out of hand. The poor kid hadn't really done anything serious and most teachers she knew of, especially the men, had students who were infatuated with them, but there was just something about this kid that bothered her.

"Except what?"

"Nothing really. Just that there's this boy in my class, Jeremy. I think he has something of a crush on me. God knows why. Not as if I provoke him or anything, but it's the way he sits there staring at me when he thinks I'm not looking. And instead of looking away, as any normal person would, he continues glaring at me, not embarrassed at all at having been caught staring. I mean, he's thirteen years old and wears trouser braces! Can you believe that? Like he got stuck in some time warp and still thinks it's the sixties or something. He just gives me the creeps, but he's an excellent student. His grades are the highest out of all of them."

"Braces? Do people still use them this day and age? Not even my grandfather uses them anymore and he's eighty! But I wouldn't worry. From the way you describe him, he probably has very few friends, has started puberty and the other girls his age make fun of him. So he turns to the new teacher instead. Leave him be, it'll pass."

Mandy hoped so. And sooner rather than later.

Chapter 11

Only one image filled Jeremy's mind from the second he saw her. It seemed impossible that this could happen to him. He didn't believe in God as strongly as his parents did, but it did indeed seem like a sign from Him. It was fate, destiny. Just when his heart had been broken by his wicked mother, believing himself destined to remain alone the rest of his life, God had listened to his pleas and sobbing, and seen fit to help. And really, he told himself, it had to be a sign from God. His new teacher could have been some young slut, dressed like a whore, flirting with everyone and showing herself off, but this wasn't the case. It might just as easily have been his own mother who walked into that classroom yesterday, the similarities were so many. All his dreams had come true.

From the moment when she walked in, Jeremy had been unable to take his eyes off her, unable to think clearly. He nearly gasped when she entered, wondering if he was hallucinating or something, that maybe Kelly had put something in his cereals that morning, trying to kill him. His heart was beating so hard and fast he was worried it might break through the confines of his chest. Not to mention his penis, throbbing and pushing against his trousers. It had taken all his will power not to pull it out there and then and furiously masturbate. He took care of that little problem at morning break. Then again at lunch time.

The rest of the day he was incapable of focusing on anything else. When English and Literature finished, and it was time to move to the next class, he'd had to force his legs to move. He could have happily sat all day at the back of the room, staring at her, watching and listening to her even though he barely registered a word she said. At lunch, after relieving himself, he had gone and hung around near the teachers' room, peeking from the side of the window to see if he could spot her. When school finished for the day, he hid and waited for her, wanting to run over to her, to say something, anything; the need to touch her was overwhelming. Eventually, when he began to worry that he'd already missed her, she left the entrance and turned left to head home. For a moment, Jeremy considered following her but decided against it. He needed to get his thoughts clear, understand what was happening to him, so he went home, completely ignored his mother and sister, locked himself in his bedroom, and spent the entire afternoon masturbating. It was only later that evening when he was fully spent that he began to assess the situation.

When he had nudged Mrs Cogsworth at morning break, she had said she liked all her students, but he had been carefully scrutinising her and it became clear that her gaze more often than not turned towards him. When their eyes met, she would look away quickly, only to return her gaze seconds later. It could only mean one thing.

She was in love with him.

Hadn't he noticed the slightest hint of a blush when he caught her sneaking a quick peek at him? Looking flushed and briefly forgetting what she had been talking about? Those were signs—he knew them well enough from personal experience.

Jeremy chuckled as he lay back on his bed, thanking God for giving him a new lease on life, for listening to his prayers. He knew already that they were meant to be together forever, and it would only be a matter of time before she came to him. He knew she had a daughter who was disabled, but she hadn't said anything about a husband. That didn't matter either; if they were meant to be together, she would renounce her marriage. The daughter could be sent to live with relatives somewhere, leaving them to themselves.

For the first time in weeks, he demanded nothing of Kelly or his mother and was happy to go and collect his own dinner and bring it to his room. He had more important things to think about than ensuring his family obeyed his instructions.

The next morning, he was at school thirty minutes before everyone else, wanting to hide in wait to see from which direction she came, maybe catch her to say good morning and hope to initiate a chat. He really needed confirmation from her, albeit in code, that she loved him, because he was too embarrassed to do it himself. He found a good vantage point from behind a parked van and scanned left to right and back again, waiting for her. When he thought he might already be too late, he finally saw her heading his way. His heart leapt into his throat, butterflies gathered in his stomach, and when he looked to her crotch, trying to imagine if it would be the same as his mothers', he instantly had an erection.

Mandy crossed the road to enter the school grounds and Jeremy moved from behind the van, trying to act as casual as possible.

"Oh, hi, Mrs Cogsworth! Seems we're both arriving the same time! Like it was fate or something, right?"

She turned to face him and Jeremy caught the beginnings of a smile on her face quickly disappear. There was the briefest flicker in her eyes. Of course, it did; she didn't want to be seen by the other kids showing her true affection for him. Had to play it cool, which was fine by him.

"Morning, Jeremy. You must be keen to start school today."

"Always, Mrs Cogsworth. Mandy. Especially English and Literature, my favourite topic."

"That's, umm, good to hear. Glad you enjoy my class. Now let's get going inside, shall we?"

She turned back towards the entrance and made to leave. Jeremy started panicking, wanting to say something to her but not knowing what. Sweat trickled down his forehead.

"I think it was meant to be, you know," he blurted.

"What's that, Jeremy?" she said, turning back to him.

"That, well, like, that you started here at this school. I mean, of all the schools, you started at this one. It's a sign, God wanted you to be here. With me… with us."

"Well, maybe you're right. I'm very lucky to work at such a good school with such bright students. Keep going as you are; I'm sure it'll pay off."

Jeremy beamed as his teacher headed into school. That was code, it had to be. '*Keep going, it'll pay off*' had to be code. Be patient was what she meant. Keep being himself, keep going, and eventually they would be united. Of course it was too dangerous for them to show any signs of affection with so many prying eyes here at school; it could get her in trouble. So perhaps she was working on a way for them to meet in secret. Maybe her husband was an obstacle. Or the daughter even. Well, Jeremy was pretty sure he could help out in that regard.

The rest of the day, he did his best to focus on the schoolwork, torn between accidently bumping into Mandy whenever he got the opportunity and not wanting to bring attention to their relationship. But when the bell rang, signalling the end of the day, he knew what he had to do.

Jeremy hid behind the same van and waited for Mandy to leave. When he was sure she wouldn't spot him, he followed behind. After just a short walk, she turned onto a side street and entered a small bungalow. Jeremy smiled.

Now he knew where she lived. Step one was complete.

For the rest of the week, he followed the same pattern, hiding near her home to see who, if anyone, entered. Each afternoon, within minutes of Mandy entering, a young woman left the property. He had no idea who she was, guessing it was a relative—someone looking after Mandy's daughter. A couple of times, he saw Mandy leave with the daughter in her wheelchair. He didn't like the kid at all. She was slightly overweight and too loud. They joked and laughed together far too often for his liking. If asked, he might have admitted he was jealous. It should be him with Mandy, not the stupid girl.

He followed after them, ensuring he kept his distance. Both times, they went to the local supermarket. Jeremy stayed outside and peered through the window, observing what they bought. Then, as they were leaving, he would ran and hid. But the worst moment came each evening at around eight, when her husband walked down the garden path and straight into the bungalow. A growl escaped his throat, hands involuntarily curling into fists. He imagined them sleeping together, her husband's hands roaming over her body, smelling her down there before touching and kissing it, as he had done with his mother. Then climbing on top of her, perhaps, entering her secret place, maybe even against her will. Definitely against her will now since she was in love with him. Jeremy had the urge to come back after dark, creep into the room and castrate the man so he could never hurt her again. As he turned and left for home, his rage becoming a hunger, it was something he thought about more and more. He would stop at nothing to ensure he and Mandy finally came together.

Chapter 12

It was Saturday morning and Jane was excited. Her birthday was the next day and together with her mother, they had made plans to go to the shopping complex nearby so she could pick out one of her gifts. She knew her parents had already bought her a ton of stuff, as they did every year—more than they could really afford—and Jane knew this to be the result of guilt. Even though they had absolutely nothing to do with her being hit by the car, she guessed they harboured some repressed sense of responsibility, as if somehow they were at fault in some way and this was how they subconsciously tried to pay for their mistake. Jane had told her parents plenty of times they didn't need to do this, that one or two small gifts was more than enough, but they never listened. Even her aunts and uncles, who she barely saw these days thanks to living some fifty miles away, mailed more gifts than they used to. At Christmas, the postman probably had to do overtime just to ensure she received everything on time.

Her dad had promised her he would be finished by midday, so Jane and Mandy made arrangements to go to the complex early, pick out a gift for herself and have lunch together with her dad. Maybe go to the cinema in the afternoon, which sounded fine with Jane. She hadn't really decided on what she wanted to buy—she had everything she needed except a new pair of legs, she often joked—but to spend the day outside, out of the house, was always something she looked forward to.

"Okay, you ready?" called her mother.

"Been ready half an hour! It's you we're waiting on, as always!"

Finally, they left to catch the bus. Fortunately, it was

a sunny day, just a few grey clouds in the sky, which for eastern England in November, was more an anomaly than a regular occurrence. If the weather permitted during the week, her carer, Nicky, would go with her around the block or to the shops to buy whatever was required but mainly it was to just get out for a while. It was the only thing Jane lamented regarding her disability—being confined indoors for such long spells. Because the street they lived on had something of an inclination, it meant going out by herself was more complicated. Having a normal wheelchair rather than an electric one meant she struggled to push herself up the steep road and required the help of others.

They arrived at the complex and began window shopping, stopping every now and again, either to get a closer look at whatever item took Jane's fancy or to enquire prices. After a while, and still undecided, Mandy called for a coffee break. They found a bar but Jane, still excited and with so many more shops to investigate, told her mother she wanted to check out a gift shop opposite.

"Okay, I'll be here if you need anything. Good luck!"

"Won't be long!" And with that, Jane headed towards the shop.

It was hard moving about freely in the wheelchair in the small shop with others absently browsing the various items on display. A couple of times someone almost tripped over the wheelchair because they weren't looking where they were going and Jane had to quickly reach out an arm to prevent them from crashing to the floor. One boy collided with her and nearly threw Jane out of her chair. It was only the quick response from another customer that prevented her from being thrown onto the hard tiles. He mumbled an apology and quickly headed to another area.

After browsing for some time, she saw something that

grabbed her attention. It was a gadget that she could attach to her Kindle with a light enabling her to read at nights in bed, something she had been looking at for some time. Often, she would submerse herself into her books while in bed, forgetting what the time was and her mother would notice the light on under the door, mildly scolding her for being up so late. This way she could happily read without having to worry about being caught. And it appeared to be her lucky day—it was the last one.

Grinning, she grabbed it and was about to go and pay when, without warning, she found herself sprawled on the floor. She never even had time to scream or grunt in surprise. Her wheelchair clattered beside her, overturned, wheels spinning furiously. Audible gasps came from customers, and the shopworker as everyone rushed over to help her to her feet. But one person beat them to it.

"Oh God, I'm so sorry. Whatever was I thinking? I didn't see you. I promise. Are you hurt?"

She looked up, dazed, to see a kid crouching over her, maybe the same age, perhaps slightly younger. He looked horrified as he reached out a hand to help her up then took it back when he saw her crumpled legs and realised he probably wouldn't be able to do it on his own, causing further embarrassment.

"I...I'm okay," she managed, feeling embarrassed and stupid, herself, with all the onlookers.

The shopworker rushed over and didn't appear to know what to do either, looking back and forth from Jane to her wheelchair. Her mother ensured she participated in lots of sports events after school wherever possible, especially the nearby swimming pool with the help of Nicky to keep her weight down. She was also very careful with what she ate, but Jane was still large. Not overweight, but one adult would struggle to pick her up unless they were trained to do so correctly.

Other customers gathered round and, between three of them, they managed to righten her wheelchair and pick Jane up, sitting her back down again. All were making a fuss of her, asking if she was okay, if she was alone or if her mother was nearby and this made her feel inadequate and useless, as much as she appreciated the help. She prided herself on being independent where possible, only asking for help if it was absolutely necessary. In this case she had no choice but to allow them to pick her up but it wasn't just this that made her feel uncomfortable. She could swear the kid who had knocked her over was doing his hardest to swipe away a grin from his face. His eyes had a sparkle to them as if he'd just done something naughty and gotten away with it. They stared at each other for a few seconds then the boy muttered something and dashed off. It was then Jane remembered the gadget she'd been holding. It was lying broken on the floor.

With all the attention and fuss, and seeing her gift to herself was broken, Jane spun around in her chair and rushed off, crying.

"What happened?" asked her horrified mother when Jane found her.

She told her everything and about her gift being broken, but more so about the boy who looked as if it had all been a clever prank. Jane was utterly convinced the boy had been wiping a hand across his face to cover that grin. The look in his eyes.

"My God, that's terrible! But I'm sure he didn't do it on purpose. No one could be so cruel as that."

"I'm telling you he was grinning. And he was such a weird looking kid as well. The last time I saw anyone with a haircut like that was grandad in one of those old photos you've got. He was like, fourteen, but dressed like he was stuck in the sixties, wearing corduroys with braces. Who wears them anymore?"

A strange look came over her mother's face. It seemed to darken as if a cloud had passed overhead. Her eyes narrowed as though deep in thought, trying to remember some event from long ago.

"What? What's wrong? You look like you just saw a ghost."

"Hmm? Oh, no nothing. Tell you what, we'll find another shop later that sells whatever you were hoping to buy. Let's go, shall we?"

Her mother rose before she could even answer, as if in a great hurry suddenly, never even bothering to ask Jane if she wanted a drink. On the way home, she barely said a word.

Later that afternoon her mother was still quieter than usual, lost in her own thoughts as they went to the cinema then to another shop to find her gift for her. It made

Jane wonder if something about the incident gave her mother more reason for concern than it should have.

"I'm telling you it must have been him," said Mandy. "The way she described him, wearing those old-fashioned clothes like he'd borrowed them from his grandfather. He's the only kid I know who wears corduroys still, brushes his hair back with so much gel, I swear it drips. It was him, Adrian."

"Okay, okay, suppose it was him. You can't tell me he did it on purpose. No one would do that to a disabled child. That's beyond wicked. It had to have been an accident, coincidence it just happened to be this kid, nothing else."

"It seems too much of a coincidence. Of all the kids

to knock her out of her wheelchair, it had to be him. And don't forget, knocking her over onto the floor isn't as easy as it seems. You don't knock someone out of that chair just by bumping into them; you do so by forcefully pushing them! There's something I don't like about all this."

"Honestly, Mandy, I'm sure you're overreacting. Tons of kids go to that shopping complex every weekend. Hell, every single kid seems to be there some days. It's inevitable he would go as well. From what you've told me about him, he doesn't appear to have many friends anyway, so he's probably bored. Wasn't looking where he was going and tripped over her, causing her to fall out."

"I admit he does seem like a nice kid and not the type to do something like that. Poor kid gets bullied himself enough as it is from the others. And his grades are pretty much perfect. He has a big future ahead of himself and I want to help him, but…"

"But what?"

"I don't know. I really want to help him however I can but the way he looks at me sometimes, it's just…I can't explain it."

Jeremy couldn't help himself. He pulled out his penis, already erect and throbbing and masturbated. Hearing those words from her, it was the ultimate confirmation. She had been on the verge of declaring her undying love for him, telling her husband she couldn't control herself any longer and needed an immediate divorce. She just needed that extra push. He could understand she probably still loved her husband on some subconscious level and this was normal; it was why he loved her so much. Such a wonderful, kind human being, but listening to those words;

I want to help him.

Loneliness is a Monster

I want to help him however I can.

Such a nice kid.

To Jeremy she was practically confessing her love for him without actually saying those magical words:

I love him.

He ejaculated, stifling a groan with his free hand as he continued listening to their conversation. His grin faltered as the husband told her to ignore the boy, that there might be something wrong with him. Jeremy had to forcefully bite down on his tongue, rage accumulating inside him like a virus. This man was going to come between them, he could sense it. He wanted to come out from his hiding place, suffocate him with his pillow, take Mandy far from him so they begin their new life together already.

"There's a chance I might be sent to Manchester on the company's next project. I was going to wait until it's confirmed before mentioning it but now seems as good a time as any. It's a big one, more money. We could go there and if we like it, stay there permanently. If everything works out it would pay for an electric wheelchair for Jane. You wouldn't have to continue teaching either, so a win-win for everyone. Whadaya think?"

"Really?! Oh my God, that sounds amazing! To be honest, while it's nice being back teaching again, I miss being around Jane all day, even though I know she and Nicky get on great. And yes, an electric wheelchair would solve so many things for her, allow her to be more independent, too. So yes, I'm definitely willing to give it a try!"

Jeremy had to stifle crying out in horror. He bit down on his tongue, this time drawing blood. This was a nightmare; it couldn't be happening. And yet, hearing their lips smacking together, a rustling of sheets, confirmed it was no nightmare. Seconds ago, she had professed her complete love for him and now she was planning on moving away. How could she do this to him?

She was confused, that's how. She didn't really want to move from him, it was just a ploy to keep her husband happy, so he didn't become suspicious. Regardless, Jeremy was going to have to do something drastic, just in case. For only the second time in his life, he was in love and there was no way it was going to be taken from him once again. From his position underneath their bed, where he'd been hiding ever since they left to go to the cinema earlier, Jeremy folded his arms behind his head and began to make plans. Plans to ensure Mandy was never going to leave him for anything or anyone.

Chapter 13

The next day Jeremy's emotions were mixed, his mind a source of conflict and incomprehension. He had heard directly from Mandy's lips that she was in love with him. Her use of the word 'help' was code. What she had really been trying to say was that she wanted to be with him, night and day. His heart felt as though it had grown twice its size the moment she said that and he was the happiest man on earth. But then the husband had ruined things by wanting to take her from him and she had even agreed. How could that be? Was she just playing along with him so he didn't become suspicious? It had to be the reason. Or maybe the husband suspected she was in love was another and wanted to ruin their plans. And this infuriated Jeremy. On the one hand he was the happiest he had ever been, yet on the other, the rage that surged through his body was like a boomerang—coming and going. One minute, he was a beaming, happy boy; the next, he could happily kill someone.

The husband preferably.

Yet no matter how he tried to convince himself Mandy was just playing along with his plans to move away, another stronger voice in his head told him that this was going to end exactly as with his mother— him abandoned and once more alone in the world, no one to love him. It was this thought that invaded his mind, haunted his soul, and refused to go away. Jeremy sat up on his bed, picked up a coffee mug and threw it at the wall, tears of anger and desolation running down his cheeks. He wished it was the husband's head smashed to smithereens instead of the mug. He wanted to go to their house now, grab the husband by the throat and slice it open, scream into his face that it was all his fault he had to die, he shouldn't have got between them. It was all his own doing. He wanted Mandy to be standing there watching as he sliced his flesh open, skinning him alive, knowing he was doing it for her, was willing to do anything to protect their love for each other.

He looked at the poster of Jeffrey Dahmer at the foot of his bed. He would know what to do. He didn't let people get away so easily from him. Jeremy must have read the book at least five times. When someone wanted to leave Jeffrey, he killed and ate them. So easy. Maybe he could learn something from this guy. Maybe he and Mandy could sit and have a romantic meal one night, feasting on her husband's succulent flesh.

Jeremy watched as the remains of his coffee slid down the wall, murky water running like the dirty tears he was shedding, making him feel childish and stupid. But he couldn't help it. Stupid and childish like his baby sister who once again had burnt his toast this morning. When he slapped her across the face for committing such a terrible misdeed, she had snivelled and sobbed, snot running down her face. It was pathetic. How was she ever going to grow into a proper woman and take care of a man's needs if she kept forgetting simple things? Perhaps she needed to be taught a lesson. One she would never forget. Perhaps he should slit her throat open so she would have two mouths to cry and scream from. He could leave her tied and bleeding outside the husband's home for him to find when he came home from work. A warning.

Stay away.

Mandy is mine.

A thud on the wall that divided his and his sister's rooms made him jump, causing him to bang the back of his head on the wall behind him. How many times did he have to tell his stupid sister not to bang on that wall? That was it. As though by banging his head something inside had been unleashed, he jumped up and stormed to her room, throwing her door open and grabbing her around the throat.

"What? What is it?" she gasped.

"You just won't learn, will you? How many times have I told you not to bang against the wall? You made me drop my favourite coffee mug. You're gonna pay for that."

She was struggling to breathe and wheezing as Jeremy dragged his sister downstairs and into the back garden. Their mother was already in bed asleep so she wouldn't be bothering them, which as far as Jeremy was concerned was completely irrelevant anyway. It was freezing outside, rain lashing down, a wind howling like some animal in great distress. Kelly was struggling and writhing to no effect whatsoever, Jeremy threw her to the soaked ground but before she could even think about getting up he tore off her pyjamas, leaving her naked.

"Jeremy, what are you doing? Please don't hurt me! It's freezing! Please. I'm sorry for whatever I did."

"Yeah, you will be."

Her frail, freezing body was now covered in wet mud as though someone had attempted to mummify her. She tried to get to her feet but her legs were so cold already they betrayed her and she collapsed. She tried to scream for help but all that came out was a wheezed cough and spluttering, her hair was plastered to her face like a spider's web.

Jeremy stared down at her in disgust. As though staring down at some ugly, squirming bug, which to him she was. Over in the far corner was a large rose bush, his mother's pride. He dragged her to her feet then threw her into the middle. Sharp, deadly thorns cut into her everywhere as she struggled to free herself. But now she was screaming and worried she was going to wake the neighbours, he quickly dragged her back out, parts of the stems sticking into her and tearing the flesh. Jeremy clamped a hand over her mouth and dragged her into the shed.

It was as if another had taken over his body, his mind clouded with rage. Instead of his grovelling sister's face it was the husband's he was seeing and hearing, begging to be released, to not be hurt, and this spurred him on even more. In the small shed were his father's gardening tools, a workbench and a wooden chair where he would sometimes come and sit when he needed some peace from noisy kids. Jeremy bent his sister over the back of the chair then grabbed a long, thin stick laying on the workbench. Kelly made to stand up, looking behind her. Her face contorted into a look of utter terror when she saw the long stick. Jeremy pushed her back down then began to whip her buttocks, long, red welts and spots of blood formed. Kelly howled in agony, but Jeremy was oblivious, whipping her again and again until his arm ached. When he stopped to get his breath back, her entire backside and legs were covered in gashes, blood running freely. Her bladder had betrayed her causing a puddle to form around her feet. This infuriated him even more so he began to whip her back, cracks like thunder resonating around the wooden shed. Kelly's legs lost all strength as she slid to the ground but Jeremy was merciless, swapping arms to give each one a rest as Kelly curled into a foetus position, trying to protect herself. He turned his attention to her bare feet, cracking the bloodied, half broken stick against her soles and toes. By the time he finished, her toes were twice the size and already purple. He suspected they were all possibly broken, Kelly barely conscious now as she lay in a pool

Loneliness is a Monster

of her own filth and blood.

Panting, Jeremy surveyed his work. Barely any skin was visible on her back and buttocks, now swollen almost twice the size and turning a deep shade of purple. He could quite happily leave her there to die and couldn't care less, another useless example of a human being. He so badly wished it was the husband laying there instead so he could continue to inflict systematic torture on the man until nothing was left. He thought of Dahmer who by now might already be chopping him up into manageable pieces, a pot of boiling water filled with spices prepared in the kitchen. It also occurred to him that if he did kill the pathetic creature before him, it might not be long before the police got involved and that would mean the end of his relationship with Mandy, before it even started. That would mean the husband winning, taking her away forever and Jeremy left to mope and lick his own wounds in a cold cell. Their mother might already be terrified of Jeremy, doing nothing that could annoy or provoke him, but it would be a totally different matter if her daughter turned up dead by his own hand.

But Jeremy so badly wanted to kill someone, anyone. Show to the world that when he said he was the man of the house and was to be respected and obeyed at all times, he wasn't joking. He wanted the kids from school, especially those two boys that harassed him relentlessly, to see what he was capable of. No one would ever laugh at him again. Just as they never laughed at his heroes either—Dahmer, Saggerbob, Parker Ray. Even his father would be proud of him finally. But as the adrenaline began to wear off, Jeremy reminded himself that this was not the time or place or person to completely fulfil his fantasises, so left his unconscious sister on the ground and turned to head back to bed. But before he did so, he unzipped his trousers and urinated on her bleeding, naked body, steam rising from the gashes in her back and buttocks.

"That'll teach you, stupid girl," he muttered and left.

Chapter 14

When Katherine stepped into Kelly's bedroom the following morning, her first thought was that the girl must have awoken early and was already downstairs preparing breakfast. A minor miracle. Katherine smiled. She never could have imagined that one of the hardest jobs as a mother was to wake up the kids and get them ready for school on time. Threats, psychological blackmail, even the legendary tickle under the armpits, if necessary, a mother needed a whole bag of tools to get their kids up on a school day. Kelly wasn't the worst of them it seemed. She'd heard other parents at school talking about the difficulties they had with their own children. Since her brother took on the role as man of the house, it was more of a struggle to get her up in the mornings. When Jeremy had demanded it be Kelly who prepared him his breakfast in the mornings, it had required Katherine to wake her and make sure she didn't fall asleep again. It seemed that not even the terror she felt for her older brother was enough to get her up and moving. And that should have been more than enough reason.

Perhaps it had been Jeremy that had awoken early himself and demanded she get up and prepare him his warm glass of milk and toast. She closed the door and headed quietly to her son's room, pressing an ear against the door to see if she could hear him awake. Instead, soft snoring came from inside the room which troubled her somewhat. It was highly unlike Jeremy to wake up, demand something from either his sister or mother then fall asleep again. When Jeremy awoke, he was up and dressed within minutes, giving orders to everyone in the house like some high-flying businessman.

Another thing that bothered Katherine was that Kelly's bedroom light was on, despite it being unnecessary, and this sent a little spark of unease to shoot up her spine. It had been well drilled into her that they were not so well off they could afford to waste electricity and it suggested the light had been on all night. So where was she?

Katherine quickly headed downstairs, after checking she wasn't in the bathroom, listening for the tell-tale signs of movement in the kitchen and hearing nothing, causing her heart to steadily increase its rhythm.

"Kelly? You awake?" she called.

When no answer came, she moved faster around the house, calling her daughter's name, checking every room until it was confirmed what she already suspected; Kelly wasn't in the house. She thought of waking Jeremy, asking him if he knew where she was or if he had punished her in some way, but waking her son was not something she did lightly—his wrath could be terrible.

Both the front and back doors were locked and Kelly's coat was hanging by the stairs implying that she hadn't left the house. It was as though she'd vanished into thin air. A knot of unease twisting at Katherine's intestines, she frantically ran through the house again, calling Kelly's name, now not caring if Jeremy woke or not. She was on the verge of running upstairs and waking her son regardless of the repercussions when she happened to glance out the kitchen window that overlooked the back garden.

Katherine gasped, clapping a hand to her mouth. For the briefest of moments, she thought it was her daughter laying outside in the cold mud until she realised it was Kelly's clothes. This did nothing to ease her panic as she unlocked the door, threw it open and rushed outside. She

Loneliness is a Monster

stopped when she saw the girl's pyjamas torn and covered in blood and mud, stems from her rose bush still clinging to them like barbed wire. Her immediate thought was someone had kidnapped her—not unheard of in this godforsaken village.

"Kelly!" she yelled, spinning wildly in circles, as though Kelly might be hiding in some hidden corner. Then she saw the muddy footsteps—two sets of footsteps—leading to the shed, and she rushed down the garden path.

When she threw the door of the shed in and rushed inside, she almost tripped over the naked figure on the floor. At first she thought it was some dead animal that had found its way inside, a dog even, because it wasn't the colour of a human being. More an animal that had been hit by a car and dragged along a dirt track a few hundred yards. But after the initial, momentary shock, recognition hit her and she rushed to her daughter's side, fearing the worst.

"Kelly! Kelly, can you hear me? Please tell me you can hear me."

Kelly was lying face down, the colour of her skin, where visible, a mottled purple colour and covered in gashes and long, deep cuts, dried blood everywhere. Such was the state of her body she was almost too afraid to touch her, as much as she wanted to. Even so, she placed a hand gently on her daughter's shoulder and shook her softly. On the verge of screaming, feeling an oncoming panic attack, she was about to scream her daughter's name again, when there was a soft murmur from Kelly.

"Oh my God! Oh my God, Kelly, what happened? Who did this to you? Don't move, okay, I'm gonna call an ambulance. Oh God, I thought you were dead!"

Now she was in hysterics, the idea of losing her

daughter something totally alien and incomprehensible in her mind, yet at the same time, another idea, not quite as alien as the previous, but still seemingly impossible to comprehend was already forming alongside it.

"Mum," came a barely audible voice.

"Yes, babe, it's me. Don't move okay, I'm gonna call an ambulance straight away, but...but who did this? What happened?"

"Jeremy."

Kelly ignored her mother's advice to not move and slowly and with evidently great difficulty, rolled onto her back. Katherine clapped a hand to her mouth. Her daughter resembled some old, manky doll or mannequin that had been run over by a car then picked up and dragged through a roll of barbed wire. Her lips were blue, eyes barely open and vacant like a cadaver, multitude of gashes across her stomach and legs. Then she saw her feet, horribly swollen, toes black and deformed, resembling rotten mushrooms. Katherine told her daughter not to move for the third time then ran inside the house, wildly looking around for her mobile phone. She found it and called an ambulance. As she screamed into her phone, begging them to hurry, she turned to see Jeremy standing at the bottom of the stairs watching her, a blank look on his face as though he had no idea what was going on.

The horrified look on the doctors' faces told Katherine everything as they rushed to attend to Kelly's many needs and bring her body temperature up again. Yet there was another look directed her way that she wasn't so sure about. When the paramedics arrived and asked her what happened, she hadn't known what to say so told the truth, that she found Kelly in this state while looking for her. A suggestion of attempted kidnapping or even rape had been made and Kelly had been rushed

Loneliness is a Monster

off to hospital. The same questions had been repeated to her by a nurse while Kelly was being attended to, then again shortly afterwards when the police arrived. Katherine told them all the same thing. The only way they would have any idea was when Kelly woke up and according to the doctors that wasn't going to be for a while. She was suffering from extreme hypothermia and her body had gone into shock. Kelly was lucky to be alive, they told her.

But the glances from doctors and nurses, as Katherine sat nervous and terrified nearby, were of suspicion. They knew immediately just as Katherine had what had probably caused most of the wounds and sure as hell hadn't been some kidnapper or rapist. And after the police spoke to one of the doctors that had attended to Kelly, the look in their eyes was exactly the same.

"According to the doctor who first examined her, he said many of the cuts contained thorns from a rose bush, as if she'd either fallen heavily into one or been pushed. Do you happen to have a rose bush in your garden?"

"Yes, I do."

"So how might she have ended up embedded in it?"

"I don't know."

"He also said the large cuts on her body were probably caused by a stick of some kind, and that her toes were beaten so badly it was impossible she did that to herself from falling. How would you explain that?"

"I don't know. Maybe the person trying to kidnap her threw her in there then got angry and started beating her. All I know is that if I hadn't found her this morning she would probably be dead right now!"

"Mrs Chan, there is absolutely no evidence to suggest someone tried to kidnap your daughter last night. No footprints in the garden other than Kelly's and another child's, assumedly your son's. Were the front and back doors locked when you went to bed?"

"Yes, I always lock them every night."

"Well, there's no sign of forced entry either, so how did she get out there in the first place? She had to have unlocked the door herself. That or you or your son did so, but why?"

"I don't know. Both me and my son were asleep. You'll have to ask her when she wakes up."

Katherine had long since realised where this was heading and the implications, but despite the immense hatred she was feeling for Jeremy right now, she was still incapable of revealing the truth. Some deep centred sense of maternal instinct prevented her, making her feel as though she would be betraying him and, by association, her deceased husband. She would cover for him for now if she had to but her relationship with Jeremy would never be the same again.

"Mrs Chan, have you ever disciplined your children before? We know your husband passed away recently and it must be tough bringing up two young children alone. The financial struggles, the constant stress, kids arguing and fighting among themselves as they do…Maybe sometimes it just all gets a bit too much."

"No! I have never laid a hand on my children before in my life. I…I love my children. I would never!"

"Okay, well, there's not a lot more we can do until your daughter wakes up and when she does, hopefully she can explain more, but in the meantime, as is the case in such matters, we will have to inform child services who will want to speak to you and your son. Then, of course, your daughter, too, when she is able."

Resigned, and knowing it would come to this, Katherine simply nodded. She'd deal with that when it happened. She'd deal with everything.

Two days later there was a knock at the door. Kelly

Loneliness is a Monster

had regained consciousness but was still incapable of communicating, so Katherine had taken a rare moment to go home and rest having barely left her daughter's side. The only time she did was because Jeremy insisted she come home to prepare his meals and wash his clothes, each day. Not once had Jeremy gone to visit his sister at the hospital and only casually asked about her wellbeing, speaking in such a manner he might have been asking what the weather was like outside. Katherine could barely look him in the eye when they spoke but said nothing about the incident.

When she answered the door, a young woman, who Katherine guessed to be in her early twenties, stood there.

"Yes, can I help you?"

"Mrs Chan? I'm from social services. The police told you I would be making a visit. May I come in?"

"Oh, yes, of course."

Katherine stepped aside and allowed the woman in. Her heart thudded a little faster in her chest as she prepared herself for the barrage of questions, any possible accusations, although she was grateful Jeremy wasn't home.

"Thank you. I'm Amanda."

Katherine led her to the living room where they both sat down, Amanda's eyes like an eagle's, scouring for the slightest sign of prey, but in that regard, Katherine was confident. She prided herself on keeping the house spotless. And then the questions began. Her relationship with her children, Kelly's with Jeremy's, Kelly's behaviour and performance at school, disciplinary measures at home. Relentlessly, like a cross examiner with a stubborn witness, Amanda plied her with questions regarding the atmosphere in the household which Katherine replied to as honestly as she could. She only faltered slightly when asked about Kelly's and Jeremy's relationship but said it was perfectly normal, and now that Jeremy was a young teen, he barely interacted with her anymore. All the time Amanda took notes, nodded occasionally and mumbled in apparent satisfaction. After what seemed hours had gone past, Amanda appeared to have run out of questions and wanted to wander around the house, starting with the kitchen. Surprised, Katherine agreed.

Amanda opened cupboards, the fridge. She nodded, taking notes while complimenting Katherine on her house being so clean. Then she turned to Katherine, looking more serious.

"Obviously, because your daughter isn't able to respond to any questions as yet, we're unable to clarify exactly what happened, but you do understand we have to take such matters very seriously. From what you've told me so far and from what I've seen, I don't see any evidence to suggest Kelly is being abused or harmed in any way. Again, I won't be able to complete my report until I've spoken to her, but for now, I'm going to assume that what you said to the police is correct; someone somehow managed to enter your home, or lured her outside, violently attacking her. Perhaps a kidnapping attempt. This isn't precisely the safest village in the world which is very sad, so all we can do for now is wait for Kelly to recover. Whoever harmed her, I hope they catch them and put them in Northgate for the rest of their life."

And with that, Amanda left.

After Katherine prepared Jeremy his dinner and left his clothes folded in his room, she returned to the hospital, still somewhat confused that Amanda hadn't outright accused her of almost beating her daughter to death. It made her wonder how many other kids were out

Loneliness is a Monster

there in toxic households and going unnoticed.

The next day, Katherine awoke with a start. There was a buzz in the room, nurses and doctors busy chatting and flitting about. She opened her eyes and immediately saw what the source of the excitement was. Kelly was whispering to a nurse sat next to her.

Katherine gasped and jumped up. She rushed to her daughter's side, wanting to hug her effusively but scared in case she hurt her. Instead, she took Kelly's hand, kissed and embraced it before leaning over and kissing her forehead. The colour had returned to Kelly's cheeks and lips, yet it was obvious she was still weak, barely able to raise her voice over a whisper. After a couple of minutes of asking how she felt, was she okay, did she need anything, the doctor politely asked her to step aside so they could continue monitoring her.

Just a couple of hours later, after waiting for Kelly to wake up from another nap, the detectives arrived, wanting to speak to her in private. And as Katherine later found out, so did Amanda. But Katherine never heard any more from either of them. It seemed the case had been closed. Something she would come to think about and regret, years later, when Jeremy's face appeared on the national news.

Chapter 15

Nothing could have prepared Jeremy for that fateful morning. It came as such a shock, for a moment he wondered if it was a sick prank she was playing on him, perhaps somehow having discovered he'd been hiding under her bed and wanted payback. It was a Monday morning, and this was not how he hoped the week was going to start. He'd gotten away with the harm inflicted upon his sister just a few days earlier and had been feeling invincible. It seemed he could do no wrong. His mother had kept her mouth shut with the police and the child services lady. She hadn't said a single word to him about it, acting as though nothing had happened, although he had caught her staring at him sometimes when she thought he wasn't looking. What appeared to be a look of hate in her eyes. But that was fine with him. As long as she did as expected of her and kept her mouth shut, there was nothing for her or anyone to worry about. He had to admit to himself, though, when Kelly finally came home and he saw the state she was in, that he had gotten a little carried away with his treatment of her. Too late now though, and besides, it hadn't been entirely his fault.

All weekend, he'd been thinking obsessively about Mandy and how he might go about ensuring she didn't leave him. Removing the husband completely from the equation had been his first thought and how he might go about doing it, but whatever he decided, he couldn't rush things. That could be disastrous. Careful planning was required.

And now this.

He had been sitting at the back as usual, ignoring the snickering and snide looks and comments from classmates, lost in his thoughts as he watched Mandy enter the room. She looked radiant as always, beautiful, meant for him. Born for him and him alone. It was clear from the moment she stepped in, purposefully avoiding catching his eye, that she was in love with him, too, embarrassed or worried about looking his way and blushing perhaps, alerting others of their secret relationship. Jeremy sat, enthralled, as she stood at her desk, cleared her throat, and addressed the class.

"Good morning, everyone. Hope you all had a good weekend. I have some news for you all today which I'm not sure if you'll be happy about or not, but this will be my last day with you. I'm kind of sad to be leaving seeing how I only just started recently, but an opportunity has arisen for my husband at work, so we'll be moving north for the foreseeable future."

A few groans resounded around the room, but Jeremy barely heard them. He sat, jaw dropped in utter disbelief, unsure whether he had imagined what he just heard or not. Maybe he was still in bed having the worst nightmare of his life. But the warm tears slowly streaking down his cheeks suggested otherwise. He wanted to jump up and call her a traitor, rush over to her and slap her across the face for playing such a cruel prank on him, but he did none of those things. His legs were too unstable anyway.

She didn't even give him the slightest glance as she spoke, looking around the room, addressing everyone except him and he didn't know how to interpret this. Was it a joke and she would grab him later, in private, to tell him she was ready to start a new life with him? He didn't think so. There was something about her mannerisms, looking very happy with herself, that suggested she was telling the truth, as though having removed a massive weight from sagging shoulders.

The rest of the day passed with Jeremy barely aware of anything happening around him, incapable of concentrating on the tasks put before him, and when the day ended, his only thought was to follow her home for what could be the very last time.

It took her a while to leave after the last bell went. Jeremy hid near the staff room, listening to the other teachers wish her all the best and Jeremy had to resist with all his will power to run to the toilet and throw up. Throw up and ball his eyes out in rage, frustration and despair. Because listening to them he now knew it was true. It hadn't been a joke, after all, she was leaving him, never to return.

Finally, she left the staff room and headed with a big smile on her face towards home. Jeremy followed, making sure to keep far enough away so she wouldn't see him. The knot in his stomach grew with each step, as if he was walking down death row, imminent finality awaiting him. He had to force himself not to call out her name, beg her to reconsider, tell her that she was making a terrible mistake, but he did none of these things. Instead, when she finally reached the gate to her house, he watched her stroll leisurely down the path, the door opening, revealing both her husband and daughter there to greet her.

He couldn't hear what was being said, only that the girl was laughing and squealing and the husband with his arm around her. He gave her a kiss on the lips, a big smile on his face. Jeremy caught the words, "finally over," and, "new life," and his nightmare was once again confirmed. He wondered if he would have time to kill the husband before they all left but knew in his heart it would be a big mistake. Being rash and impatient was how most of his idols had been caught and that was not going to happen to him.

Jeremy watched all three enter the house, the door close, signifying the closure on another dream of his. The door slamming shut might as well have been his dreams and ambitions locked forever from him, the key thrown down a drain. Dejectedly, Jeremy turned around and headed back home. He might have taken out his frustrations on his sister but right now, he didn't even have the energy for that. But should Mandy and her family ever return, she would never be leaving him again. Of that, he would make damn sure.

It took time, a long time, but Jeremy's thoughts and dreams slowly turned in other directions. For the first few months after Mandy's departure, he could barely concentrate in class. Mandy's replacement was another woman, much younger this time, and he resented her with all his heart, as though it was her fault Mandy had left in the first place. She wore makeup, blouses that showed too much cleavage and skirts showing too much thigh. He hated her, privately calling her Miss Slut when talking to himself at nights. His grades dropped because school didn't matter anymore. Nothing mattered.

He didn't even care that the bullies continued their relentless onslaught. The girls took delight in making fun of the acne that now ravaged his face. The boys cornered him behind the bike sheds, asking him if he was still a virgin, how many times a day did he masturbate. Did he masturbate while fantasising over having sex with his mother, as if they could read his mind too, know his secrets. On one occasion, one kid pulled his trousers and pants down at the entrance to school, snapping the braces holding them up. On full view to all the boys and girls passing by, he was subjected to horrific torment for weeks over the size, or lack of, between his legs, to the point they questioned him as to whether he was really a girl in disguise.

This infuriated him, sparking a new rage as his masculinity was called into question. Especially as he still considered himself the man of the house at home, above everyone else. Sometimes he took out his frustrations on Kelly, beating her with a stick or whip, but always careful not to leave marks on her where they might be visible. His mother still said nothing, regardless.

But six months later as the others in his school became more interested in the opposite sex, his depression began to lift, and he started focusing more on his schoolwork. Jeremy decided he was going to dedicate himself fulltime to getting the best grades possible, and when he finally finished school at sixteen, would move on to university, study business management and get himself the best job possible. Move away from this village and start fresh.

And so he did.

And when some three years later, at sixteen, he was top of the school in almost all grades, a new sense of accomplishment filled him with pride. He was ready to move away from home, leave his stupid mother and sister behind and prove to the world what he was really made of.

Until he overheard the two teachers talking to each other towards the end of term.

Mandy Cogsworth and her family were returning.

Chapter 16

"Welcome home!"

Adrian opened the car door then parked Jane's wheelchair beside it so she could ease herself in. Normally, Adrian and Mandy would have helped her but now she refused, saying she was perfectly capable of doing it herself. Which, Mandy had to admit, she was. Now fifteen, she was even more independent and determined than before. She was stubborn and insisted she could do everything alone, even easing herself into the bathtub which previously had been impossible without risking a nasty injury. Both Mandy and Adrian were beyond proud of her, confident she was going to lead a productive and happy life. She'd even met a boy while living away, also in a wheelchair, and they had promised to stay in touch. They had often left together in the afternoons to go to the local specialised sports centre, playing basketball or building their muscles up at the gym. Jane hardly even needed the help of a carer most times, being able to cook herself now, too. When they gave her the news that Adrian's job had finished and they planned to return to Bradwell, they expected her to be upset now that she had a new best friend. She was but she fully understood. Such was her father's job. She expected it and already made plans to visit her friend in the summer if she could get a part-time job somewhere and save some money. Mandy and Adrian had almost cried at her understanding response, such had been their nervousness before giving her the news.

A big smile was on Jane's face as she took in her new home. It was a bungalow just as they had before, with a ramp so she could enter and leave of her own accord. Another step towards total independence.

"Nice touch, Dad! Thanks!"

"Thought you'd like it. Even the kitchen has been modified so you can reach the cupboards and cook for yourself any time you like. Means me and your mother have to squat but hey, what are friends for?!"

Jane laughed and pushed herself up the path and inside, leaving Adrian and Mandy alone. Adrian kissed his wife on the cheek as they took in their new surroundings, a quiet road near to the school where Mandy planned on attending, once they were settled. A specialised bus would come and pick up Jane in the mornings to take her to nearby Belton High School and Adrian had a big job awaiting him nearby, that would hopefully mean he would be coming home earlier in the evenings.

While Mandy had enjoyed her time down south, she had been glad they were returning to Bradwell. It was a small village, the nearest town was five miles away so there was no danger of it encroaching on them, and not too far away was Fritton Woods. A place they could go at the weekends, follow the river and enjoy the countryside, perhaps have lunch at one of the bars while taking in the scenery. Mandy had never been much of a city person; too many people, too much noise and congestion. This was the perfect place to settle down—Adrian's job permitting—and with any luck, Jane would agree. She was even looking forward to going back to teaching again.

"I love it!" exclaimed Jane as she looked around her new bedroom, bars on the walls beside the bed so she could help herself in and out each night and morning. Her writing desk to study in the corner, complete with new monitor and keyboard, everything set at the perfect height. From her window she could look out onto the back garden, spacious and tidy with a barbeque over in

Loneliness is a Monster

the far corner.

"Thought you'd like it," said a beaming Adrian. "And we got one more piece of good news. As soon as I get paid, my bonus for finishing the last job on time, that motorised wheelchair should be arriving sooner rather than later!"

Such was her excitement Jane squealed in delight and almost fell out of her wheelchair as she reached to embrace her father.

With Jane not having to start school until the following Monday, Mandy awoke early and checked in on Jane, as was her custom, regardless of whether she had to get up or not. Even though she was a teen girl, strong and independent, Mandy still couldn't shake the idea that perhaps something might have happened to her during the night. Fallen out of bed maybe, banging her head, leaving her with concussion and unable to call for help. Adrian had tried to reassure her countless times she was just being paranoid and needed to leave the girl alone, but years of worrying about the slightest thing had instilled in her a protective instinct that wouldn't go away. The day Jane eventually left for college or university on her own, caused chills to skate up Mandy's body.

Jane was fine, so Mandy headed downstairs to make coffee and prepare breakfast before starting her first day back at Bradwell High School. As always, she was nervous, never quite sure what kind of class she was going to be dealing with. This, coupled with leaving Jane on her own all day, despite once more trying to convince herself she'd be fine, made her struggle to eat her toast. She considered calling a friend to come by and check on Jane a few times but forced herself to put her phone down and focus on the day ahead. Jane wouldn't be happy knowing someone had been sent to spy on her throughout the day.

It was because of all these doubts running through her mind as she headed off to school, she failed to notice the person watching her from a distance.

Jeremy had barely slept the night before. The excitement and anticipation had been too much. A day he thought was never going to come, he had submersed himself in his schoolwork, seeking to get the best grades possible so he could leave this shitty house and start elsewhere. He had already made up his mind, he was going to open a home security business, installing cameras in people's homes and businesses. One of the reasons for deciding on such a career was because he would be in high demand. Belton and the surrounding villages had seen more than their fair share of horrific crimes over the last few years, Northgate Hospital for the Criminally Insane looming in the background like a curse, so more and more people were having cameras installed in their homes. The demand far outweighed the supply.

But this wasn't his major reason. Putting cameras in for a living, especially for the most vulnerable—women living alone—it gave him the perfect opportunity to investigate, snoop and maybe even set up a few secret cameras here and there, as well. The law of averages dictated that somewhere was another woman like Mandy and his mother, who he could use all his charm on, that would fall in love with him. And by hiding cameras in their homes, he could watch them in private, fantasise about sleeping next to them. He would know everything about them and could use the information as bait. It had been reading about the BTK killer that gave him the idea and he loved it. The idea of spending his whole life alone was not one Jeremy contemplated.

So to hear the news, yesterday, that the woman he had dreamt about being with was finally coming back, meant sleep had been all but impossible. It had been through overhearing teachers talking about Mandy's return to work today, that he discovered the date, but as much as he had tried, he had been unable to discover her new address.

Which left him with only one option.

His heart was beating manically in his chest when he saw her finally approach the school. Such were his nerves, he thought he might throw up if he didn't somehow control them. He'd rehearsed everything he was going to say to her, had imagined a thousand scenarios where she'd apologise profusely for having abandoned him, that she never really wanted to go but had been left with no other choice. That she promised it would all be over soon and they could finally be together. Forever.

When she was a few yards away, he stepped out from behind the large oak tree he'd been hiding behind, and grinned. At first, she didn't even notice him, seemingly lost in her thoughts. Jeremy coughed and blocked her path, yet even then she almost walked straight into him.

"Oh, sorry," she said, and made to walk around him. A pang of doubt and unease clawed at his still manic heart.

As she tried to walk around him, he shifted, blocking her path again.

"Sorry, I'm late for work, would you mind letting me pass?"

Okay, three years have passed. You're bigger, stronger. She's nervous about starting work again. Don't panic.

"It's me! You don't recognise me? I know it's been a long time, three years, and I'm bigger now, but you look exactly the same as when you left. Fortunately!"

She looked at him for a few seconds, frowning as though trying to find some long lost memory. Then she shook her head. "No, I'm sorry. I think you've mistaken me with someone else. Can I please get past?"

Jeremy's shoulders sagged, he felt his stomach drop, despair creeping into his system like a poison. "Jeremy. Jeremy Chan. I was in your class. The one at the back. We...we were friends."

Then, as she looked him up and down, it seemed to dawn on her, but instead of a smile appearing, a look of shock replaced the frown. She took a step backwards as though he might attack her.

"Oh. Oh yes, Jeremy, I remember now. Nice to see you. Look, I really have to go, okay? Take care."

And before he could stop her she hurried off, constantly looking behind her until she entered the school grounds. Jeremy watched her go, once more feeling sick but for a different reason. Time seemed to stop as she disappeared into school, everything around him becoming fuzzy and distant as though he was wearing the wrong glasses. His legs wobbled as if the bones had suddenly turned to rubber, and he had to grasp onto the tree to stop himself from collapsing to the ground.

Jeremy replayed the whole incident, which had lasted less than two minutes, in his head, wondering if he had missed some secret code between them. But he knew he hadn't. Mandy didn't have the slightest idea who he was and when he told her, instead of being elated and overjoyed at being reunited with him, had seemed almost terrified of him. She hadn't been waiting for him all this time, hadn't been secretly in love with him, planning to leave her husband to be with him. He had been a nobody in her life, just another kid, but, judging from her reaction, one who had given her the creeps.

Despair slowly turned to rage. His hands instinctively curled into fists, drool ran down his chin from a twisted sneer on his face. All this time, she'd been lying to him, leading him along, unable or unwilling to face her true feelings for him. A coward. Well, he was going to change all that. Forget college and university, he was going to prove to her the undeniable truth. Make her see and understand that she couldn't hide her real feelings from him, or anyone, anymore. And the first thing he had to do was get rid of the husband, the person responsible for Mandy failing to think straight.

Sobbing quietly to himself, Jeremy returned home and began preparing. By the time he was finished, Mandy would be begging for his undivided attention and love.

Chapter 17

The sound of screaming caused Adrian to grunt, and for his eyes to flutter. He absently rubbed the stubble on his chin and resumed snoring again until a further scream awoke him from his lethargy. He grunted again and this time his eyes opened fully. He looked around the room, confused until he realised he must have fallen asleep on the sofa. It had been a late night at work, going over the plans at his new job with his boss. When he got home, rather than head up to bed, he had decided to curl up on the sofa with a beer and watched a movie. When the scream came again, this time his senses were alert, his immediate thought something having happened to Jane until, blinking several times to wipe the sleep from his eyes, he relaxed when he realised the screaming was coming from the TV. Some horror movie was playing, and it was a girl in the middle of being stabbed multiple times by her assailant. Annoyed, he fumbled for the remote and turned off the TV.

Adrian figured it must be late, but he was so comfortable, he wasn't sure he really wanted to get up and climb the stairs to bed. He would surely end up spending an eternity trying to get back to sleep again. But at some point Mandy would wonder where he was and come get him, anyway. Groaning, he slowly pushed himself up. Then it hit him; something wasn't quite right. Still half asleep and groggy, putting the blame on the four beers he'd had instead of the one he had planned on, he tried to stand, gripping the side of the sofa to stop himself falling. That was when he realised the problem; he couldn't walk. Something was stopping him from moving his feet. Adrian tried to take another step forward then had to quickly grab onto the sofa with both

Loneliness is a Monster

hands to stop himself falling over.

Now, fully awake, he looked down at his shoeless feet.

"What the fuck?" he muttered.

His feet were tied together with a piece of rope. His initial thought was maybe he'd gotten drunk last night and had played some stupid game with Mandy or Jane but he knew full well he hadn't been drunk and besides, neither of them were into the kind of games that involved tying someone up. They'd been in bed asleep anyway. The trouble was he also knew full well he hadn't done it himself, either. His heart taking a sudden leap into his throat, Adrian spun around.

"Hello, thief," said a voice, and suddenly Adrian found himself on the floor, a terrible, dull ache in the back of his head.

"You stole my bride. You took her from me, far away, so I couldn't have her. You're a thief and you're going to pay for ruining our relationship."

His vision blurry, teeth gritting against the pain in the back of his head, Adrian tried to think who the hell this person might be, and what they wanted. It had to be a case of mistaken identity. What this person was saying made no sense, even if he did know about them having moved away. There was absolutely no way Mandy was the type of person to have an affair with anyone or even so much as flirt with another man.

"What? Got nothing to say about it? Feeling sorry for taking her from me, are you? Yeah, I bet you are. I bet you didn't even want to come back here, keep her as far away from me as possible. I know. I was listening to you discuss it one night in bed. I heard you two fucking."

"Wh-Who are you?" he said. "What do you want? You've gotten us mistaken for someone else. I'm sure—"

107

"You think after all these years I've mistaken you for someone else? Are you really that stupid? Your stupid face has been on my mind for years. I could never forget. Mandy was mine, you bastard and you tried to take her from me!"

It was then Adrian realised he might be in serious trouble. Whoever this person was, they were obviously mentally disturbed and unless he figured a way out of this, it might not end well for him or his family.

"Look, listen," he said, as he tried to rise slowly, attempting to undo the rope around his ankles. The darkness was his ally right now. "I don't know who you are or what you want, but I swear I don't know what you're talking about. Why don't we just put this down to a misunderstand—"

Before Adrian could react, the intruder rushed around to his side of the sofa and delivered a kick to his face, shattering two of his teeth, and, he suspected, fracturing a cheekbone. But despite the pain, saving his family was his total priority, so he ignored it and tried to grab the person. He was too late, though. Before he could react, a length of rope was wrapped around his wrists and tied so tightly, it almost cut off the circulation to his hands. Then before Adrian could scream for help, warn his family to call the police, a strip of duct tape was placed over his mouth. Writhing and struggling, Adrian tried to make sense of this new horror, when the intruder headed over to the light switch and turned on the light.

Adrian had absolutely no idea who the person was in his living room but the very last thing he expected was to see a kid standing there, barely out of school. Such was his shock, he forgot about struggling. The idea it was a mistake was still strong in his mind until an idea slowly formed in his muddled brain. A comment from his wife a few years ago when she was teaching at Bradwell High

School. What had been the suggestion he might be in serious trouble, suddenly transformed into outright terror. This wasn't some burglar who had mistakenly gone to the wrong house, but someone who was very disturbed and dangerous. For him to still be obsessed over his wife after all this time meant he was to be taken very seriously indeed.

His mouth full of blood, Adrian tried to reason with him but the way the kid was staring down at him, utter scorn and hate etched into his face, told him he was going to have to use force if he wanted to get out of this alive.

"Kid, listen to me. You're wrong. I didn't try to take Mandy from you or anyone. My job, I work all over the country. She…she's not even here right now. She went back to where we were staying to colle—"

Another kick, this time to his groin, caused him to double over in agony before he felt himself being dragged to his feet and led away. The wind had been taken from him such had been the force of the kick and he was utterly incapable of resisting, even though he was much bigger and stronger than the kid. Feebly, he tried to punch the kid using both hands as a makeshift fist, but he might as well have been swatting away a fly.

Adrian could do nothing as he was dragged towards the back door and then outside. The kid, barely struggling with the bigger man, stopped when they reached the shed at the bottom of the garden. He used his foot to kick the door open then bundled them both inside. With no idea what to expect, yet praying the boy left his wife and daughter alone upstairs, Adrian was once again stunned when he saw the state of his shed. Not only had this intruder broken into his home and had been standing over him, waiting for him to wake up, but it seemed that beforehand, he had been preparing the shed for when it occurred.

In the middle of the spacious shed, a chain and pulley had been set up, attached to a thick wooden beam that ran across the middle. Adrian's heart dropped, as did his stomach. This kid had been planning for some time and didn't appear to have been worried about being caught. He must have broken into their home, saw Adrian fast asleep on the sofa, then gone to the shed and prepared things with no concern at all. A series of gardening and building tools and accessories, were also carefully laid on a workbench in the corner. This simple fact, that this wasn't some enraged kid acting on a spur of the moment thought, but one with a callous, calculating mind was what caused claws of panic to grip into Adrian's body, sending him writhing and panicking like never before. He tried to headbutt the kid, knee him in the groin, anything to get away, but no matter what he tried, he failed. The kid simply stepped aside any advances he made. Then he grabbed a screwdriver, wrapped an arm around Adrian's head and pointed the head of the screwdriver mere centimetres from his eyeball.

"I will do it, you know. Don't think I won't – if you don't stop struggling. And then I'll ram it up your invalid daughter's dirty, little pussy."

This was all it took for Adrian to stop resisting. The mention of his daughter reminded him it wasn't just his safety at risk here. He would do anything the kid wanted as long as he left his wife and daughter alone.

"Good, that's better," he said, then proceeded to wrap the hook of the pulley around Adrian's wrists and started hoisting him into the air. He stopped when Adrian's feet were dangling just off the ground, Adrian's arms feeling as though they might be torn from their sockets at any moment.

"I don't suppose you know me, do you? Just an

insignificant kid from school with a crush on your wife? But you are so wrong. My name is Jeremy, and your wife was—is—in love with me. From the moment we first set eyes on each other. Ours was a secret relationship and our plan was to elope together but you had to ruin it, didn't you? Take her away from me. Steal her from me. You ruined my life! Everything was carefully planned out for her to leave you and take me instead. I even thought about killing myself, you know that? That's how distraught and depressed I was.

"Nothing mattered anymore, I just wanted to die. But guess what? God must have seen my suffering because He brought her back to me again. It's meant to be, you see? The only problem is you."

With the duct tape across his mouth he couldn't speak, but even if he could, Adrian had no idea how he might respond to Jeremy's obvious delusions. This was taking the idea of having a crush on someone to a whole new level. The kid was mad, obsessed, and it seemed nothing would make him see sense in the madness. The thing that worried Adrian the most, though, was what was he going to do to him. The grimy lightbulb to his left didn't give off much light but he could still clearly see Jeremy's face, scrunched into a sneer, eyes that showed complete and utter contempt and hate for him, as though confronted with something foul and grotesque that must be annihilated immediately. And this was what made Adrian fear most for his life.

As though Jeremy could read his thoughts, he turned around and produced a Stanley knife from the workbench. Adrian whimpered as the kid began to cut through his clothes leaving him completely naked. Immediately, goosebumps covered his body and not just from the intense cold in the wooden shed. Jeremy was staring at his groin as if seeing a penis for the very first time. Sweat now started pouring from Adrian's forehead and armpits, despite the cold. He whimpered again when Jeremy turned around and started searching for something. Adrian was not the kind of person that endured pain easily. He frowned when Jeremy turned around again and held a rubber band in his hand.

"You dared to continue violating my beautiful lover's body even when she made it clear she wanted to leave you for me. With that thing dangling there. You poisoned her with it."

His whole body trembled and shook when Jeremy gripped his balls with one hand then wrapped the rubber band around them, causing them to double in size. He thought about trying to wrap his feet around Jeremy's head, squeeze as hard as he could until the kid fell unconscious but such was his terror, he could barely move them. Adrian winced and involuntarily jerked when Jeremy flicked his balls with his fingers sending an intense shudder up his body, his balls as though someone was squeezing them tight and twisting as hard as possible.

"You won't be doing it again, I can promise you that. She's mine now," said Jeremy as he searched for more items. Adrian's eyes widened in horror when he saw the drill in Jeremy's hand, a long, thin drill bit protruding from the end. Adrian tried to beg to be let down, using his tongue to loosen the tape, squirmed as hard as he could, hoping to snap the chain holding him up, not caring anymore if he angered the kid, even trying to kick him with both feet but all attempts were worthless. A sinister grin crossed Jeremy's face as he easily avoided being hit by Adrian then grabbed his throbbing balls. The pain that Adrian was subsequently submitted to was like something he could never have imagined in his whole life. In that moment he would have happily died as the

Loneliness is a Monster

drill bit pierced the soft sac and continued probing until it popped out the other side like an emerging worm. It was as if his whole body had been set on fire and Adrian was barely aware of the fact his bladder had betrayed him. He writhed and struggled to no avail, muffled screams of agony as the drill bit was pulled out. When he looked down, a colourless, thick secretion was dripping onto the floor from the two holes and Jeremy was giggling to himself like a naughty schoolboy.

With his finger, Jeremy flicked Adrian's balls again, sending another white-hot bolt of agony up his spine. Then he introduced the drill again, this time drilling directly through his testicles, wiggling the drill bit as though trying to enlarge the hole he was creating before crudely pulling it out again. Adrian was on the verge of passing out, tears running down his face, eyes barely seeing anymore yet was still aware of Jeremy laughing, seemingly having the time of his life. When Jeremy returned the drill to the workbench, the tip dripping the same secretion, he prayed this was the end of his torture.

He wasn't so lucky.

It had only just begun.

"I think the punishment should fit the crime, you know. My father taught me that one. And I've learned so many things in the years since you took my love from me. That's a lot of suffering I had to go through. I wish I could keep you here suffering for the same amount of time, but unfortunately, it's not possible. My wife will probably wake up in around an hour's time to use the toilet as she does every night at the same hour. I've been watching you, see. And well, we don't want her stumbling onto this, do we? She'll get upset. So even now you're still getting off lightly. Which is a shame, really. But still…"

Adrian's wish to die right now increased tenfold

when Jeremy produced a can of lighter fuel, poured a generous amount over Adrian's ruined sack then set it on fire. Adrian was writhing so furiously he dislocated his shoulder in the process but didn't even realise it. His focus was on the destruction below rather than above. It was as if a thousand burning needles were being stabbed into his sac at the same time or someone had decided to try their hand at acupuncture and gotten too carried away. Adrian grit his teeth so hard, he felt some of them chip. Jeremy had his hands out in front of him as though warming them against an open fire, then after a few seconds of unfathomable agony, Jeremy grabbed a rag and gripped Adrian's sac to put out the flames. It did nothing to quench the torment though. The room quickly filled with the stench of burning flesh and hair.

"Well, I don't suppose you'll be using that again, will you? You should have left my wife alone to make her decisions."

Such had been the force with which Adrian grit his teeth and shook his head from side to side that the duct tape across his mouth came loose.

"Help!" he yelled as loud as possible, tiny pieces of enamel spat across the room. "Please! Please stop. I'll leave right now. I'll go away and never come back, but please stop!"

"Too late."

"Hel—"

But before he could finish screaming another plea for help, Jeremy grabbed a pair of pliers from beside him on the workbench and jabbed them into Adrian's mouth, firmly gripping his tongue. He pulled hard, Adrian's head jerked forward. Then he grabbed a Stanley knife, also from the workbench, and in one deft move, sliced it off. A gush of blood spurted from his mouth, a fresh bout of agony shooting down the back of his throat, followed quickly by a river of crimson.

"Scream now."

As much as Adrian wanted to, he couldn't. his mouth was too full of blood that he failed to spit out quick enough. It was clear that his life as he knew it was over. All he wanted was for this to end quickly and for his wife and daughter to be spared. He tried to say as much but this too was impossible. A fresh stream of urine ran down his legs as his body jerked against the spasms of agony throughout his body.

"See, this is all your fault. If you had just let her follow her true feelings none of this would have had to happen. And now we must finish this, I'm afraid. As much as I'd like to stay and continue, my wife will be waking up any second."

Adrian was barely aware he was being lowered until his body slapped hard against the wooden floor, his ruined testicles smashing against it, a feeling as though someone had stomped as hard as possible on them. His face hit the floor hard too, sending shockwaves through his brain.

Sensing this as his only chance to save himself, ideas of dying temporarily abandoned, he tried to push himself to his feet, using whatever remaining strength he had to knock the kid out, but every attempt to move his legs felt as if someone was kicking him in the groin again. But still he tried.

"Going somewhere?" asked Jeremy, as he turned around and toe-punted Adrian in the mouth, shattering more teeth.

Jeremy held something in his hand but with Adrian's blurred vision, unconsciousness blissfully close, he was unable to see what it was.

"You know, reading about some of my heroes gave me so many ideas. You know what they used to do in asylums years ago? Probably at Northgate too before they had a change of heart. I'm going to show you. I'm not entirely sure how it works though, but I think I have an idea."

In Jeremy's hand was the power drill again. Adrian could only watch in horror as the kid squatted beside him, raised his legs with one hand and crudely inserted the drill bit into his anus. Then turned it on.

It roared to life. Jeremy wiggled and made a circular motion with the drill, tearing open the entrance, blood and flesh splattering the walls and floor around them, even covering Jeremy who seemed oblivious. Yet again, it was as if someone had impaled him with a white-hot poker. He could feel internal organs rupturing, moving around inside him as the drill bit smashed everything inside to smithereens. Barely conscious, Adrian was aware the drill seemed to have gotten stuck, Jeremy using both hands to try and free it. When he did, he fell backwards, such was the force required to do so.

"Well, it works!" said Jeremy, a smile on his face as though trying out a new toy. "Now to finish things off."

Adrian swiped feebly at him as the boy straddled him and directed the drill bit at one of Adrian's eyeballs. It punctured it easily, tiny pieces of the gelatinous material spraying Jeremy too, sticking to his face like bits of jelly. It was the last thing he saw and the last thing he felt was the drill bit easing its way into his skull like a burrowing worm then finally his brain.

Mandy groaned. Why she had to go through this ritual every single night she didn't understand. It wasn't like she drank gallons of water or anything, so why the need for her bladder to torment her every time? She tried to resist, ignore it and hope to fall asleep again, but her brain refused to accept the challenge and she was left with no choice. Groaning louder, she opened her eyes, and threw the blanket back, but before she got up, she turned on the little lamp her side of the bed, not wanting to stub a toe on her way to the toilet.

Adrian was beside her and it made her jealous every time how he never seemed to suffer this way, despite the beers he liked to drink in the evenings. Sometimes, for fun, she liked to nudge him when getting out of bed on purpose. A little game they played back when they were much younger. She grinned, deciding to do so now, and looked over her shoulder.

"Hello, my love, we're finally together. I took care of everything."

It took Mandy a few seconds to understand what was happening, but through the blood-splattered face she eventually understood it wasn't her husband lying next to her but the creepy kid from school. Before she could scream, he clamped his hand over her mouth and wrapped an arm tightly around her neck.

Chapter 18

Mandy's body stiffened with fear, even her bladder that seconds ago had called desperately to be emptied. Jeremy's face was inches from her own, his warm breath smelling of rotten meat, splashes of dried blood across his cheeks and forehead, and small blobs of something sticky dotted everywhere. That Adrian wasn't here beside her made her fear the worst and instinctively her thoughts went to Jane in the room next door. What had this maniac done and what was he planning were the other thoughts colliding in her scrambled brain. It was as if the mythical bogeyman had come to life and was sharing her very own bed with her, nefarious thoughts in its mind that would never end well.

"It's okay, my love, you don't have to be scared. I would never hurt you. Why would I?" he murmured, then kissed her cheek.

Dozens of other thoughts ran through her mind. What had he done to Adrian? Was he even alive or dying slowly in great agony downstairs somewhere? For surely it had to be his blood and whatever else it was that adorned his face. Did the same fate await her and more importantly her daughter? This boy obviously had some sick, twisted crush on her and was not well in the head. How was she ever going to get out of this? Would he rape her? Jane?

"I know you're scared right now, but honestly, you don't have to be. From now on, everything is going to be just fine. It's what we both wanted, right? To be together forever. And now we are. Your husband can't bother us anymore or get in the way. It was his fault we weren't together sooner, taking you away from me like that. On purpose.

"My guess is he knew about our secret and wanted to stop us. Well, he underestimated me, didn't he. Nothing could ever come between us, and it won't."

A sob escaped her, despite the bloodied hand still covering her mouth. One of her questions had just been answered. Her husband, the one and only true love in her whole life, first and only boyfriend, was surely lying dead somewhere and this maniac hadn't even bothered to clean the blood from his face before getting in beside her. And the more she looked at his face with bulging, terrified eyes, the more she thought she knew what those little blobs were. Jeremy's whole body stank of coppery, dried blood.

"Now, I'm going to remove my hand okay, so you're not going to scream for help or do anything stupid, are you? No one would be able to hear you anyway, just Jane, and I'm sure you wouldn't want her to wake up and do anything stupid, either. Because that would make me angry and as the man of the house, it probably wouldn't be a good idea to make me angry. My sister can testify to that."

All Mandy wanted was this kid as far away from her as possible so she could call the police. Part of her was listening to what he was saying, another part of her brain was remembering every little detail it could about this boy and as she went through the history of their lives together, the more terrified she became. This kid had been infatuated with her for years. She could picture him now as an adolescent glaring at her when she started work as a teacher for the first time. She remembered taking Jane to buy herself something for her birthday and someone tipping her from her wheelchair in the middle of the shop. She knew now that it had been Jeremy and most likely had not been an accident at all. Bumping into him again after returning to Bradwell the other week and the look on his face when she didn't recognise him. He looked as though he might burst into tears, then very shortly afterwards, there had been something in his eyes that scared her. This was not a boy who had developed a sudden crush on her but someone who had had that crush for years. And had just killed her husband because of it.

His hand slowly came away from her mouth. She gasped, catching her breath. For one fleeting moment, she considered trying to run. Maybe to grab a knife or something, or just run out into the street and scream for help, but this quickly disappeared. Instead, her brain, acting in survival mode, suggested it would be in both hers and Jane's interests to do everything she could to not upset him, try and stall him and hope to get help later. If her maths were correct, he wasn't old enough to have a driver's license yet so he couldn't take them somewhere secluded, especially given Jane was in a wheelchair and she was in her own home. What could he do? Tomorrow, if she didn't appear at work or Jane at school, people would come looking for them.

"Good. I knew you wouldn't scream anyway. I realise it's hard to come to terms with one's true feelings and well, I know there's an age difference between us, but that shouldn't come in the way of true love, right? I accept it may take a little time for you to accept your true feelings but I'm patient. If anything, I'm extremely patient! I've had to wait a long time for this to happen!"

He kissed her again, this time on the lips and all she wanted to do was vomit. When she dared to glance down and saw him naked beside her, an erection brushing her belly, a whimper escaped dry, cold lips. The boy had to be around sixteen by now, old enough to have sex.

Please, please don't. Please don't do that.

The very idea that he might want to have sex with her, rape her, caused bile to rush to her throat. She might have told herself to comply with what he asked of her, tell him how handsome he was if necessary, that yes she would love to be his girlfriend, was one thing, but to allow him to do that to her was something completely different. She would fight to the death rather than let that happen. And the gleam in his eyes, plus the fact that with his free hand she could feel him stroking his erection suggested this was exactly what he wanted.

"Jeremy, listen. I understand you have certain feelings towards me, and I'm really honoured you should think that way, I really am, but…but this, this is different. I'm a happily married woman. I'm old enough to be your mother. My daughter is probably almost the same age as you.

"You need to…to be with girls your own age, and look, you're really attractive, I'm sure there are plenty of girls out there that would love to be your girlfriend, but not me, okay? You really need to understand that, because—"

"Shh. Don't. I get you're struggling to come to terms with how things will be from now on, but it's okay. I did it for you, so you didn't have to. I know this is awkward and going against everything I was taught growing up…See, my mother always said sex out of wedlock was a sin, but I've been waiting for this moment for so long. I've tried with other girls, even my own age, and it's just not the same. I'm not built that way. You're the only one, Mandy.

"So, as much as we shouldn't, I think we should start our relationship now. I think it will help you accept things as they are now. I'm sure you want to. All these years wishing it was me sleeping beside you instead of him. Well, now we can!"

He ran a hand across her breast then slowly began to lower it. Her pyjamas were thin, it being a warm evening, she shuddered and swiped his hand away roughly.

"No, Jeremy. And I mean it. I'm being very serious. You'll get into a lot of trouble unless you stop. Besides, look at you, you're covered in blood and...I don't know what. Why don't you go home, get showered and we can discuss things in the morning? I'll wait for you. I'll take the day off work so we can chat about how we move on from here. What do you say?"

Jeremy snatched his hand back as though she'd bitten it. His eyes widened, warped smile twisting slowly into a sneer. Drool ran from his mouth turning a pinkish colour as it met with the blood on his chin.

"Do you really think I'm stupid? Do you honestly believe I'm going to fall for that? Don't tell me you're just like all the others who took me for an idiot. The stupid girls at school who were so horrible to me. Me! The man of the house! No, I can't accept you're like them. No, you're confused. And yes, I admit, with all this blood on me I probably do look a little scary. I'll pretend I didn't hear that.

"So shall we, before Jane wakes up?"

He tried to run a hand across her breasts again, but she pushed him away even more violently this time and pulled the blanket up tighter to her neck. "Get your hands off me."

His eyes widened again. "You...you were being serious. You don't want me to touch you. You were lying all this time. Just like my mother. Just like all the others. You bitch. You lying little slut."

Now foam was forming at his mouth, as though rabid, eyes bulging unnaturally. "Mandy, I haven't waited all this time for you to deny your feelings for me. We both know we're in love and I'm not going to stop until you accept it."

Loneliness is a Monster

He pushed himself off her and for a moment Mandy thought he'd finally seen reason. Instead, he produced a length of rope from the floor and tied her wrists to the headrest, then stuck a piece of duct tape across her mouth. Mandy writhed and struggled but to no avail— she wasn't going anywhere. The terror invading her mind now, though, was about what he planned on doing with her. And her daughter.

"I'll be right back. Just have to get some things and we can start all over again."

He leaned over, kissed her forehead, dressed, then hurried out. When she heard the front door close, she struggled, desperately trying to free herself from her restraints. Ten minutes later, she was still struggling when she heard him return.

Her eyes widened in horror when she saw what he'd brought with him, a tripod and an old-fashioned video camera. Mandy's panic increased as she watched him set it up, the lens pointing directly at her, then began to undress, not even having bothered to wash the blood from his face as though he'd forgotten it was there. The lecherous grin on his face, plus the throbbing erection confirmed her suspicions. He turned on the camera.

Mandy's biggest fear in life, aside from anything happening to Jane, was to be raped. The idea of a man, a stranger, forcing himself on her, potentially getting her pregnant in the process, was her worst nightmare. And it looked like it was about to become reality. She tried to kick out at him with her feet, hoping to connect with his groin, but he was too far away and too quick. The grin on his face changed to a scowl, but his erection remained intact.

"Don't struggle, Mandy. You're just delaying the inevitable," he said as he climbed onto the bed.

But before he forced himself upon her, he spread her

thighs and simply knelt there staring at her vagina, a lecherous grin on his face, eyes sparkling, looking at her privates as though he never seen one before. Then he bent over, his face inches from her vagina and began to sniff, using the fingers of one hand to pry her pubic hair to one side. She could feel his nose brushing lightly against her, still sniffing like a hungry dog. Such was his shock she momentarily forgot about struggling, watching him as he probed and stroked her, mumbling to himself. A finger tentatively entered her. He pulled it out and sniffed it before running his tongue over his finger. He looked to be drooling as she watched, eyes now wide and bright.

"Wh…what are you doing?"

"So beautiful. Just like mother's. So pretty. We're going to have to shave you, though, to see it in all its glory. But first…"

Despite all her best efforts, she was powerless to resist as she felt him enter her. She thrashed and writhed, trying to squeeze her legs together, but he held them tight with each hand, forcing them back. She imagined her daughter wheeling herself into the room and Jeremy doing the same to her. She thought of her husband, probably lying dead downstairs, or maybe still alive but slowly dying from loss of blood. But most of all, she visualised being set free by Jeremy and grabbing whatever makeshift weapon she could find and beating him over the head again and again until he either died or fell unconscious. Mandy had never wished harm on anyone in her life before right now as he continued grunting, kissing her thrashing face, and thrusting inside her. She hadn't seen him put on a condom either.

Finally, after what seemed like hours, she felt him ejaculate inside her, that might as well have been poison he was injecting into her, Jeremy panting and shuddering

Loneliness is a Monster

as he did so, a massive grin on his face that she wanted to slice off with the biggest knife she could find. Instead, she sobbed at how powerless she was, hating this kid with every fibre of her body, feeling dirty and nauseous.

"There, see, it wasn't so bad, was it? I knew you'd enjoy it. Thank you for letting me. I'd been wanting to for so long. Next time it will be much easier, I promise.

"Now, I have to go home and get showered before my mother wakes up. I'm going to tie Jane to the bed too, just in case, but I promise I won't do anything to hurt her. Not to my daughter, never. See you shortly, my love. We're going to have the best life together, just the three of us."

Mandy thought of trying to break free once again, but by now was too weak and dejected, for some reason also feeling shame for not having resisted harder. As if a part of her believed the madness Jeremy had been spouting. But instead, she did her best to keep calm and figure a way of getting Jeremy to let her go. Before he did anything worse to her or her daughter.

Chapter 19

The only nightmare Jane ever had begun shortly after the accident she suffered. It was a recurring nightmare too, one that would see her bolt upright in bed, sweating and panting, then throwing back the blanket to see that in part, it hadn't just been a nightmare. Part of it was real.

In it, she would be walking along the street with her parents when a car came swerving around the corner, tires screeching. The driver was drinking from a bottle of something, not looking where he was going. Before either of them could react, the car suddenly swerved, aiming directly at Jane's parents. There was a loud screech and when she turned around her parents were flying through the air. But not just this, both their bodies had been severed at the waist, their legs flying in opposite directions as though a bomb had exploded, seriously maiming them. As Jane screamed and ran towards them, she found it harder and harder to run, and it felt like she was sinking, growing smaller and smaller. It was only when she looked down to see that both her legs were missing too, she would wake up, a scream bubbling away at dry lips, then throw back the blanket and remember that instead of being a nightmare it had also been a cruel reminder.

She opened her eyes now, trying to think if the thuds and noises she had been hearing were part of her recurring nightmare or some other source. But she hadn't had the nightmare for years, having since come to accept her disability and adapting to getting as much out of life as she could. Despite the occasional pang of regret or jealousy when she saw friends running around on a sports field or doing things they took for granted though she would never be able to, she refused to dwell too

Loneliness is a Monster

much on the matter and carry on with her life. So if it hadn't been the nightmare, what had caused her to suddenly waken?

Jane glanced at the clock beside her bed. It was four in the morning almost, pitch black outside and not a sound to be heard except the occasional gust of wind. Maybe it had been her bladder that caused her to awaken but there was no dull throbbing and she had learnt a long time ago not to drink too much in the evenings for precisely this reason. Going to the toilet in the middle of the night was just one of many minor issues she had been forced to deal with.

Then she heard a voice, a man's voice but it didn't quite sound like her dad's which was deep and gruff, often joking he sounded like a dog barking when he spoke. This was more high-pitched, almost that of a woman's. Her first thought was either her mother or father were having one of their own bad dreams, or maybe her father had developed a loud snore, but she didn't think so. A bang came on the wall opposite, exactly where her parent's bed was, which caused her to grin then immediately grimace. Surely they weren't having sex at this time of night?

During the inevitable chat her mother had with her when she reached thirteen, her mother's views on sex and men in general had been unwavering and unapologetic; men only wanted one thing when they reached a certain age and sex was pretty much a taboo subject. Jane would go to hell if she lost her virginity before wedlock. So for them to be doing that this late at night seemed unlikely.

She decided one of them or both were having some kind of dream and would turn over and go back to sleep, when she realised something was terribly wrong. While trying to figure what had woken her in the first place, she tried to put her arm under her chest and that's when she found she couldn't. Neither could she move the other, as if she'd suddenly lost the use of them as well as her legs. Now more awake, she frowned when she saw her wrists were tied to the headrest. Her initial thought was she was still dreaming after all, but when she pulled her arms and the knots tightened causing her wrists to hurt, she knew she wasn't dreaming.

Wide alert, Jane tugged on the rope, panic and bewilderment tugging at her nerves at the same time. She was about to yell for her parents when the door opened. But it wasn't her father or mother that stepped inside; instead, it was a kid, perhaps her age, who for some reason seemed vaguely familiar.

"Hey, you're awake! Sorry if I woke you, I didn't mean to, I promise." The kid sat at the foot of the bed as if he was a regular member of the family.

"Wh-who are you? What are you doing in my home?"

"Well, good question. I don't suppose your mother bothered to tell you. It was always meant to be a secret anyway, until the right time came along. Which thankfully it has!"

"What are you talking about?" The way he was acting completely normal, as though he lived here, was making her even more nervous than if he was threatening her. And the fact her wrists were tied to the bed suggested this person had been in her home for some time.

"Well, umm, you see, for the last few years your mother and I have been having a secret affair. And, actually, telling you about it like this is kinda embarrassing, but now, well, I guess you could say it's not so secret anymore! Your mother and I are now officially a couple. Isn't that great? So I guess you will have to start calling me Dad from now on."

Jane couldn't believe what she was hearing. Was this

some kind of sick joke? Where was her father? Her birthday had passed months ago and it wasn't either of her parents' either so it being some kind of prank was impossible. And when the kid had told her this news, he had blushed, as though confessing to something naughty he'd just done. Given the way he was acting so naturally, she wasn't sure whether to scream for her parents or go along with what he was saying. Maybe the kid had mental issues and had escaped from Northgate Hospital for the Mentally Impaired. Better not to make him angry, but she needed answers. If ever Jane was conscious of the fact she was paralysed, it was now. She was at his complete mercy.

"Oh, umm, really? So…where's my mother now? And…my dad?"

"Well, your mother is in bed. I think she's tired. It's been quite the night. As for your father, well, he won't be interfering in our relationship anymore, so you don't have to worry about that. I, umm, took care of that, too. So as I was saying, from now on, as the man of the house, I'd appreciate it if you called me Dad."

Panic was starting to worm its way up Jane's body. The way he said he'd removed her father from the equation in such a nonchalant manner caused her heart to flutter in her chest. The idea that something terrible might have occurred was now a very real possibility. She considered screaming for someone to call the police. But what if no answer came? Tears welled, she noticed her hands were shaking. How had he got into their home? Dozens of questions ran through her mind and she had no answers for any of them.

"Umm, why are my wrists tied to the bed? Did you do that?"

"Yes, afraid so. I didn't want to risk you waking up and, well, catching us while we were in bed together, you know…"

"Well, can you please untie them. My arms are aching and my hands have gone numb. Please?"

"I could untie them for you, but you didn't say the magic word."

"Yes, I did. I said please."

"That's not what I'm talking about. You have to call me Dad from now on, I told you."

Despite the situation she found herself in, there was no way she was going to comply with his demands. The realisation that something terrible had happened to her father was growing with each second. The kid had no blood on him, but if he'd already been in the house for some time, tying her wrists while she slept, he would have had plenty of time to clean himself up. Her phone sat beside her on the bedside table but might as well have been a million miles away.

"No, I won't. I want to see my mother right now. Mum!" she yelled.

Something changed in the kid's expression. The smile vanished, the sparkle in his eyes was replaced by a darkness that seemed to obliterate all light around him. What sounded like a growl came from tightly pressed lips. Jane had never felt so vulnerable in her life as right now.

"Are you disobeying me, Jane? We've only just started out as a new family and you're already disobeying me? I know and understand about your disability but that's no excuse when it comes to showing respect to your father."

"You're not my father! You're some kid barely older than me! Mum!"

His eyes widened and his lips curled upwards. Before she could even prepare herself, he slapped her hard across the face.

Loneliness is a Monster

"Mum! Help! Someone, help!"

"You disobedient little bitch. I should have taken care of you too, I knew it. You call me by my title or you're in serious trouble, little girl."

"No, never! You freak. You bastard! Where's my dad? What did you do to him?"

"What did you just call me? You dare to insult your dad? On our first meeting?"

It was in that moment she truly understood he'd done something terrible to her father, who was a light sleeper by nature. By yelling out her mother's name, he would have awoken and come running by now. So would her mother. But Jane was determined not to give in to his demands. Unless he was completely deranged, she had to assume her mother was okay, probably tied to her own bed, too. Exactly what his plans were she couldn't begin to imagine, but at some point in the morning, people would start wondering where they all were. Giving him the pleasure of calling him Dad was not going to happen.

"You are not my dad. I don't know what you think you're doing but you're ill. You're sick! Freak!"

The kid gasped, then slapped her again, even harder this time. His face was bright red, eyes bulging. "Right, you little whore. You're gonna pay for that."

He left the room, slamming the door shut behind him. Jane once more tried to loosen the rope, screaming for her mother to come and help, but only silence answered her pleas. Until she heard the sound of quick thuds along the hallway. Jane braced herself for whatever he had in mind.

And when she saw what he held in his hands, she still had absolutely no idea, but her terror increased exponentially.

"If my father ever taught me anything, it was that one should respect their elders. Discipline and respect must go hand in hand. If you can't respect me, how can you ever respect yourself? You should ask my sister about it, she'll tell you what it means to disobey and disrespect me. Others too."

As he approached the bed, she saw he was carrying a cordless drill, a long, thin drill bit attached to it, covered in a suspicious dried, red colour. There was also something else attached to it and that was when she began to writhe and scream even louder. At first she had assumed it was some kind of punctured ball but as he grabbed one of her hands she realised she was very much mistaken. The punctured pupil right in the centre, wormlike, red tendrils hanging down meant it could be only one thing.

The kid leaned over and Jane took the opportunity to try and bite him, anything to get him to stop whatever he was about to do but he ensured he was always just out of reach.

"Please, please don't! I'm sorry! I'm really sorry! Please!"

"Too late now, Jane. You have to learn your lesson. You'll thank me in the long run."

Gripping her finger tightly, Jane could only watch in horror, her body tense in anticipation of what was to come, as he placed the tip of the drill bit against her fingernail and turned it on. The pain was excruciating, nothing she could ever have imagined before in her short life. Slowly but surely, it cracked the tough layer and worked its way through the nail until it reached the flesh then the hard bone of her finger, the kid twisting the drill to open the hole up bigger. When he pulled it out it was as if someone had set fire to her finger or simply cut it off. She sobbed, screamed, then begged harder when he took the next finger and repeated the process. He only stopped when he'd drilled through every fingernail of both hands, bits of nail, flesh and bone, flying everywhere, landing on her face like confetti. On the verge of passing out, she barely heard him telling her it hurt him more than it hurt her to have to do this.

"I have to go speak with your mother now. We have a lot to discuss. I'll leave you to think through what I told you. You should try and get some sleep too, you look stressed. I'll come and see you in the morning. If you've been a good girl, I'll let your mother make you breakfast. Goodnight."

He leaned over and kissed her forehead as if nothing had happened before he left, leaving Jane in utter agony and completely incapable now of moving any part of her body at all. For the first time in her life, she really did want to die.

Chapter 20

Jeremy sat in the living room sipping a glass of whiskey. He didn't like alcohol much, especially hard liquor, but figured that now he was the man of this house too, he should make an effort. The liquor cabinet was well stocked which meant the husband liked to enjoy a tipple now and again, and maybe Mandy did as well. If he could get used to the taste and the sensation of his stomach on fire when it reached it, they could share romantic evenings together here as they watched a movie or discussed their future.

And yet, judging from their first night together, it seemed it might take longer than he expected for her to come around to his way of thinking. To understand her true feelings for him. The more he thought about it, the more he was coming to realise he just didn't understand women at all. Not as much as he thought he did anyway. So unappreciative, just like his sister and mother. He'd gone to the trouble of removing the husband, getting himself dirty in the process, had shown her how much he loved her by giving her the best love making session she could ask for, and how had she responded? By rejecting him. Telling him it was all a mistake. Even to the point of insulting him, calling him the kind of names he detested. How could he possibly deserve such treatment after doing all that for her? He'd planned everything meticulously. And if that wasn't bad enough, the stupid bitch of a daughter had to start screaming and yelling, too. It appeared he was going to have to be a little bit more disciplined with both of them if this was going to work out as intended.

Unfortunately, though, he hadn't quite planned everything as well as he thought he had. There was a little problem he hadn't taken into account. His mind had been focused on one thing and one thing only—getting Mandy to understand why he was doing what he was doing and making her understand and accept it. After killing the husband last night then making love to his new wife, he'd been so tired he'd fallen asleep on the couch, leaving them both tied to their beds. When he woke up it was almost eight and there were missed calls and messages from his mother, asking him if he was okay, where was he, had he been in an accident? For this, he had already planned things out, telling her he had made some new friends and would be hanging out with them now and again—last night was his friend's birthday and they were having a party. This seemed to satisfy her, but it was when a mobile phone on the living room table began to ring shortly after eight, he realised his mistake. The first time, slightly panicking, he had answered it but said nothing, listening as someone asked Adrian why he hadn't arrived at work and where was he. Jeremy quickly hung up. A short time later Mandy's phone rang, which he had taken from her bedside table, just in case she managed to free herself and call for help. Again, he answered it but said nothing.

"Mandy, it's Christine. You didn't come to work today. Is everything okay? Mandy, you there?"

He quickly hung up just as before, then leaned back on the sofa and held his head in his hands. It was then he poured himself a shot of the husband's whiskey to calm his nerves. Of course, he'd forgotten all about their workplaces. Friends who would want to know where they were. His daughter's phone would surely start ringing at any second too—how was he going to deal with everyone who came looking for the husband and, more importantly, his new family? Really, though, for now, an immediate solution was quite easy. The whiskey causing his vision to blur slightly and for him to stumble as he quickly rose from the sofa, he headed to wake his wife taking both phones with him. Jeremy entered the room and was surprised to see her wide awake, eyes puffy and bloodshot. The second he walked in she began pleading with him once again which he was not in the mood for.

"Jeremy, listen, please, you have to stop. You have to untie me. I can't feel my arms. Where's Jane? Where's my daughter? Tell me you haven't done anything to her."

The questions and demands came in quick succession. Jeremy held up his arms for her to stop.

"Shh, stop. Our daughter is fine, she's asleep in her room and—"

"What was all that screaming last night coming from her room? You hurt her, didn't you? You bastard! I swear I'll kill you if you—"

"She's fine! We just had a little chat, that's all. She got a little upset when I told her she had to call me dad from now on, but she finally understood. Everything is going to be okay, don't worry. I'll take you to see her shortly, but I need you to do something for me first."

"Jeremy, please, I'm beggi—"

"Shh!" he said more sternly. "I'm going to untie you, yes, because I need you to do something. You have to phone some people. Do as I say, and don't do anything stupid, everything will work out perfectly. Do something stupid, say the wrong thing and I'm afraid I'll have to punish you both again. Does that sound fair? And once it's done, you can make us all breakfast! You must be hungry by now."

"Okay, anything, but promise you'll let me see my daughter."

"I promise, Mandy. A man must keep his word."

A relieved sob escaped her. Jeremy felt sorry for her

Loneliness is a Monster

in that moment—her pillow was wet from where she'd been crying so much, no doubt all night. Her arms and wrists must indeed be aching badly, too, he figured. Now he regretted having fallen asleep and leaving her alone. He went around to the other side of the bed, leaned over and kissed her forehead, then untied her. She groaned as her arms flopped beside her. He waited until the strength returned to her arms and wrists again, then handed her Adrian's phone.

"I need you to call his workplace—they've phoned once already today—and tell them he's ill. Covid or something, I don't care, but he won't be coming to work for a while and is asleep in bed. After that, you have to phone the schools and tell them the same about you and Jane. We can't have folks knocking on our door and disturbing us, can we?"

Hesitantly, Mandy agreed to dial all three places. Jeremy listened intently, in case any of those she phoned asked the wrong question or sounded like they might not believe her, but everything seemed to work out accordingly, even if her voice and excuses weren't the most convincing. Once she finished, he kept to his word. Both the front and back doors were locked and he had the keys, in case she tried to run, and he also took the phones and switched them off.

When they entered Jane's bedroom, Mandy let out a loud gasp and rushed to her daughter's side.

"Oh my God, what happened to you? What did he do? You bastard! You promised you didn't hurt her!"

Jane had been asleep when they walked in but on hearing the door open her eyes had shot open. Knowing at some point Mandy would want to see her, he had put rubber gloves on her hands to hide the injuries, but blood splattered the sheets.

"It was a misunderstanding, that's all. Right, Jane?"

Her mother hugged her, showering her with kisses while inspecting her for further damage.

"Are you okay, Mum? Did…did he hurt you? I think Da…he's dead."

"I'm fine. Don't worry, everything will be fine. Tell me you're okay. Why are you wearing gloves like that? What did he do to you? Let me see."

"It's…it's nothing. I'm okay," she said as her mother tried to pull the gloves off.

Both burst out crying, casting uneasy glances at Jeremy as if he might suddenly attack them. But he had no intentions of doing so. He was happy to see his wife and daughter like this, showing each other such affection. He hoped it wouldn't be too long before they treated him the same way. He left them like this for five minutes or so before telling Mandy she should prepare breakfast. Neither wanted to be separated.

"I need to go to the toilet," said Jane.

Last night after drilling through her fingers he'd moved the wheelchair across the room so she couldn't get to it and potentially escape. His idea had been to dispose of it or put it in the shed, not fully trusting of the girl, but he was confident he had everything under control and besides, it was true, she had to use the toilet somehow. There was no way he was carrying her there.

Once finished, he told Mandy to prepare breakfast while he sat with Jane at the kitchen table.

"This is so nice," he said. "Just as I imagined it would be, the three of us all happy, eating together, planning our future together. I think we're all going to be very happy!"

But neither Mandy nor Jane said a word.

It was the next day, after once more tying them to their own beds that night, despite their protests, that the first problem arose.

Loneliness is a Monster

It appeared that Mandy hadn't been convincing enough when it came to telling her boss she wasn't well. It was around ten in the morning as they were having breakfast when there was a knock at the door. Jeremy's heart jumped to his throat. Both Mandy and Jane visibly tensed, too, their eyes widening as they looked at Jeremy to see what he would do. He caught Jane giving her mother a sly glance and knew immediately what she was thinking. But it wasn't going to happen. He grabbed a large kitchen knife and hurried to the living room, peering out from behind a curtain then rushing back. He had two choices; ignore the woman at the door or answer it. If he ignored it, this would raise further suspicions so he gently grabbed Mandy by the arm and took her from the kitchen.

"It's a woman, permed, grey hair, about sixty."

"That's my colleague from work, Kirsty. She must want to see if I'm okay."

"Then you open the door, tell her you're really ill with Covid so she can't come in, then make her go away. Do anything stupid, you'll both regret it. Okay?"

Mandy nodded then Jeremy let her go answer the door, making sure he was close by but out of sight. He listened as they had a brief chat, nothing coming from Mandy that might cause him to panic and smiled as she made to close the door.

But it was when he heard Jane screaming for help at the other end of the hallway his smile vanished.

Fortunately, Mandy had closed the door at the exact same time so hopefully the woman never heard Jane's pleas for help, but he learned a lesson that day; Jane could not be trusted and he would have to ensure she never got the chance to try that little stunt again.

Chapter 21

The tears wouldn't stop falling after Jeremy raped her the first night. She had never felt so sick and dirty in her life. He'd even filmed the event. What was he planning on doing with the videos? Uploading them to some sleazy website? But even then, with Jeremy on top of her, her greatest fear had been the kid doing the same to Jane. Despite being raped being her biggest fear, she would have accepted it without question as long as he didn't touch Jane. When Jeremy promised her, he would do no such thing and the girl was quite safe, did the full horror of what he had done hit her.

After several minutes of sobbing, for her, Jane, and her husband, undoubtedly dead somewhere, she had begun to replay everything Jeremy had said in her mind. If it had been some intruder wanting their money and valuables, that was one thing, but this was infinitely worse. Homes got burgled all the time, it was almost a part of life, but this was completely different. This wasn't some unfortunate desperate for money, this was personal. Premeditated down to the last detail. He had to have been planning this for years and the most shocking and scariest part of the ordeal was that the kid really believed the mad things he was saying. No amount of bargaining or pleading on her behalf was going to change his mind; somehow this kid had gotten it in his head she was in love with him. To the point he'd murdered her husband. What else was this maniac capable of or willing to do?

Despite her utter terror at what he might do to her, or Jane, should either of them anger him, and what may lay ahead, she forced herself to calm down and think with a clear head. It wasn't easy but by panicking she wasn't

Loneliness is a Monster

getting anywhere. The first thing that struck her was Jeremy appeared to have overseen an obvious scenario. At some point, people were going to wonder where they were. Friends, family, colleagues from work. It wouldn't be long at all before they started getting worried and suspicious something had happened to them if all three weren't answering their phones. The very next day, in fact. She had only just started teaching again at the school so if she failed to turn up and not phone in to say she was sick, they would be immediately suspicious. Adrian was one of the most relied upon people at the construction site; his presence was imperative and his bosses would be demanding to know where he was. Same for Jane's school. So many people concerned meant that surely tomorrow morning after their calls and messages were not returned, they would come looking for them. How was Jeremy going to deal with that?

The simple answer was, he couldn't. If no one answered the door, someone would call the police. They would kick the door in if necessary and their nightmare would be over, Jeremy arrested and sent to prison for murder.

Another sob caught in her throat. Her poor husband, the kindest man she had ever met. The one who had been strong for all of them after Jane's life-threatening accident. She couldn't help wondering where he was right now, maybe still clinging to life as he bled out. Maybe, if she prayed hard enough, he would still be conscious when the inevitable help came tomorrow. She'd heard of lots of cases where people had been through unfathomable torture and injury yet miraculously survived the ordeal. Adrian was strong— she just had to pray and keep her hopes up. When Jane suffered her accident, they had both prayed she would survive, and it had worked. When they were at church or at the hospital, praying Jane wouldn't have too many lasting scars or trauma at losing movement in her legs, these pleas had also been answered. Now was the time to ask Him for one more favour.

At some point, she had managed to drowse for a short time until she was awoken by the sound of screaming. Her daughter screaming. When she opened her eyes, she tried to jump out of bed and go running to Jane to see what was wrong; maybe she'd fallen out of bed and hurt herself. It took several seconds for her to realise why she couldn't get up.

"Jane!" she yelled. "Jane, what is it? Jeremy, don't you dare touch my baby!"

Another long-winded scream came which was abruptly cut off. What sounded like some kind of power tool replaced it. What the fuck was he doing to her? She screamed again, thrashing in her bed desperate to free herself. The sound of the power tool seemed to last forever, as if someone was drilling right through the walls of her house. Finally, it stopped and silence resumed. Now, the only thought running through her mind was if Jane was dead, too, Jeremy having broken his promise not to hurt her.

It had been several long, excruciating hours until Jeremy finally returned to her room and he agreed to take her to Jane.

The second she saw Jane's hands, she knew he'd done something terrible to her. He was evil, a monster. Her heart had almost broke in two when she saw the damage to

Jane's hands, the obvious pain she was in, yet even then, trying to convince Mandy it wasn't too bad. If Mandy had been able to get her hands on any kind of a weapon she would have killed him there and then.

Then, another setback that made her reconsider

Loneliness is a Monster

everything she'd contemplated last night. It never even crossed her mind he would use Covid as an excuse for their absence. And it was totally feasible. She'd had Covid just a year before and had been ill in bed, unable to move for nearly a week. When she made the phone calls the temptation to blurt out what was really happening was so strong she had to bite her tongue. As far as she was now concerned, instead of being rescued this very day, their nightmare could continue for several days more, at least. The thought of being raped by him every night until they were freed made her want to scream. That her husband would now surely not survive, made her want to attack Jeremy right now with everything she had in her. Her daughter's hands curled like talons; fingers unable to bend. Just when she thought she couldn't keep any form of control over the situation and do as promised in keeping calm, there was a knock at the door.

Mandy's heart, which had almost broken in two, on two separate occasions, now threatened to jump out of her mouth, thudding manically in her chest. This could be her only chance. When Jeremy told her it was Kirsty, her colleague from work, her mind raced to think of any and all possible ways to warn her they were in danger.

And it worked.

As Mandy used all her will power to not raise Jeremy's suspicions, pretend she had Covid, she winked at Kirsty just before she closed the door. And not smiling in the process. Kirsty had given her a funny look, had opened her mouth to say something, and then Jane had made possibly the biggest mistake of her life. Little did Mandy know it would be the last time she saw Jane for a very long time.

143

Chapter 22

Everything should have been perfect in Jeremy's life. He had the wife he'd been desperate for. The ex-husband now well and truly out of the picture, and the daughter, too, had been taken care of, too, after her foolish act the other day. Two days had passed since he moved in with them. He had returned home to collect fresh clothes, give dirty ones to his mother so she could wash them, and also so she could prepare food. At lunch times, it was too risky to have Mandy anywhere near the kitchen which looked out onto the back garden, in case someone spotted her, and Jeremy had no idea how to cook. He could just about manage to cook eggs and bacon. When shopping was required, he would leave Mandy tied and gagged then use her credit card, only buying absolute essentials so as not to alert anyone. But he couldn't expect his wife to survive on eggs and bacon every day, or simple sandwiches, not if he wanted to win her over completely, so he told his mother to prepare food for him. When she asked why he needed so much food to take with him, he said it was for his new girlfriend. Somewhat delighted, she asked when she could meet the new girlfriend, but Jeremy was always quick to say the girl was shy and not ready yet. But he promised she would be soon.

It was important to stop his mother getting suspicious because he discovered he was having enough problems as it was with others. Even though Mandy had told everyone the whole family had Covid and were quite sick, people still kept coming around to visit, to see how they were. The phone rang several times a day, friends, work colleagues, all wanting to know how they were. Could they speak with Adrian, and he was having a hard

Loneliness is a Monster

job getting Mandy to act convincing and keep them at bay.

It was too late now but he was furious with himself for not thinking it through properly. How long could he keep up the pretence of them having Covid? The more he thought about it, the more he realised he was going to have to get them out of the house, and this meant finding the money to rent somewhere else. As he sat in the living room, with Mandy tied to her bed, still too soon to fully trust her yet, he decided he'd speak with his mother and see if she could get him a job at his father's old workplace. He'd always said he wanted Jeremy to carry on where he left off so it should be simple. If he could just stop the troublemakers from bothering them for a few more weeks, he could start the job, and find somewhere cheap to take his wife and daughter.

One thing that would definitely have to be taken care of, though, was the husband's body, which was already beginning to smell foul. Jeremy had gone to the shed this morning to look at it and could smell it from outside. It wouldn't be long before neighbours noticed it, too. After some consideration and recalling something he'd heard a few years before, Jeremy had the perfect answer to his dilemma.

That evening, he headed to Mandy's room, carrying her dinner, his mother having explained to him how to prepare it. As always, she flinched and drew her naked body up into her chest, as though trying to make herself smaller. Jeremy smiled.

"Hey, darling. I've brought dinner. I hope you're hungry."

He sat beside her and removed the gag covering her mouth. She let out a deep breath and pulled herself further from him.

"It's okay. You don't have to be scared. Everything's

going to be perfect, I told you."

"Where's my daughter? I want to see her. What have you done with her?"

"Mandy, my dear, I explained to you. You know how important it is to respect one's elders. To not deceive or lie. I can appreciate these are slightly worrying times for you both and she's still just a child, but it's better to learn the hard way sometimes when we step out of line. My father taught me that one. So many times as a child when I misbehaved, he would lock me in my room for hours on end. Often without supper.

"It was hard and I cried a lot, but I learnt my lesson. Jane must learn hers. I was very specific about not screaming for help and that's exactly what she did, so she's been left on her own for a little while to think about the error of her ways. I promise, I'll take her dinner as soon as you finish yours. Look, it's soup! My mother helped to make it!"

He unlocked one of the handcuffs, he'd bought the day before, attached to her right wrist so she could eat properly. Her arm flopped beside her.

"Why are you doing this, Jeremy? It has to stop, don't you see? We can't live like this forever. You must let us go before…before something happens you might regret. I'm not angry, honestly, I'm not, but Jane needs me. She has to exercise. At least bring her in here with me."

"I'm sorry, dear. But she needs to be alone for a while. I promise you'll be together again soon. So we can all be one big happy family. Now eat before it gets cold."

She looked hesitant as he laid the bowl of soup on the bed beside her. She hadn't eaten all day, also as punishment for arguing with him earlier, so he figured she must be starving by now, and if Jeremy was honest, his first ever preparation did indeed taste good. He'd followed his mother's instructions perfectly and this was the reward for doing so. If she ate it all, he decided he'd make love to her again as a treat to them both.

Mandy ate it all, evidently ravenous. If she allowed him to make love to her, he'd let her have another bowl—there was no way he was going to eat it all himself. He'd made enough for several days, just in case.

Once she'd finished, he handed her a glass of water to wash it down with, then took both the bowl and glass from her.

"Was that good? Did I do okay? Not too much salt?"

"It was fine, Jeremy, but listen, you can't leave me like this all day and night. I have to go to the toilet, shower, do laundry. It's almost time for my period, Jane's too."

"I know. I thought about that and had an idea. If you do your duty as my wife, I'll let you do all those things tomorrow."

He stood and began to get undressed, putting his braces on the bedside table, just out of her reach. He was rapidly coming to learn that women were so moody and unpredictable. One minute they were all smiles; the next they was trying to strangle him with the braces as they made love.

"No, Jeremy, no. I refuse. Don't you dare put your hands on me. I'll scream so loud the neighbours will hear. Jeremy, stop, right now!"

Always playing hard to get. He supposed it was a game she liked to play, which was fine with him. He liked games too. Once naked, he went to the corner where the video camera was still set up and pressed record. He'd been fascinated when he read about serial killers keeping souvenirs of their crimes. After a long thought, this was his souvenir—recorded for ever so he could rewatch in private.

Mandy visibly tensed, pressing her thighs together to

prevent Jeremy from spreading them. She writhed and struggled, trying simultaneously to kick him with the balls of her feet, but Jeremy knew this game all too well and dodged her easily. But as he raised her legs and slowly entered her, she lifted her head and spat in his face.

"You bastard! I fucking hate you. Get off me, you pig. You dirty, fucking monster!"

If there was one thing that Jeremy despised, found utterly disgusting, it was being spat upon. His sister had made that mistake one day after he slapped her and he had been so shocked, found it such a foul thing, he had beaten her with a stick until she fell unconscious. The bruise on the back of her thighs had lasted for weeks.

Immediately, his erection was gone. Furious, he stood up, head spinning with rage. In all his planning of all possibilities, he had not allowed for this hypothetical situation; that she would insult and refuse him. Maybe at first, but after a few days, he had been positive she would eventually come to terms with things. He was going to make love with her then give her more soup as a treat. Perhaps a piece of the baguette he'd bought earlier to soak up the wonderful sauce. A meal he had sweated over for hours, and this was how she responded.

Well fine, if there was one thing he knew about it was discipline. She didn't want him inside her, he'd give her something else instead. Jeremy attached the other handcuff to her wrist, locking it to the headrest then rushed to the kitchen and grabbed the baguette. When he returned, he forced her legs apart and rammed the whole thing inside her, roughly nine inches and wider than his wrist. Now, until she apologised for her actions, that was going to be her meal for the rest of the week. Piece by stinking, wet, soggy piece.

Loneliness is a Monster

Jane heard the screams coming from her mother's room but was too tired and in too much pain to react. She wanted to yell as loud as she could for Jeremy to leave her mother alone. Instead, only weak croaks came. Her throat was parched, as though someone had forced her to swallow a cup of dry mud. Her stomach was a constant rumbling, spasms of pain shooting up her immobile body, causing her to wince every time. Since yelling for help two days ago, when someone knocked on the door, she had barely eaten or drunk anything. One glass of tepid water a day and a stale piece of bread at midday, another in the evening. Several times he had come to her room, occasionally just standing there, glaring at her as though undecided what to do with her. Other times, he would bring her the piece of bread and glass of water, watch her finish them both, then just turn around and leave without saying a word. The first day she was left here she refused to apologise, preferring to be stubborn and not give him the satisfaction, but that was then. Now, as the sores under her back and thighs increased, along with her hunger, she pleaded with him every time he stepped into the room.

But her pleas fell on deaf ears.

She winced when another spasm shot up her back. Having not moved at all in the last two days, her hands just as useless as her legs, the sores underneath her were a constant source of agony, a throbbing that felt as though someone had set fire to her. It wasn't just here either. Having not used the toilet, she had no choice but to soil herself. Urine and wet and drying faeces clung to her buttocks and vagina causing a stench to fill the room, slowly rolling out across the bedsheet like an outgoing tide. Even though she was barely being fed, twice a day her bowels and bladder betrayed her, despite attempting to keep it in.

And now, even more worrying, were the flies that had started landing on her, her incapable of swatting them away.

Chapter 23

Kirsty Walker sat at the plastic chair and fidgeted with her hands, unable to keep still. The interrogation room was bare, only an old table with suspicious scratches carved deep into it and two chairs. The walls were a pale grey, like the sky outside, dreary and bleak like her mood. In the corner hung a camera pointing directly at her. As she waited for the detective to come, she wondered what kind of interviews and interrogations might have gone in here before. Horrific confessions, revealed in all their sadistic, twisted glory from psychopaths more than willing to go into minute detail of each crime they'd committed. Victims or witnesses, sitting right where she was now, either in great distress or fear, as they recounted what they'd seen or heard, perhaps wondering if they were making a terrible mistake and the perpetrator would be waiting for them outside. Decided to seek revenge for daring to come to the police with information.

She felt like that now, not knowing if she was doing the right thing, perhaps exaggerating and what her gut was telling her, and she might be reprimanded or even arrested for wasting police time. But regardless of whether she was or not, she felt it was her duty to come here and tell the police her suspicions. That something was not right and she had a terrible feeling in the pit of her stomach, eating away at her like a parasite, that something was wrong. Kirsty had spoken to her husband about it, and a few colleagues at work, and they all agreed it just didn't seem like Mandy to act this way, Covid or not. She would at least be replying to their text messages; surely, nothing to do all day at home except precisely that.

It was true that Kirsty had also had Covid and there had been days she had been unable to get out of bed, let alone answer the door or chat with friends, but something told her there was more to this than just a nasty virus. Before she had closed the door last week on her, Mandy had winked at her, but not in a funny way, as if sharing a secret joke between them. Mandy's face had been gaunt, dark circles under puffy, bloodshot eyes which suggested to Kirsty that what her friend had been telling her about everyone in bed with Covid was not entirely true. It suggested that Mandy was trying to warn her it was much, much worse.

Her husband had told her she was probably overreacting, that Covid could knock down the strongest of people, and if it wasn't Covid, what exactly was she suggesting anyway? It wasn't as if the family were rich and had a house full of valuables someone wanted to steal. The woman was probably busy trying to do everything she could to keep things running in the household and was exhausted. It was only when Kirsty mentioned that Mandy had replied just twice in the last week with simple, one-word texts he agreed it wouldn't hurt just to check up on her colleague again. Sandy had gone to visit her the next day, knocked several times, and was about to leave when she caught movement in the living room. When she looked, whoever it was quickly disappeared as though they didn't want her to know they were home. So after trying to phone her three more times and asking colleagues at work if they'd spoken to her, she decided she had no choice to report a possible…what, she didn't know.

Finally, after what seemed like hours had passed, and she was beginning to worry if they were checking up on her instead, the door opened and a man entered. Wearing a grey suit, he smiled reassuringly as he closed the door.

Loneliness is a Monster

If that smile was meant to soothe Kirsty she didn't know, because it did anything but. The detective's features, balding dark hair and hard, hazel-coloured eyes suggested he had long since lost any ability at soothing anyone. Perhaps he'd been in this room too many times with people who were required to be handcuffed as they spoke and another officer present just in case. They hadn't even said a word to each other yet and Kirsty was already starting to feel as if she'd done something wrong.

"Hi, I'm Detective, Chris Sutton. You wanted to report a possible kidnapping if I understand correctly?"

When Kirsty had entered the station and said she wanted to talk to a detective, the duty sergeant had insisted she tell him the nature of her visit first. With nothing else she could come up with except a possible kidnap, she had no choice but to voice her suspicions.

"Umm, yes. I think so. I'm not sure. I just…it's all so very strange and I didn't know what else to do. It all just seems so…*off* and not like her at all."

"Okay, not to worry. Just tell me what you think is going on."

Kirsty took a deep breath and did so, also mentioning that neither Mandy's husband or daughter were answering their phones either—she'd tried.

The detective took notes, nodded now and again but said nothing until she'd finished. "And you last actually saw Mandy almost a week ago? You haven't been able to speak to her or anything since?"

"No! I mean, her daughter is disabled, in a wheelchair. Which is what really concerns me. I kept texting asking if she needed me to go shopping for them or help with their daughter Jane in any way, but she just replies with a simple, '*no, we're fine.*' I mean, if they're that bad they can't answer the phone or come to answer the door, surely, they need help with stuff, right?"

"And as far as you're aware, no one has been able to speak with her, her husband or daughter?"

"No, no one. A colleague's husband at work is friends with Mandy's husband. He spoke with Adrian's—Mandy's husband—company and they haven't heard from him since he first told them he had Covid. It's like they've all disappeared from the face of the earth. Only replying occasionally to text messages is the only way we know they're still alive."

The detective took more notes, then looked up. "And you think they've been kidnapped? In their own home?"

Here it comes, she thought. "Yes, I know it sounds stupid, saying it like that, but it's just not normal. When she winked at me, it was like she was trying to give me a warning. Like there was someone standing there behind her and she couldn't say anything. We've only recently gotten over that child kidnapping thing that was going on here. Making them vile videos for the internet. What if...what if someone is holding them prisoner in their own home to do something similar? It can't hurt just to go check on them. If a detective or policeman answers the door, they might be more inclined to answer."

The briefest flicker of a grin twitched on the detective's face as he took down Kirsty's address and phone number. Whether he was taking her seriously or not, there was no way of telling.

"Okay, thank you for informing us. Given that a minor is involved, yet there's no actual evidence of a crime having been committed, the best course of action will be to inform Child Services, and ask them if they can at least speak with the girl. I'll be in touch to let you know the results."

And with that, it was done. Kirsty didn't know whether to be glad or not; he didn't seem too interested and that little smirk on his face…

She prayed he kept his word about investigating though, not just brushing it off as a waste of time. She prayed her friend was okay; she didn't know anyone who deserved to lead a happy life more than Mandy and her family.

Ashley Gibbs knocked on the door and took a step back. She'd only been working for Child Services for six months and had already heard plenty of horror stories from more experienced colleagues about what she might expect now and again. One guy had revisited a house again after further complaints from neighbours about the welfare of the owner's daughter and he had been greeted not by the parents, but by a bucket of freezing water poured on him from an upstairs window. In no uncertain terms, then told to mind his own damn business.

Another had demanded to see a child reported as being out all hours of the night and often wearing bruises on his face and arms. When this colleague knocked on the door, a woman threw it open, stinking of alcohol and nicotine, eyes bloodshot and told Ashley's colleague to fuck off then flicked her cigarette at her face. There were many other cases Ashley was informed of and told to always be vigilant when visiting whether it be the first time or a repeat visit. The Child Services were not the favourite service by many parents she soon came to learn.

After waiting a few minutes and neither seeing nor hearing a response, she knocked again, then checked her watch. It was almost five in the afternoon already and she still had four more houses to visit before she could finish for the day. Just six months into the job and she was already beginning to wonder if she'd made the right decision. It seemed that every time one case was closed, another ten were waiting for her. Ten for her, ten for each colleague. In the short time she'd been working for them, seven colleagues had already resigned due to the stress, lack of appreciation and lack of appreciation on pay day either. Of the seven that resigned, only three more had been hired. Less employees but more cases for them all to check out. Not to mention the paperwork.

She checked her watch again and peered once more in the living room window. *Come on*, she begged, *just answer the door, let me see the kid, and I can go*. All she had been told was that the daughter hadn't been seen in a few days. Just ask to see her, make sure she's alive and okay, and go. But at this rate she wouldn't be done until at least eight and her boyfriend had arranged to pick her up at eight-thirty for a drink. They'd only been dating three months and already the stress and long hours were causing rifts between them. If only she didn't need the money...

Ashley was about to knock for a third and final time when the door answered. She instinctively tensed, not knowing what to expect but the person that answered the door looked totally incapable of harming anyone. A frail and ill-looking person stood there wearing a face mask that did little to hide the blotchy skin on her face or tired, bloodshot eyes. But all Ashley cared about was seeing the kid and getting out of there. Adults were not her problem.

"Hi, umm, Mrs Cogsworth?"

"Yes," came a soft, croaked reply.

"Umm, yes, good. I'm Ashley, from Child Services. We had a report that your daughter, Jane, hasn't been at school in some time and no one has seen or spoken with her either."

"She had Covid. Like I do now. She's getting better. Hopefully, she'll be back to school next week. Thanks."

Loneliness is a Monster

She made to close the door already, but Ashley, now slightly more confident that she knew who she was dealing with, put a hand against the door.

"Sorry, I haven't finished yet. I'd like to see Jane if that's possible? Just to make sure she's okay."

Mrs Cogsworth hesitated, as though debating with herself. "Well, she's not here right now. She recovered then went to visit her aunt and uncle over in Norwich for the rest of the week. But I'll be sure to let you know when she returns."

"Really? That's a shame. Okay." Ashley produced a business card with her email and phone number on it. "Here's my card. Please contact me when she returns just so we can close the file. Thanks!"

And with that, she left. If the other four visits were as quick and easy as this, she could be home by seven. Smiling, Ashley got in her car and drove off. Ten minutes later, Mrs Cogsworth was totally forgotten about.

Deborah leaned back in her chair with a fresh coffee in her hand. It was the third one already today and she still felt half asleep, like she hadn't slept all night. Which wasn't true at all; she'd been so exhausted she'd slept almost nine hours, not even the cat managing to wake her for breakfast which was theoretically impossible.

It seemed that no matter how hard she worked, how many arrests she made, there was always another case waiting for her. Like a nasty cold that won't go away, always in the background just waiting for the right moment to spring out at her and ruin her day.

She'd spent the morning in court, giving evidence about Kyle Thompson, convicted of kidnapping a thirteen-year-old and forcing her to perform sexual acts that he would then upload to the dark web. Kyle had been a friend of a previous arrest she'd made, Daniel Radcliffe, who had been convicted of blackmailing young girls online. This particular case, instead of relief and jubilation for catching another paedophile, had caused Deborah a lot of heartache and a feeling of immense grief. It had been a year since Daniel's arrest and they had been sure of Kyle's involvement somehow but had been unable to prove it. Kyle had been allowed to molest and kidnap young girls right under their noses and had gotten away with until just recently when an anonymous tip informed them of his activities. If only she had kept investigating harder, she repeatedly told her colleagues. A lifetime of trauma for the poor kids might have been avoided. Yet despite her colleague's constant reassurances that it wasn't her fault, the sleepless nights suggested otherwise.

Her only hope now was that there was enough evidence to send Kyle to the same prison as his buddy, Daniel. Assuming Daniel was still alive that was; child predators were not welcome in any prison. On the drive back from court, she had been contemplating requesting a week's holiday. Just stay at home all week, barely leave the house except to do shopping and cuddle up with the cat and a good book. She hadn't had any time off since the Radcliffe case. And that had been two days with strict orders to visit the police psychiatrist.

And now this.

After going to collect her second coffee, she'd overheard a fellow detective talking to another about a case. They were joking about it; a woman had come forth to say she hadn't heard from her colleague in over a week, and no one had heard from the husband or daughter who it seemed was disabled and in a wheelchair. They were joking over the fact that if they responded to every call like that they'd be millionaires with the amount of overtime they'd have to do. But to Deborah, it didn't sound funny at all.

In theory, it sounded like a simple case of a family suffering from Covid, not wanting to infect others with it, so they were hiding up at home for a few days. Perfectly normal in the current climate, but there was something about the fact no one had heard from the daughter. This was rather ominous and not a good sign, but even so, technically domestic issues weren't her problem anymore—since arresting Daniel she had been assigned to the child exploitation department, charged with investigating any and all cases of abuse involving minors. It was something she relished, but it came with a lot of stress and heartache.

The only moment of happiness came when she went to visit Angela, the girl rescued from the clutches of her own uncle. Multiple therapists trying their best to get Angela to speak to them, share with them her thoughts had proved almost impossible. Angela, perfectly understandable, didn't trust adults anymore, only Deborah, who visited her home several times a week. They would sit in her bedroom, often quiet, saying nothing, just letting the poor girl know she was there for her. That she wouldn't abandon her. Angela was even nervous around her own father, refusing to let him hold or embrace her. But the girl did trust Deborah and soon the girl began to open up to her revealing her inner thoughts and fears. Now, a year later, Deborah had become the girl's Godmother and of this, she was extremely proud.

She took another sip of her coffee, going through the notes she'd made, trying to decide what to do. She wanted to go home and take a long shower, but what if something nefarious really was going on in that home? According to the detective, there was a teenager in there confined to a wheelchair. Under normal circumstances, it would be inconceivable that anyone would use a disabled child for their sick practices, but if there was anything she'd learned over the last few years, it was that absolutely no one was safe from their grasp. In fact, the tech department had discovered through their infiltration of dark websites, it was something members demanded more and more of.

"I dunno," she muttered to herself, finishing her coffee and throwing the Styrofoam cup in the wastebin. Someone else could go knock on the door, demand that Mandy or her husband opened it, Covid or not. Just a quick check, ensure everything was okay, then let the Child Services officer know. A ten-minute job.

But what if...

"Ugh."

It was almost like a curse. Every case she looked at or heard about, if there were children involved, she couldn't help but think the worst. And it was no good relying on Child Services either; these, she had also learned, seemed more interested in avoiding any form of investigation rather than doing their job. Only a few weeks ago, a young boy had been rescued from a toxic household after his mother had been repeatedly abusing him for months, starving and beating him, then leaving him tied up in the wardrobe all night, completely naked and freezing. Apparently, every time he complained about being hungry she forced him to eat raw peppers, the hottest she could find, then when he was sick, she'd make him eat that too. Three times Social Services had visited, three times they had closed the case.

"Okay, what the hell, let's do it. I can shower on the way home afterwards," she muttered to herself.

Deborah arrived at the Cogsworth's home and parked directly outside. She paused to take in the scenery first

Loneliness is a Monster

for a few minutes before getting out of her car. Nothing looked out of place, except perhaps the front garden where the weeds were starting to push through. Perfectly normal and understandable if the whole family had Covid. She wasn't quite sure what she was supposed to be looking for, and felt a little foolish for doing so. As though she half expected to find something resembling an abandoned, haunted home, like in the movies, blood dripping from broken windows, ominous shadows lurking by torn curtains. But inside, nothing moved.

Deborah got out of her car and headed down the garden path, putting on a clean mask just in case. She knocked loudly on the door, guessing those inside were asleep. After a few seconds she knocked again, then went to peer into the living room window. Seeing or hearing nothing, she headed back to the front door and knocked again. When once more no one came to answer, she lifted the letterbox and called for Mandy, informing her she was a detective and needed to speak to her. Being a bungalow, she should be able to hear the tiniest sound, even if it was a large home, and after just a few seconds, she did. What might have been whispering, a soft thud, as if something had fallen over.

"Mandy Cogsworth, are you there? I'm a detective, I need to speak to you please."

Deborah stood back and waited. When no one responded she banged harder, then peered through the letterbox. A rank smell greeted her, like stale sweat and something else. Rotten vegetables or something. She yelled again, but no one came to greet her. She was sure someone was there though, but why ignore her calls?

Not to be deterred, she tried the door. Locked.

"Mrs Cogsworth, if you're deliberately avoiding me, it's not wise. I can return with a search warrant if necessary."

This was something of a lie. If she believed someone was in danger in the house she didn't need one, but right now, she didn't have the necessary evidence to do so. She hoped the threat would prove enough, but after a few more minutes and no signs of life, she was forced to give up.

As she headed back towards her car, she made a mental note to keep in touch with Child Services and to continue trying to contact the family herself. But for now, a thousand other cases demanded her attention. Shaking her head, she drove off, a nasty feeling in the pit of her stomach that unfortunately, was not something new to her.

Chapter 24

"What do we have to do to get people to stop fucking coming around here or phoning, for Christ's sake?" yelled Jeremy at Mandy. "You told them you all have Covid. Can't they just leave us alone and let us get on with our lives?"

He looked to Mandy for suggestions but again, she was being unresponsive. She lay on the bed, one wrist handcuffed, but she wasn't even looking at him anymore, let alone speaking with him. Unless it was to beg him to let her see her daughter or to scream and fight when he made love to her each night. It was just her being moody, he knew this now. Women were moody creatures, getting in a huff when they didn't get what they wanted. Admittedly, she wasn't looking so healthy and pretty these days, and she was beginning to smell. He made a point of letting her use the toilet twice a day,

while he watched, of course, but he wasn't quite so willing to let her shower alone yet. She might do something stupid, like scream for help from the bathroom window.

Patience and time, that was all they needed, but they weren't going to get that if people kept knocking on the fucking door all day!

Now it was the Social Services and a detective who came checking up on them, thanks no doubt to the nosy bitch of a colleague from the other day. Jeremy had been shocked and horrified. At first, he decided not to respond but after how hearing how insistent she was being, and realising it would probably make things worse if they didn't, he had forced Mandy to answer. He had been standing right behind her, large kitchen knife in his hand, and he would have used it if necessary, too, but fortunately, Mandy had been a good wife and gotten rid of the social worker. But that didn't mean the problem was gone for good. If none of them returned to work or school in the next week, more questions would be asked, no matter how many times he made Mandy reply to text messages and phone calls.

"You still in a bad mood? I've told you a dozen times, Jane is fine. Her punishment will be lifted soon. I've made a stew, so if you eat it all up like a good girl, I'll consider letting you speak to her. How does that sound?"

Finally, she turned her head to face him. "You've been saying that all week, you lying bastard. Just let us go, for God's sake! Can't you see it's not working out like you thought? The police will come, it's just a matter of time, and you'll go to prison. You can still stop this if you want to."

"I'm not going to prison, Mandy. Never. I'll kill myself first, I promise. Besides, I have some good news. I finally got a job! How about that? I start work in the morning, working for a security company that installs cameras. Now I can start looking for a place to rent for the three of us! We can tell your friends you've moved away. London or something. How does that sound? Isn't it exciting!"

The look on Mandy's face did not suggest she shared the same excitement, though. Instead, she started crying. She'd cried so much these last few days; Jeremy was surprised she had any tears left to shed.

"But...but Jane needs to go to school! She has her friends here, special needs facilities she must go to. You're going to keep us locked up forever?"

"No. I told you. Once she's learned a little discipline and accepts me for who I am, her father, then I can start trusting her more. She's fine right now, she really is. Just a day or two more, I think."

"But it's been nearly a week already! I haven't seen my baby in over four days! You can't do this to me. I need to see if she's okay. And…and if you're at work all day, who's going to take care of us? You're just going to leave us tied up all day without being able to use the toilet or anything?"

"You'll be fine! I'll let you go to the toilet in the morning before I leave and I'll come home at lunchtime, so stop worrying. Now, are you going to eat this stew I've prepared?"

It took her a while to respond, tears still trickling down her blotchy, thin face but she nodded, then looked away as though embarrassed. Jeremy beamed. She was going to love his new recipe. He hurried to the kitchen, poured a healthy portion then carefully carried it on a tray to her room. In the other bedroom, he could vaguely hear Jane sobbing and talking to herself. Such a bad girl. It was annoying him now, hearing her constant sobbing and moaning as though it was his fault for her current predicament. She could wait to eat, as further punishment. Maybe then she'd shut up for a while. Jeremy lay the tray on the bedside table, unlocked Mandy's wrist and allowed her to sit up. She groaned, rubbing her wrist, and arm which slumped back on the bed. When she picked up the spoon, it fell from her hand.

"Shall I do it for you?" he asked.

"No, I'll be fine. You are feeding Jane, too, right?"

"Of course I am! Once you've finished I'll prepare her a bowl. Now eat up before it gets cold."

She tried again. Jeremy could hear her stomach rumbling. Poor woman had barely eaten the last few days, refusing to unless she could see her daughter, but eventually, she had been so hungry, she relented. Mandy ate a little, chewing slowly on the tender meat. Jeremy watched eagerly, hoping she enjoyed it. But then, she suddenly stopped. Her face scrunched up, as if she'd just swallowed something nasty and she spat the contents onto the floor.

"Hey! What did you do that for? You don't like it?"

Her eyes widened as she glanced at the remains on the floor. So did Jeremy's when he saw what she'd spat out. He grimaced, silently disgusted with himself for not having taken more care with the preparation.

"What is that? What have I been eating the last few days. Oh my God, tell me that's not what I think it is."

Horrified, she looked to him for answers, but it was obvious what it was without him telling her. On the floor, mixed with pieces of chewed potato, were three teeth.

Human teeth.

Mandy leaned over and threw up everything she had just eaten.

Jeremy wasn't sure what to tell her. His initial thought was she would be impressed by his clever thinking, that he had taken care of a nasty problem. He thought of lying and saying it was lamb he had cooked but knew she wouldn't believe him.

Mandy finished retching and spluttering and looked Jeremy hard in the eyes. "Tell me what we've been eating these last few days, Jeremy. Tell me now."

"Well, it was starting to smell and was covered in maggots and flies. I couldn't just throw it in the bin, could I? And well, I got the idea from reading about Jeffrey Dahmer. He was cool!"

"Oh my God." She retched again. "You cooked my fucking husband! You monster. You sick, fucking monster. Oh my God! You've been feeding us Adrian. And Jane has been eating it, too?"

"Yeah, a little," he replied sheepishly. "But not all of him! Just…the face mostly. I got sick of seeing his ugly face staring up at me every time I went in the shed to

Loneliness is a Monster

check on his body. I boiled it to tenderise the flesh, but I guess I forgot to remove the teeth. I have pretty much the rest of him cut up to make stew with, too, in the freezer. There's a lot of it."

She stared at him as though seeing something repulsive, an alien creature, then after dry heaving once more, Jeremy was caught off-guard when she suddenly launched herself at him, screaming and howling, desperately trying to sink long fingernails into his eyeballs. Trying to bite him, kick him, anything. Such was the speed at which she attacked him, he wasn't prepared, and they both fell to the floor, Mandy on top of him, spitting, snarling, and screaming obscenities at him like a wild beast. She tried to smash him over the head with the soup bowl, hot liquid burned his face. Only then did he retaliate rather than just trying to defend himself.

The pain to his face caused a rush of anger-fuelled adrenaline to surge throughout his body, he easily threw off a much lighter Mandy, brought back his fist and punched her in the face as hard as he could. Two of her teeth joined the ones already on the floor. Having stunned her, he quickly jumped up, grabbed her roughly by the arm and threw her down on the bed, making sure both wrists were tied securely to the headrest with the handcuffs.

"You ungrateful little bitch. You women are all the fucking same. You don't deserve shit. Especially not me. All I ever wanted was to make you happy and this is how you respond, you whore!"

Mandy responded by spitting in his face again, a wad of bloody saliva that landed on his stinging cheek. Beside himself with rage, Jeremy rushed out of the room. Seconds later he returned, straddled Mandy on the bed then thrust the pliers into her mouth. Once he'd managed to grip one of her teeth, he squeezed the handles closed as hard as he could with both hands, tugging so hard that he brought her head up off the pillow. The tooth snapped in half, revealing the nerve. Not satisfied, and with Mandy screaming and writhing in agony, he proceeded to remove the rest of the tooth. Once it came free, he dropped it onto the floor and started with the rest. The same thing happened with almost all her teeth, snapping off in places, never coming free in one piece. He was sweating by the time he finished, massive spasms from Mandy each time the pliers connected with one of the nerve endings.

Once the last tooth was pulled, he stood up, panting and observed his handiwork. Mandy was barely conscious now, eyelids fluttering as she moaned. Then, as he surveyed the multiple teeth laying on the floor like miniature dice, he saw something else among them. He picked it up with the pliers and pushed it down Mandy's throat, snapping her mouth shut so she was forced to swallow it. It was half an eyeball, something he had also neglected to remove while boiling the head. Tired and thirsty, Jeremy left her and headed to the kitchen to grab a drink. He was sick of women, sick of Mandy, sick of everything and everyone. Why couldn't people just do as they were told?

Later, as further punishment, he dragged Mandy to the shed, threw her to her knees and told her to scrub all Adrian's dried blood clean until nothing remained. He sat in a chair with his feet up on her bare back as he watched, smoking a cigar he'd found in the house. Then when she'd finished, he fucked her, thrusting into her as hard as he could until he finished. He stubbed his cigar out inside her anus.

Chapter 25

Kelly had never really believed in God. When she had to go to church each Sunday with her parents and Jeremy, rather than be in awe of the things she was hearing, she had been quite scared. The massive figure of Jesus nailed to a cross, face a mask of agony and suffering while blood ran down his palms, gave her nightmares. The main nightmare consisted of being caught by her father, committing some kind of sin, like stealing food from the fridge at night, and being punished the same way as Jesus. But hanging from the ceiling, her palms nailed there as he whipped her, his booming voice telling her what a wicked, sinful girl she was. She'd wake up screaming and her mother would come running to see what was wrong. Even then, Jeremy would taunt her in the mornings, telling her she was a baby.

But when their father died and Jeremy took on the role of man of the house, a part of her thought that the punishments her strict father would often subject them to would stop. At church, she had been taught that violence was a sin, thus could never fully understand why her father would beat her with his belt, often for the most innocent of reasons. Accidently wetting the bed, getting poor grades at school, dropping a glass and breaking it. Nobody had told her it was a sin to wet the bed or drop a glass, so why did her father feel the need to contradict what he'd taught her and hit her so badly? When she asked her mother, she was told not to make a fuss and they should never question her father's actions.

Two years later, her beliefs hadn't changed. She was constantly being told she shouldn't hurt others, either verbally or physically, both at school and at church, yet she was constantly being punished with violence. She would never admit it to anyone but when the man died, a part of her was relieved. Jeremy, while stupid, and a little mean at times, surely wouldn't hurt his own sister when he took on his father's role. So, for things to get even worse for her, was yet another nightmare, but this time it was real.

She hated Jeremy. There was no other word for it. She hated him and was terrified of him at the same time, terrified of making the slightest mistake so he would find reason to punish her, and as time passed the punishments became steadily worse. She'd never been so cold in her life when he forced her to sleep naked outside when it was pouring rain or even snowing, convinced she wasn't going to wake up in the mornings, having frozen to death. She even hated her mother, in a way, for allowing him to get away with it. It was only when Jeremy was at school and Kelly, too injured to go, would her mother take care of her, make her favourite meals, help bathe and soothe her. Secretly, Kelly thought she was a coward.

But now, it seemed it was finally over.

For the last two weeks, she had barely seen her brother, and this was just fine with her. Curious, and hopeful it would remain this way forever, she eavesdropped on conversations between Jeremy and their mother, when she asked where he had suddenly disappeared to. It seemed utterly impossible, that such a horrible, nasty person could ever find someone who found him handsome or nice, but it appeared he had a girlfriend and was staying at her place, most of the time. When she first heard the news, Kelly had run to her bedroom, jumped on her bed and screamed in delight. It was the best news she had heard in her life and prayed the brother she hated and feared with all her heart would

Loneliness is a Monster

move in with this girl, permanently, and if she was lucky, she might never see him again.

No more massaging his smelly, filthy feet, being forced to clean the toilet with her bare hands after he'd finished using it, purposefully making a mess in the bowl. Sometimes being forced to drink from the bowl without it having been flushed. No more sleeping naked outside in the garden or shed, no more beatings. Many times, she cried herself to sleep at nights—if the latest beating allowed her to do so—wishing he was dead. Wishing he suffered the same fate as their father. But this, this was the next best thing.

"Is it true? Does he really have a girlfriend? Will he be moving in with her?" she asked her mother the day before.

"Well, I don't know if he's going to be moving in permanently, but it certainly seems like he has already, doesn't it!"

"So it's serious? He might move in with her?"

"As I said, I don't really know. He doesn't talk about it too much. Only that he has a job so is hoping to rent somewhere soon. Maybe...perhaps she'll help to curb his temper a little and he'll be happy."

Kelly's little heart thudded rapidly in her chest with delight. As far as she was concerned, he could move to the other end of the earth and it wouldn't be far enough, but this would do. So long as he wasn't here tormenting her, it was fine. She also thought her mother was secretly pleased, too. Many times, Kelly had heard her crying in bed at night when she thought Kelly was asleep. She'd seen the look on her face when Jeremy would come home from school. The tension was so thick it seemed they were both temporarily blinded when Jeremy was around.

In the last week, she had seen Jeremy maybe four

times. He came home in the evenings to shower and change his clothes, then spent some time in his bedroom. Often, she would dare to stand outside his room and listen in because there were strange noises coming from inside, as though he was watching a horror movie. The funny thing was that it sounded like his own voice, interjected among screams from a woman. And when he left his room, if she caught him on the landing, his face would be red and he'd be sweating.

But today, Saturday, he had apparently started his new job and would be out all day. For Kelly, it was the perfect time to snoop a little in his room, discover what it was that made him look so funny every time he left.

Her heart thudded in mischievous apprehension as she opened the door to his room and peered in, a room she hadn't been inside for weeks. Before now, nothing on earth would have convinced her to go inside without his permission, for fear of being caught. The room was pretty much as she last remembered. Posters on the walls, now slightly tatty and torn, of men she didn't know but who looked nasty. His bed perfectly made, barely used anymore, and his writing desk, a new laptop sitting there. Kelly headed over to the desk and sat down, turning on the laptop. It came to life immediately. She hoped that Jeremy wouldn't think to use a password because he figured no one would dare to touch anything of his without permission.

Not knowing exactly what exactly she was looking for, she went straight to his history, clicking the keys she'd learned in IT class. A long list came up of strange pages and websites. She clicked on one that Jeremy had obviously visited many times. A video came on, somewhat blurry. She hit the play button. She gasped loudly. The video depicted a naked woman who had to be her mother's age, perhaps older, judging from the

Loneliness is a Monster

wrinkles on her body and sagging breasts. With her was a boy she guessed to be around Jeremy's age, skin flawless. The woman got on her knees and put the boy's erect penis in her mouth. Kelly cringed and pulled a face—this was disgusting. She quickly turned it off.

Kelly tried another one, this one also viewed multiple times, and immediately clapped a hand to her mouth to prevent yet another gasp from escaping. She leaned in closer, trying to determine if what she was seeing was real. A part of her couldn't believe it; another knew it was what she suspected. On the video, somewhat fuzzy, was a woman laying naked on a bed, screaming and shaking her head from side to side, using her legs to try and kick the naked person on top of her.

Her naked brother.

Even though he had his back to the camera, it was obviously him. She recognised his haircut and voice, yelling at the woman to stop moving and screaming. His voice high-pitched like a girl's—every time Jeremy got angry his voice would rise in that way. She knew that too well. The woman's wrists were in handcuffs, bound to the headrest. Jeremy started doing something to her which she assumed to be sex—something she'd heard older girls talking about, sometimes. The woman still resisted, screaming for help and for him to get off her, but he clamped a hand over her mouth and continued. After a few minutes, he abruptly stopped and climbed off the hysterical woman, who was sobbing uncontrollably. The video went blank.

Kelly only had a rough idea of what sex entailed before she saw this video, but she knew full well now. And she also knew that the woman had not been a willing participant. Was this Jeremy's new girlfriend? she wondered. If that was the case, something seemed very wrong about the whole thing. She tried another video and saw the exact same scenario played out; the woman screaming and howling, trying to resist while bound to the bed. She started calling him names, insulting him, using foul language, until her brother clamped a hand over her mouth. When it finished, he turned to face the camera before switching it off, a lecherous grin on his sweaty, red face.

Kelly was stunned and confused. This didn't seem in any way how a boyfriend and girlfriend should behave, even if they were adults. She knew adults often did weird things, but to her it didn't look like a game at all. The woman looked genuinely terrified and in pain. Why would he tie her to the bed and do that if she didn't want him to? At one point she even spat at him which was disgusting, and she knew full well this was something Jeremy utterly detested. As she scrolled through his history, she counted another nine more videos with the same link.

Kelly didn't know what to do. This was something that seemed just wrong and she was sure she recognised the woman from somewhere. Maybe an old teacher from school or a neighbour, she couldn't remember. Jeremy had been hurting this woman and evidently enjoying it. She thought of all the times he had hurt her, doing horrible, spiteful things to her, enjoying that too—the same malicious grin on his face as he did it. So many times, she had silently begged for something to happen to him so he couldn't hurt her anymore, or, somewhat guiltily, to find someone else to punch and kick and whip. Well, it appeared he finally had. What if he was in fact keeping her prisoner somewhere and it was all a lie about them being boyfriend and girlfriend?

If Kelly had often daydreamed about something bad happening to Jeremy so he couldn't hurt her anymore, she didn't really want him doing it to someone else

Loneliness is a Monster

instead. It was only in moments of pain and terror she had selfishly wished it upon another. But now, seeing this, she realised there was only one thing to do.

"Oh my God, Kelly, what are you doing watching this? What's wrong with you? You can't watch this filth. What on earth has gotten into you?" exclaimed her mother after Kelly told her she had something she needed to see.

"Mum, don't you get it? It's Jeremy! He's hurting that woman! I was looking for something on his computer and accidently clicked on one of the links. What's he doing to her?"

Her mother's face drained of blood, her hand shooting to her mouth just as Kelly's had done. She quickly slammed the laptop shut and took a step back as though she was confronted with some nasty, poisonous bug instead of a computer. She shook her head, as if trying to deny what she had just witnessed.

"Oh my God," she muttered.

"We have to do something, Mum! He's hurting her really badly!"

"Just…just get out. Don't ever come in here again."

She grabbed Kelly's arm and dragged her from the room, slamming the door shut behind her.

"Ow! You're hurting me! Are you going to call the police!"

"Don't you ever talk to anyone about this, do you hear me?"

"But—"

"I said, do you hear me? Never! Now go to your room!"

Katherine sat shocked and in disbelief on the sofa downstairs. Very rarely did she drink alcohol except a glass of wine on special occasions but right now she needed a shot of something stronger. She rose and poured herself a second shot of whiskey from the cabinet and sat down again, her face already flushed from the potent liquor. Even though it was a tiny glass, she still had to be careful not to spill any.

She took a sip of the foul stuff, winced, and shook her head, her mind reeling from the horror she had just witnessed. It couldn't be real, just couldn't be, she kept telling herself. People nowadays could do all kinds of fake stuff on computers; to the point no one knew what was real or not anymore. Surely, it had to have been faked by Jeremy, some video he'd pulled from somewhere and added his own features. But if so, why would he even do that?

But she already knew the answer to that question. She'd always known there was something wrong with him from the moment he took over the house. Ever since he'd been able to talk, he was so demanding, wanting everyone's attention all day and night. Then as he grew older and Kelly was born, his jealousy had been evident, often making her cry for no reason, or stealing her sweets so he could eat them himself. She would never admit to anyone—barely even to herself—but since becoming the man of the house, she had been scared of him. Scared of her own son. Her husband, Reginald, had been strict and a feared disciplinarian, but he was nothing compared to Jeremy. So often had she wanted to do or say something every time he punished his sister so cruelly, but she had been brought up to obey, watch and not speak, and her heart broke every time.

That was one thing, though, but for him to turn into what amounted to or appeared to be a rapist, was something completely different. She'd had a feeling things might not turn out well for him, but this was despicable, beyond words. When he told her he had a girlfriend she'd been as surprised as anyone. Maybe he had changed, after all, she told herself, had discovered a part of himself he never knew was there, and she would later feel guilty for harbouring such nefarious thoughts about her own son.

Now she knew different. This woman, who, from the very little she saw, appeared to be the same age as herself, was not acting as though complicit with this disgusting behaviour.

Then her mind invariably went back to when he was a young teen, going through the turbulence of puberty. Waking up to see him with a flashlight staring at her vagina after pulling down her pyjamas, pulling almost tenderly at her pubic hairs to see the flesh beneath. After those incidents, she had been sick in the toilet, horrified at his actions, but told herself it was just a normal boy's curiosity. As she finished the second shot of whiskey, a sob caught in her throat. Her son had gone from a curious pubescent boy to a rapist, violating a woman practically her age. Then she remembered Social Services coming to her home, after a particularly brutal beating he had inflicted on Kelly, and after doing practically nothing, closed the file on him.

By not saying anything herself, though, she was just as guilty as they were.

Now, the question was what was she going to do about it now?

Nothing. Don't say anything. It was a game they were playing. That bondage thing or whatever it's called. She wanted to be tied up.

Katherine wasn't so naïve she didn't know certain kinks existed for some men and women. She'd heard lots of stories in her time about what some couples liked to get up to between the sheets. And as long as they weren't hurting each other, while she didn't fully understand it, she kept her opinions to herself.

That woman was not faking, Kate. You know full well she wasn't. Not with that language she was spouting, and she spat at him! She was screaming herself hoarse, and the terror in her eyes was real.

So, what are you going to do about it?

"Nothing. I can't," she muttered. "It's my own son!"

What if he kills her? He's been seeing her for nearly two weeks now. In her own home—he's been raping her. Does she have a husband? What if she has kids? You going to be responsible for something happening to them, too?

Katherine burst out crying, a war waging inside her head that threatened to explode with a guilt-ridden shrapnel fallout. If she went to the police and it turned out to be one of those perverse sexual games they were playing, Jeremy would be furious with her. Wanting to know how she found out in the first place. He'd surely take it out on Kelly. The punishment dished out to her would be like nothing else she'd ever known. And that would be on her too.

But if she didn't do something and he really was keeping this woman against her will in her own home, how could she ever live with herself. How could she go to church on Sundays and hold her head up high? God would send her to hell, and rightly so.

No. I refuse to accuse my own son of something that might not be real. The woman's friends and family must surely be checking on her. Let them take care of it.

Even so, Katherine barely slept that night, unable to contain the feeling she was doing something terrible and the devil might be preparing a room for her right now. A special suite where he kept all his best guests.

Chapter 26

Jane had no concept of time anymore. She might have been laying here in the exact same position for two days or two weeks. What was going on around her and the condition her body was now in, suggested the latter. She spent hours screaming for Jeremy to please help her, she was truly sorry and would do anything he asked of her. She started yelling 'Daddy' instead of his name in the hope this would please him and he would come free her. Feed her even, get her off this filthy, stinking blanket, help to turn her over at least. But he never came.

In the mornings she heard him moving about the bungalow, entering her mother's room and mumbling between them, but when she prayed he would then come to her room, she would hear the front door slam and wouldn't see him again until later that evening. Then he would come in, smiling at first, which would then change to a grimace, scrunching his nose, sometimes coughing as he gave her a glass of water to drink through a straw, then fed her. Sometimes, it would be a sandwich he made himself, the contents often stale and mouldy but which she would devour as eagerly as though it was her favourite food ever, begging for more. Other times, it might be a Big Mac he had bought from the McDonald's just down the road, a few fries to accompany it while he ate the rest. Sometimes he'd torment her, dangling a fry in front of her mouth, letting her parched tongue touch it before eating it himself. Jane detested pickles, but she devoured those too. She was so desperate she would eat a whole jar of pickles right now if he brought them to her.

Once she finished drinking the glass of water, she would plead for another, just one more, knowing she might not get another drink until the following day, but he would completely ignore her, often not even bothering to look at her, disgusted by her presence, breathing through his mouth so as not to be bothered by the foul stench coming from her. Other times, she tried a different tactic. Instead of pleading and begging, she would insult and threaten him, do her best to raise her head and try and bite his fingers as he fed her. She thought that if she could clamp her teeth on one of his fingers and bite down as hard as she could refusing to let go, he might untie her. Be so angry and fed up with her he might even return her to her mother. But every time she attempted such a thing, he seemed to know what was coming and pulled his hand away. The result was being fed even less, Jeremy standing beside her bed and eating the food himself or pouring the glass of water all over her or onto the floor. Then she would scream in anguish, the torture too much to cope with. She would cry until the tears dried up, even using her tongue to try and catch them—anything to quench her thirst with.

And yet, as much as the hunger pains and dehydration were such that she could barely swallow, her stomach sending spasms like lightning bolts up her body, this was nothing compared to everything else she had to suffer. It paled in comparison.

Unable to move an inch for days, her whole body, every single inch of it, was in utter agony. Her body converted into a single organism of suffering. Not a human body anymore but a malignant tumour slowly eating away flesh, blood, and skin. When Jeremy entered the room, he would not only cough at the pungent stench inside but would also swat away the cloud of flies with their incessant buzzing, something that also threatened to send Jane mad with delirium. Yet even this wasn't the worst of her situation.

Slowly but surely, powerless to do anything but watch, the flies had found a home in her rotting, decaying body. The boredom, pain and suffering she found herself in, so many hours laying on the bed, unable to move, gave rise to Jane having nothing to do but watch as she was slowly eaten alive. The flies had begun as just one or two bluebottles buzzing around her body until they found somewhere to their liking to land. At first Jane blew and spat at them but she stopped when they soon got used to it, and she didn't want to waste valuable saliva. Two, became five, became dozens until the room was alive with them. She watched as they landed on her, crawling over her, tickling her, but knowing something worse was surely coming. And she wasn't wrong.

Confined to her bed, immobile, she was now riddled with bedsores. What started as small bruises and sores that even then had throbbed and stung as though she'd been stabbed, were now pus-leaking, open sores. Her skin had cracked, revealing the raw red flesh beneath, a perfect invitation to infection and a perfect nesting area for the flies.

And they made themselves at home.

Jane watched as, one after another, they landed on whatever sore appealed to them the most and nestled down comfortably to lay their eggs. The pus from the open wounds dribbled down her legs and such was her delirium at times that she would stick out her tongue to try and lap it up, as though it might offer a respite from dehydration.

Then the eggs began to hatch.

Jane watched in horror and defeat as the maggots delighted in finding their perfect food source. They wriggled in multitudes, eating the decaying flesh of her body, burrowing their way inside, further and further, until in some parts of her thighs, the bone could now be seen.

And still they grew in numbers.

On her bare stomach, they wriggled and squirmed, feasting on decaying skin. From her greasy, unwashed hair, they fell onto her face, some finding their way into her nostrils. Or landing on her lips. She was so hungry that when they did, she opened her mouth and ate them. When a bluebottle approached and landed on her face she tried using her tongue to snatch them like a hungry frog. There were times she hoped for them to land on her lips, such was her hunger.

Beneath her, a pool composed of faeces and urine gradually formed. It stunk of potent ammonia and rotting, foul meat, working its way up her stinging back into the bed sores that she couldn't see, but she could feel. Such was the decay and rotting matter of her own flesh, combined with that of her waste, the bed was slowly sinking, as if she was putting on weight rather than losing it. Hundreds of maggots fought to escape the fetid pool but died instead. They were quickly replaced by new ones. When she was forced to urinate or defecate, which she now didn't even bother trying to prevent, it stung so much, she cried out in pain. Dried faeces had stuck to the walls of her anus, spreading to her vagina, meaning both were virtually glued together, just a tiny stream able to seep through the fine gap, making it ever more painful. If there was a way to somehow catch her urine and drink it, she would have done that too.

Sleep was virtually impossible due to the agony she was going through. When sheer exhaustion did finally cause her to close her eyes, she was soon woken by a stabbing pain somewhere on her body, often in multiple places at the same time, as the maggots fed slowly and lazily on her rotting flesh. The rotting stench her body gave off, continuously attracted large amounts of flies

Loneliness is a Monster

which found a way into the enclosed room.

Yet still Jane clung to life, not wanting to die, instead, wanting to see this sadistic, warped kid brought to justice. She didn't know if her mother was suffering the same fate. Or something even worse. It was only occasional muffled cries and the headrest banging against the wall that told her she was even alive at all. But in what condition, Jane didn't know. The first few days, when Jeremy wasn't there, her mother would call out to her, tell her to stay strong, that soon someone would come looking for them, but that stopped some time ago. Jane still couldn't understand how no one had come checking on them, the police, anyone. It had been the only thing she clung too, a tiny morsel of hope, but as the days passed, it appeared as though this was being savagely consumed by the maggots, too.

Jane's failing heart began to beat harder when she heard the front door open. She had been reduced to whimpering instead of screaming, now, despite the agony her body was being subjected to. She heard her mother's bedroom door open, Jeremy saying something to her she couldn't hear. Maybe Jeremy had come with fast food again, something she craved so badly, she started drooling but quickly sucked it back up, precious liquids that couldn't go to waste. After a few minutes and he still hadn't come into her room, panic began to spread to her throbbing brain. He had forgotten about her, or just stopped caring? Was he going to let her starve to death? If the maggots didn't eat their way through to her heart or brain first. But when she was on the verge of mustering all the strength she could and call out to him, her bedroom door opened and Jeremy stepped in, carrying a tray in one hand.

Such was her desperation she momentarily forgot about her predicament and tried to sit up, ready herself to eat, but was crudely brought back to reality when a massive spasm shot up her insides, causing her to howl in pain. Jane greedily eyed what he was carrying, ignoring Jeremy, as he winced and coughed, quickly covering his nose with his shirt, swatting away the swarm of flies disturbed by his intrusion. As usual, he ignored her, saying nothing, as if embarrassed and guilty of his own actions. Careful not to sit in her waste and the massive pool of maggots surrounding her, he set the tray down and held the glass to her mouth. She sucked up the water through the straw, almost wanting to cry from how good it tasted, despite being lukewarm. She did sob briefly when she finished and there was no more, but this stopped when he held the soup spoon to her mouth and she sucked in the contents.

She was so hungry she tried to swallow the lumps of meat mixed in with the soup without chewing, ravenous like a starving animal, but as it went down, it lodged in her still-parched throat.

"Easy now," said Jeremy. "Wouldn't want to choke to death, would you?"

She did as she was told, using all her willpower to eat slower. Each morsel was gold, the greatest thing to have ever been cooked. She would eat a hundred more bowls, if possible. She stopped, startled and horrified, when she took a bite and saw a long strand of hair on the spoon and what looked suspiciously like a toenail. But her hunger overrode any thoughts of complaining or disgust she felt, and she swallowed it down. More hairs and toenails followed. When the bowl was empty, she begged for more.

"Please," she whimpered, "more water as well. More water. Please."

"I can't do that, I'm afraid. Look at the mess you're making already. I'll be back again tomorrow after work.

You should get some rest."

He stood up to leave and once more Jane tried to sit up. She wanted to grab him with both hands and beg and plead for him not to go, to bring more food and water, but the only thing she could manage was to twist and turn her head.

"No! Don't go. Please, just a little more. I'm so hungry and thirsty. I need more!"

The soup giving her slightly more energy, she screamed at him to come back, but he was already gone, the flies once more settling back on the bed, on Jane. Regardless, she yelled his name again and again, shouted for help, for her mum and dad, until exhaustion took over and she was left with nothing else to do except watch the maggots eating away at her putrefying flesh. For the first time in her life, Jane wished she was dead.

Chapter 27

Despite her overload, several cases of child abuse to investigate already, Deborah's thoughts kept returning to that family of three not too far from where she lived. Everything about it screamed something was not right, very wrong in fact and she found herself thinking about it as she sat on the sofa at night stroking her cat while sipping a glass of wine. Several days had passed since she visited and absolutely nothing made sense about it. Yes, she knew many people had gone down with Covid in a bad way, confined to bed in many cases, unable to leave the house, but something didn't seem right about it here.

There was a young teen in that house which more than warranted her involvement in the case, but until she had hard evidence abuse of some kind was taking place, or even kidnapping as Mandy's friend had suggested, there wasn't a lot she could do. Besides, the husband and daughter were apparently visiting relatives so until they returned if this was the actual case, she would have to wait. She'd already phoned the school to see if Mandy had returned and the answer was negative; they'd barely heard a word from her and patience was wearing thin. When she phoned Mandy herself, she had to do so two or three times before she answered.

"We're much better, thanks. I'm sure we'll be returning to our jobs and Jane to school when she gets back from visiting her aunt. Thank you, bye."

Then she would hang up before Deborah could ask any more questions.

She managed to track down Adrian's workplace phone number and tried that.

"Listen, I don't know what the hell is wrong with him.

When he at least bothered to reply to my messages, he said Covid. But that's no excuse. Not once has he answered the phone, only his wife with some vague crap about he's too ill to speak to us. So you can tell him from me, seeing as he doesn't want to answer the phone or show any interest in his job, that he's fired! He's already been replaced by someone else," said an angered boss.

Now, Deborah was more than just concerned. She knew that he had a very important job, was one of the few deemed unreplaceable and whose presence was practically obligatory to ensure everything went according to schedule. No one at his workplace had heard from him in almost two weeks. She'd have to find his parent's phone numbers and check with them to see if they'd heard from him. She phoned Jane's school and asked to speak to the headmaster. He said pretty much what she feared. No, she hadn't been to school at all, didn't answer her phone, and when they phoned her mother, they received the same information—she'd been ill with Covid, was now visiting relatives and would return soon.

Somebody else nobody had seen either.

Deborah sat at her desk sipping a coffee while going through a case file. A nasty case of a young boy having been locked inside his wardrobe all week, completely naked and with barely any food. He'd been punished by his mother because he accidently tore his school shirt while out playing with friends. The poor kid had been finally rescued suffering from dehydration, starvation and multiple beatings. Deborah was expected to testify in the trial next week. She couldn't help asking herself if Jane was now in a similar situation.

"Fuck it, she muttered, picked up the phone and dialled Mandy's number. If she refused to answer, she fully intended to return right there and then and not leave until she was able to see the girl for herself.

As expected, no one answered. She tried again, let it ring for a while and was about to hang up when, to her surprise, Mandy responded.

"Hello?"

"Mandy, is that you?"

"Yes, who is it?"

Strangely enough, it didn't sound like Mandy at all. That or she was eating or something, her mouth full, which she took to be a good sign.

"This is Detective Inspector, Saunders. I visited your home recently. I was wondering how you and your family were doing?"

"Oh. Umm, we're better, thanks."

That was all she ever said. She was about to tell her she intended on passing by personally when it occurred to her that if something nefarious really was happening, there could be someone listening to the conversation, so quickly came up with an excuse to drop by.

"I visited Jane's school yesterday—we're teaching kids about the dangers of the internet—and the headmaster asked if I could drop some stuff by. Homework for Jane to do. So I'll be coming around shortly to drop it off."

"Oh. Umm, you can just leave it outside. I'll pick it up afterwards. I don't want to give you Covid."

"It'll be fine, I'll be wearing a mask."

She thought she heard the faintest sound of a whisper on the other end. Was that someone telling Mandy what to say?

"Just...just leave it outside. Thank you."

She hung up.

Mandy's voice was all wrong, she could have sworn she heard whispering in the background, and this woman absolutely did not want anyone to see her. Was she beaten up, face badly bruised, and whoever had done it didn't want anyone to see? Could it even be her husband with a bit of a bad streak to him? Wouldn't be the first time. Especially since the lockdown just a couple of years earlier. Deborah had been stunned when the results came out from Social Services. Reports of sexual abuse and violence had more than tripled that year. Families stuck at home unable to leave, unable to seek help. Husbands frustrated at not being allowed out and taking it out on their wives and kids. Social services unable or unwilling to investigate because of the risk of catching Covid themselves or because they were quite simply prevented from making house calls. Abuse to children and even toddlers had risen by more than fifty per cent.

If it was up to Deborah, she would go to the house and kick the door in, demand to see Adrian and Jane. Instead, she'd have to speak to her boss. She was sure she could persuade him there was something highly suspicious about the whole thing.

"Fuck it, I'll do it now," she told herself and went to find him.

"Just because no one has seen the husband or daughter for a few days is not reason enough to demand to enter their home and see for yourself. They've been answering their phones so it's not as if they've completely disappeared. Unless you think the woman killed her family which sounds highly unlikely," he said.

"The husband has been fired from his job because he didn't once phone his boss to inform him how he was. That's suspicious on its own. His was a high paying job, a lot of responsibility. According to his boss, it's not like him at all to just suddenly stop answering his phone. No one has spoken to the daughter either. I think they could be in serious trouble."

"But how? You've spoken to the woman on the

phone. Says she has Covid. My wife had Covid and could barely get out of bed for days. She's probably being overly protective. Call Social Services again if you're that worried about it, because I need you on a dozen other cases which are far more important.

"The husband won't be the first or last to lose his job because of it. Unfortunate, but it is what it is."

The tone from his voice suggested he wasn't going to listen to her anymore about it. She had two choices; investigate on her own terms or call Social Services and get them to send someone else. And from what she knew about Social Services, she might as well ask the pizza delivery guy to check on them. Her decision was made.

Chapter 28

Jeremy sat on the sofa counting all the money he'd just received from his first ever wage. The second he finished work he rushed to the bank and removed every penny, paranoid that somehow it might disappear. He trusted banks as much as he trusted people—not at all. In the back bedrooms he could hear his wife and daughter banging against their walls, no doubt hungry. Well, this time, if Mandy behaved, he might treat them to takeaway. McDonald's would be nice—he had a soft spot for that. But if Mandy misbehaved, it would be soup again. The same they'd been eating all week, hairs, teeth and whatever else floated in it. There were still leftovers from the husband in the freezer, too.

The notes felt heavy in his hand as he counted them once again. He'd never even seen that much money before, let alone held it. The journey from work to the bank was less than ten minutes away, but he'd already mentally spent it a dozen times. He could eat in fancy restaurants and enjoy barking at the waitresses, demanding they attend to him by snapping his fingers in the air, enjoy the control he had over them. A better video camera to record his sessions with Mandy. He fantasised of buying a gun, hunting down all those that tormented him when he was younger and shoot them all in the face. Or take them back to his place and torture them, just like his heroes used to do. He would need bigger freezers to store their meat.

But no, despite the thousands of ideas running through his mind, there was one thing that far outweighed all his other desires. And he figured he shouldn't take too long in seeing his idea come to fruition. Things were starting to get a little too dangerous. Nothing had quite worked out exactly as he had planned and unless he was careful it could all come crashing down on him, and fast.

Starting with that bitch of a detective and her snooping where she didn't belong.

As much as he would like to spend his money on other things, it was time to find somewhere else to live. Sooner or later, the police or friends of the family would come around demanding to see them and there would be little he could do to stop it. With each passing day, the phone was ringing more and more often. The husband and Mandy's parents and other family, Jane's friends. It was never ending. At least six times a day someone knocked on the door, waited a little, sometimes shouting through the letterbox, before leaving. He was already annoyed with himself for having smashed Mandy's teeth out; it meant anyone that did come around would see the damage for themselves. And how was she going to explain to her relatives or friends where her teeth were? Covid? It was harder now just for her to speak when she had no choice but to reply to the incessant phone calls, as he listened next to her. The excuse of Covid could not last much longer.

But fortunately for Jeremy, it seemed luck was on his side. On his way to the bank, he had seen a sign for flats to rent on a council estate. He phoned immediately after withdrawing his money and there were still two available—both well within his budget. He could get his mother to do all the complicated paperwork for him, of which he had no experience and they could move in as soon as it was done. A couple of days the woman had said it would take. There was only one problem.

Jane.

Moving her would not be easy, and not just because of the unfortunate smell she was giving off. Given how thin she now was, it wouldn't be a problem moving her if he pushed her in the wheelchair, but the stupid girl wouldn't stop screaming. That wouldn't do at all if he pushed her along the streets to their new home, but he couldn't exactly leave her where she was, either.

Or could he?

More banging from the bedroom disturbed him from his thoughts. Sighing, he rose and went to see what Mandy wanted. He grimaced when he opened the door. The acrid stench of stale sweat accentuated by the fact the window was nailed shut and hadn't been opened since locking her in there, smacked him in the nose. Mandy tried to sit up, wincing as she did so.

"Please. My daughter. Let me see my daughter. I'll do anything, I promise," she begged, drool dripping from her mouth due to the lack of teeth.

"Shh, calm down. All in good time. Jane is fine. You know I wouldn't do anything to hurt our daughter. I have some good news! Guess what, I've found us a place to live! Start all over again. Isn't that great?"

"Just let me see her, I'm begging you. Please, she's my daughter. I need to see she's okay." She was sobbing, her one free arm trying to grab onto him, fingers pathetically trying to latch onto his arm. He swiped it away.

"Didn't you just hear what I said! Christ, what is it with you women, you never listen to anything I say!"

"Jeremy, please. Listen to me. Just…just a second. Just let me open the door and see her, that's all. That's all I ask. Please."

She reached out for him again, stretching her arm, as far as possible, hand waving back and forth as though trying to swipe a pesky fly away. Disgusted and annoyed he pushed her back onto the bed.

"You know what, I was going to treat us all to

MacDonald's takeaway if you behaved, but your behaviour disgusts me, Mandy. Never thought I'd say that, but it disgusts me. So instead, you get soup again. Cold. You ungrateful, little woman."

He turned around and left, ignoring her wails and pleas, shaking his head. He thought she would have been happy to know they were finally getting their own place to start fresh. Women were such weird creatures. At this rate, he figured he'd never understand them.

Jeremy headed to the kitchen and filled two bowls with the remaining soup, not bothering to heat it up this time. A thick layer of scum covered it, dead flies sitting on the top because he hadn't bothered to put a lid on the pot. He grabbed a wooden spoon and mixed it all together then poured two large amounts into each bowl. Bits of hair dangled like worms from the sides of the bowls. When he'd sliced the husband's face and scalp, chopping it up into smaller pieces, he thought the hair would have come out and fallen away. It wasn't as if he could have asked his mother why it hadn't, so he left it there rather than trying to remove it himself—it was too complicated a task. He put both bowls on a tray with two glasses of water, and carried it first to Jane's room.

He winced and gagged as he entered the room, a swarm of flies so dense, he could barely make out his daughter's body on the bed. His eyes watered at the smell and was sure he could actually see stench fumes rising from her. It really was going to be a problem deciding what to do with her. There was so much waste accumulated beneath and around her that the bed was starting to sag in the middle. When she saw him, she began to murmur and mumble something he couldn't quite hear. Here bloodshot eyes widened when she saw the bowl of soup and glass of water, mouth dripping copious amounts of drool. Careful not to stain his trousers, he sat on the very edge of the bed and began to feed her. She swallowed it down greedily, strands of hair clinging to her chin which she seemed completely unaware of. Good. Last thing he needed was her complaining about his cooking skills right now. When it was all finished, she eyed the other bowl as well, begging him for more, but instead he gave her the water, putting the straw into her mouth. She drained the glass instantly. Jeremy could hear her stomach rumbling, she farted. Maggots squirmed around her, some falling from her hair into the glass. He tutted and tipped it upside down onto the floor.

"I thought you should know that I've found us somewhere new to live. We'll be moving any day now, but I'm still undecided whether you should come with us or not. You were a very bad girl, Jane. I'm not sure I should forgive you for what you did. I'll have to discuss it with your mother. Now, get some rest, I'll be back tomorrow."

He stood up. Jane's whimpers grew louder. She started pleading with him again for more food, more water, but he ignored her. He winced when he saw the deep holes in her thighs, bone visible, maggots burrowing their way further into the yellow-purple flesh that oozed pus down the sides of her legs. Flies started landing on him and, disgusted, he rushed from the room.

The state of Mandy's room wasn't much better. Again, the stench of dry sweat assaulted his nostrils, although this was nothing compared to Jane's room. If only they behaved, he could open the window at least. As before, Mandy tried to sit up and reason with him, plead to see her daughter, but he refused. Her phone, in his pocket, began to ring. He checked to see who was calling and was annoyed to see it was Mandy's mother again. She fortunately lived the other side of the country and he ignored the call and put the phone back in his pocket. It was a sign that he needed to get that new flat sorted quickly, before Mandy's family started showing up or calling the police, too.

He fed her the soup, that, even Jeremy admitted, was probably quite disgusting, but she slurped it down, hairs and all. All the while trying to convince him to let her see Jane. He shook his head, considered making love to her again but decided against it—she really was in quite a pitiful state. It had been a week since he last let her shower, two days since he had sex with her, and, because of her disobedience, her body wasn't as attractive as it used to be. Large bags sat under puffy eyes, skin blotchy and dirty, drool constantly running down her chin. She was starting to get bed sores under her thighs, large purple bruises slowly growing outwards. He made a mental note to buy some fly spray; last thing he needed was the same thing happening to Jane to his wife.

Jeremy gave one last thought to making love to her then decided there were more important matters to deal with so returned the empty bowls to the kitchen sink which was now piled high with dirty dishes and cups and then he headed home.

"Mother, I need you to do something for me first thing in the morning," he said, as soon as he found her. She was in the living room watching TV.

She looked up at him as he entered, visibly tensing. He'd noticed there was something off about her lately. Whenever he appeared, she seemed more apprehensive than usual, barely looking him in the eye as though afraid of him and he didn't know why. He'd never laid a hand on her since becoming the man of the house, knowing that he needed and relied on her to do the chores he was incapable of doing himself. And he hadn't been around much lately to do anything to Kelly that she might not

Loneliness is a Monster

like. She used to go out of her way to please him, always making him his favourite food, ensuring his clothes were clean and ironed, but over the last few days, he'd noticed a definite lack of interest in doing so anymore.

"Oh, what's that?"

"I've found a place to live. I'm going to be moving with my girlfriend as soon as the paperwork is done. I need you to sign it. I'm not old enough."

She eyed him suspiciously, making him feel slightly uncomfortable. "With your girlfriend?"

"Yes. Why?"

"And…is she okay with that?"

"How do you mean? Of course she is. Why wouldn't she be?"

"So why haven't you introduced her to me yet? I should meet her. I want to meet her, especially if you're going to be living together."

"She's shy. All in good time. I just want us to get settled down in our new home first."

"Is that so? I could refuse to sign it, you know, unless you let me meet her. I'm still your legal guardian."

Jeremy was stunned. Was she threatening him? Never, since his father died, had she questioned let alone flat out refused to do something he asked of her. It made him wonder if she knew something she shouldn't.

"If I tell you to do something, you do it. You understand?" he countered, trying to sound authoritative, but his voice faltered.

"I didn't say I wouldn't do it; I just want to meet your girlfriend first."

"No! You'll come with me tomorrow and you'll sign the lease," he said, his voice rising, almost a squeak, which embarrassed him immensely. Hearing the arguing, his sister poked her head around the corner.

"Get to your room!" he yelled at her. "Or you'll be

sleeping outside again."

He looked back at his mother, who was staring at him with what resembled a grimace on her face.

"I'm going to my room to sleep. First thing tomorrow morning, we go to sign the paperwork. If you don't, there will be consequences."

He left before she could reply. Furious, he sat at his writing desk, hands shaking, unable to believe what his mother had dared to do. He shook his head. Four women in his life, if he included his sister, and all of them daring to question his decisions, his authority. His father would never allow this type of behaviour.

Relax, Jeremy. You have a big day tomorrow. Relax and get a good night's sleep.

To try and take his mind off things, he turned on the laptop and scrolled to where he kept the videos that he made. He found the one he wanted and was about to hit play, when his hand froze. He stared at the keyboard, not believing what he was seeing. There were crumbs there, no doubt from a biscuit. Jeremy kept his laptop spotless. It was his prize possession. Someone had been sitting at his desk, using his laptop. His heart racing, he clicked on the computer's history. There he saw, a couple of days ago, someone had clicked on several of his videos—and it sure as hell hadn't been him.

Jeremy leaned back, heart racing, hands balling into fists. Someone had watched the videos as recently as yesterday, but his sister hadn't been at home all day. She had been at a friend's birthday party. But he could guess what had happened. His sister, always munching on biscuits, had dared to snoop on his computer, somehow found his private videos, and had told their mother. Then his mother had watched them yesterday while Kelly was out. This was why his mother was acting so strange around him lately.

She knew.

His immediate thought was to go drag them both into his room to confront and then severely punish them. Lock them both in the shed for the rest of the week with no food or water, but his rational brain reminded him he still needed his mother to sign the lease. That was fine. Not a problem. His mother hadn't phoned the police or told anyone and he was sure his sister hadn't told anyone, other than their mother, either. He would get the flat, get Mandy in there and then he could decide what to do with his snooping mother and sister. By the time he finished with them both, they'd regret snooping for the rest of whatever short time he allowed them left to live.

Chapter 29

Mandy had totally lost track of time since being kidnapped. Whether it had been a couple of weeks or two months she had no idea anymore. For the first few days, she had kept herself motivated by believing it was just a matter of time before someone came looking for them, the detective deciding something terrible was going on and barging into the house with a search warrant. Any one of their friends or relatives demanding the police come inside so they could see them. She kept her hopes up and refused to give in to blind panic, by telling herself she had to be strong for Jane. She knew her daughter wasn't dead because she occasionally heard her groans and weakened screams.

When they were finally rescued, Jane would need her mother's help to get over this terrible ordeal. Had Jane been fed her dead father's flesh, too? It seemed impossible to believe otherwise. The therapy Jane had been through after her accident was nothing compared to what she would need after this. It was what prevented Mandy from simply breaking down and waiting to die, begging to die so this torture could end. She tried not to think about it, but there was also the possibility Jeremy had been violating Jane as well, the girl might even be pregnant right now. In Jeremy's twisted, sick head maybe that was what he wanted—to have a child with Jane so they'd never leave him again. Raise his own family.

Mandy had come so close to just giving in from the constant agony of the hunger pains and dehydration, and the incessant aching and throbbing from her destroyed mouth—every time she opened or closed it, exposed nerves would send lightning bolts to her brain. She had

Loneliness is a Monster

started telling herself, albeit briefly, that Jane was probably dead by now, anyway, and she kept imagining she could hear her daughter's wails and sobs. Didn't Jeremy want Mandy for himself and not have anyone else get in their way? It was a constant battle working to banish these thoughts from her head, she refused to allow insanity and madness to accompany the agony within.

Her hopes of rescue were almost as depleted as her will to survive. With nothing to do all day except contemplate possible outcomes to this nightmare, her mind was slowly but surely working against her, her body slowly failing, rotting away. When Jeremy allowed her to go to the toilet when he came home from work, he had to help drag her there, the muscles in her legs atrophied, feet dragging behind her as she groaned and whimpered. To make matters worse, she wasn't even allowed the dignity to use the toilet in private. Jeremy would stand and watch, saying she still couldn't be trusted to be left alone, without the use of handcuffs. There was a window just above the toilet she could use to call for help. It made Mandy wonder just exactly how Jane was coping with her toiletry needs. Was Jeremy carrying her to the toilet then standing over her, as well? Mandy found it hard to believe he would go to such lengths as to carry the girl in his arms. Which meant…

Another sob escaped her, tears falling that she couldn't afford to waste. She'd even given up believing in God, at times, for surely He wouldn't let this happen to such innocent people. Other times though, she willed herself to keep believing. Any second now, any day now, help would come. But then another day would pass, another day of being violated by this evil, sick kid while he recorded it on his video camera. Was he uploading the videos to the internet for everyone to watch?

It was thoughts like this that slowly whittled away at

her morale, as her body slowly consumed her muscle tissue and body fat. But tonight when Jeremy had come into her room, he had been unusually subdued, barely speaking as he fed her as though something was consuming him, too. He looked worried, lost in thought. To the point that when he half carried her to the toilet, he didn't even bother watching, instead, he looked at the floor, scratching his chin, and mumbling to himself. For the first time in days, hope returned to her like an old friend.

There was something else, too, something far more important she'd noticed as he handcuffed her wrist to the bed again before leaving again.

This time he hadn't wrapped the cuff around her wrists as tightly as he normally did.

On the one hand, she was terrified to even try to break free in case he came back and caught her, but on the other, desperation, like a howling beast, was screaming at her to do it now. She relented and pulled on the cuff. Being so depleted of energy, she barely even tugged, but the metallic cuff still cut into her skin, her arm muscles incapable of finding the strength to tug harder. But she reminded herself that unless she at least gave it her all, she may never get another chance. She owed it to her daughter.

Mandy took deep breaths, ignoring the spasms in her wasted stomach, gave a silent prayer and tugged again, wanting to grit her teeth against the pressure on her wrists yet unable. Then she was free.

For a second, she wasn't quite sure what had happened. Then slowly but surely the pins and needles in her arms faded and the blood began to flow again to her hands. For the first time, when Mandy lifted her arms, there were no constraints preventing her from doing so. She let out a sob of relief, of disbelief. Her hands were shaking so badly she couldn't stop it as she stared at them. Her mind was suddenly fully active again. She tried to sit up and jump out of bed, a desire to run to Jane more powerful than any desire she'd had in her life. But as she did so, her back creaked and a million muscles screamed in agony.

Slowly, Mandy. Take it nice and easy. Don't panic. You'll end up on the floor, unable to move and when Jeremy returns...

She listened to her own advice, first rubbing her arms together to get the blood flowing properly. She flexed her ankles, bent her knees back very slowly then straightened them again. Confident she had strength in her arms, she gradually pushed herself up, ignoring the cramps in her stomach. Then she stopped, taking deep breaths, counting to ten. She bent her legs again, rubbed her thighs with her hands, waiting for the rush of blood to her head to subside. Then finally, after what seemed like so long, she was convinced Jeremy was going to walk in at any moment, she swung her legs over the side of the bed and eased her feet onto the cold, tiled floor.

Again, she forced herself to go easy. Instead of trying to stand, she counted to thirty, her brain still telling her she was going to get caught at any moment. Then, she gradually pulled herself to a standing position, gripping the side of the bed in case she fell. Her legs screamed, she wobbled, on the verge of falling, legs about to betray her at any second, but then, she dared to put one foot in front of the other. She repeated the process until she found herself gripping the bedroom door handle.

She told herself it was bound to be locked and all this had been for nothing. Hardly daring to look, holding her breath, which caused more spasms, she turned the door handle and pulled.

It opened.

A loud sob escaped her, not believing escape could really be within her grasp. Her brain screamed at her to just run, run outside and scream for help, run to the neighbours, anyone, until someone came and helped her, but her desire to see her daughter overruled those thoughts.

Mandy hobbled to her daughter's room instead, sobbing profusely, yelling Jane's name.

She opened the door and burst in, almost falling over in her desperation to see whether Jane was indeed alive or not. But what greeted her was nothing she had imagined in her worst, most fearful moments.

Mandy was so stunned that she froze. Her jaw dropped, several flies inadvertently flying into the toothless hole. She was so focused on trying to understand what the thing on the bed was, she didn't even realise it happened. It was like trying to see though a dense, thick fog, some shadowy figure beyond, but the impenetrable wall preventing her from fully seeing what or who it was. And whatever it was must obviously have been lying dead for a long time because when the stench hit her, it caused her to wobble on her legs, and grip the walls for support. She coughed and spluttered, retched, more spasms from her stomach, but she barely noticed. It was as the flies began to land on her body, nose and cheeks that she jerked and some of her faculties returned. She frantically swiped and waved away at the swarm and rushed to the bed, screaming her daughter's name yet not knowing if it was even her or not.

"Jane! Jane, can you hear me? Oh my God what has he done to you?"

Now that she had broken through the swarm, she could clearly see the emaciated state of what was left of her daughter. Jane was whimpering which meant she was at least alive, but this did nothing to alleviate

Mandy's horror. She wanted to hold her, kiss and hug her but was too scared to do so in case she broke something. She looked Jane up and down, hands hovering over her body, taking in the terrible state she had become. There were large purple-yellow bruises covering almost every inch of her body and in the middle of these bruises were gaping holes. In places all over Jane's legs, Mandy could see bone poking through. She couldn't tell how deep many of the holes were because they were filled with maggots, squirming around inside, worming their way into the rotting, stinking flesh. The holes were slowly getting bigger from the inside out.

Dead flies accumulated on her belly, in her matted, clumped hair, maggots crawled over Jane's face, occasionally falling into her mouth which she greedily swallowed. Jane tried to say something but it appeared she didn't have the strength for that anymore, her body was so thin her ribcage protruded, along with the rest of her bones. Beneath Jane's body was a growing mass of dried and wet faeces, urine that had spread, covering the complete length of the bedsheet. It was plastered over Jane's buttocks, thighs, and her whole back and neck, even spreading as far as her cheeks. Mounds of dead flies and maggots in a cesspit graveyard.

"Oh, Jane. Just...Just hold on a little longer. I'm going to phone the police. We're going to be okay, I swear!"

"Mum," she mumbled.

"It's okay, don't say anything," she replied. "I'm going to go call the police, get help."

She desperately wanted to pick up her daughter and carry her out, despite her own frailty, Jane must weigh so little it shouldn't be a burden at all, but she was worried a bone might snap. Instead, she brushed the maggots off Jane's face, gagging at the stench coming from her body. With no time to think about the potential repercussions of Jane's terrible ordeal, she looked wildly around for a mobile phone, swearing when she didn't see one. She rose and Jane whimpered again.

"It will be okay. I promise I'll be back. I have to get help. I...I can't carry you like that." Not wanting to waste time, and conscious Jeremy could return and see Jane untied, she left her daughter tied to the bed still and hurried to the door to go find help.

Sobbing hysterically, not wanting to imagine the hell Jane had been through, she staggered to the front door and cried in relief when it opened. Mandy almost tripped over her feet as she headed outside, not even caring that she was naked and ran down the garden path.

Just as Jeremy came walking down the road.

He was walking with his head down, but the second she saw him, she panicked and began running in the opposite direction, screaming for help, but she only managed to shout twice before she felt an arm wrap around her face and mouth. She was lifted off her feet and dragged back to the bungalow. She tried to bite down on his arm, forgetting she had no teeth, then tried to kick him, squirming and struggling as much as possible, but she was no match in her condition for the strong teenager. When the front door closed, she realised it was all over, her one chance at rescue was gone.

"What have you done, Mandy? Just what have you done? I knew this might happen. Women just can't be trusted. You have to just fuck things up every time, don't you?

"After everything I've done for you, this is how you repay me. I just rented a flat for us! We were going to start a new life together and you had to fuck it up."

Jeremy dragged her to Jane's room and threw her to the floor. Somehow, Jane seemed to find strength and began to scream at Jeremy to let them go while flies buzzed around them all.

Mandy thought about pleading for help, begging for forgiveness, but knew it wouldn't make any difference. There was only ever going to be one outcome from her thwarted attempt at rescue.

"Just…just let my daughter go. You've done enough already. Just don't touch her. She's just a kid, for God's sake. Please, Jeremy."

His reply was a hard punch in the mouth, the exposed nerves sending unbearable lightning pain to her brain. She collapsed onto her side, not even having the strength to cry anymore.

"Those that misbehave must be punished, that's what my father always taught me. You're going to regret this, dear wife."

Jeremy picked her up and threw her onto Jane's bed, face down. The angry swarm rose into the air. She felt a hand on the back of her head push her face down into the watery, fetid puddle between Jane's legs.

"Eat it. Lap it up and I might let our daughter get off lightly. All of it, maggots included." "No, Mum, don't… He's lying."

Wet faeces filled Mandy's nostrils and entered her mouth, along with a host of squirming maggots and dead flies. Mandy vomited onto the whole mess, spewing out bile and everything she had just swallowed.

"Well, that wasn't very clever was it? Now, you've got even more to eat. Eat it."

Her face was pressed down even harder into the vile pool. Faeces and urine smeared all over her face, splashing into her eyes. She didn't know if Jeremy was lying or not, but felt she had no choice. Surely someone would have heard her scream when she rushed outside just moments ago. A police car could be on its way right now. All she had to do was stall for time.

Mandy began to lap up the filth, swallowing chunks, maggots sticking to the back of her throat before falling off and squirming down into her stomach. She gagged constantly, vomiting up some of what she swallowed. A fly desperately tried to escape from one of her nostrils, tickling the inside of her nose. It eventually fell out and she ate that, too. Lumps of dried faeces clung to the insides of her mouth, like mud, meaning she had to use her tongue to prise it off so she could swallow. She continuously vomited and lapped it all up over and over, until finally, Jeremy told her she could stop, her face caked in shit while he giggled and laughed at her.

Panting, having to clutch her stomach from the constant spasms and dry heaving, she fell back onto the floor. She felt like she'd been drowning in a sewer, having to breathe through her mouth because of a blocked nose.

"Now you have to keep your word, Jeremy," she said, the words coming out as though she had a mouthful of food.

"Sorry, but it's not going to happen. Now let's get you back to bed, you must be tired."

Mandy hurled insults and abuse at Jeremy until both she and her daughter fell asleep exhausted.

Chapter 30

"I'm telling you; it was him. I know my brother when I see him."

"But you think he was, like, raping her? Like, doing stuff? And he has her kidnapped somewhere?"

Kelly nodded, looking around the school playground wildly, as if Jeremy might be hiding in wait, listening from somewhere. Such was her paranoia and terror, she wouldn't put it past him.

"Wow, that's sick. You gotta tell someone, then. Like the police. Does your mother know?"

"Yep. I showed her the videos and she told me never to say a word to anyone. But now I think he knows we know. He came home the other night, went in his bedroom and I heard him shouting and swearing to himself. Saying the word 'bastards' over and over."

"Then tell the police! Tell 'em, they gotta arrest him or something."

The same thought had occurred to Kelly many times over the last couple of days. Her mother refusing to even discuss the subject, Kelly, in desperation, had gone to her best friend, Jody, swearing her to secrecy and telling her everything about the abuse over the years. At first, Jody thought she was joking, some sick idea of a prank but the look on Kelly's face and the old scars that covered her body convinced her otherwise.

It had taken Kelly a long time to build up the courage to even tell her, as if by doing so she was inadvertently converting her friend into a co-conspirator but her mother's refusal to even discuss the matter had left her with no choice. It had been bottling up inside Kelly's head all day and night and when she did finally grab Jody, the words spurted out so fast, she could barely keep up with herself. And yet, now that she had told someone, she was left with the same problem. What to do?

There was no way the police would believe a young girl, she told herself the second her mother made her keep quiet, which left her with few options. She considered telling one of her teachers, showing her old scars as proof she wasn't lying, but what then? What if the teacher phoned her mother and somehow Jeremy found out? He'd kill her. Literally. She was positive of that. And if he didn't, the punishment would be severe. Since he'd been with this woman, he'd practically ignored Kelly. For the first time in years, she felt safe when she returned home from school. The idea of things reverting to how they were before terrified her.

Because she felt this woman needed help, she formed a plan.

On Sunday when Jeremy left after lunch, she figured there was only one place he was going. Even though she was terrified that he might spot her, she followed him. Kelly felt she had no choice but to do so if she wanted to help that poor woman.

There were several short alleyways, that joined the streets together, around the area which people often used as shortcuts. High brick walls that hid gardens on either side, offered nowhere for her to hide. She followed a short distance behind him, on the other side of the road, using parked cars to her advantage when she could. She peered through the car windows to keep sight of him. Kelly was fully aware that she couldn't look more conspicuous if she tried. She knew that at any moment she could be spotted by a friend or neighbour who might shout her name and give her away. But fortunately, no one saw her.

Jeremy, barely looking where he was going, walked on auto pilot. When he turned down one of the

Loneliness is a Monster

alleyways, Kelly rushed to the other side of the road, daring to peer round the corner, then dashed into the alleyway once Jeremy exited. The horrifying idea that he knew she was following, occurred to her several times. She worried that as soon as she exited the alleyway, he would suddenly grab her around the throat and demand to know what the hell she was doing.

But he never did.

She had been following Jeremy for ten minutes when he stopped outside a bungalow. After glancing around, he quickly hurried down the garden path and entered the home. He even had a key with which to let himself in, and Kelly knew, without a doubt, this was where he was keeping the woman. She considered creeping down the garden path herself and peering in through the letterbox or the window to see if she could spot the woman. But the idea of that was harrowing. The threat of more physical abuse from Jeremy overrode any acts of bravery.

Instead, she decided to wait a while to see if the woman made an appearance at the window. If he really was keeping her handcuffed to the bed then that wasn't going to happen. So she gave up on that idea and went around to the back where she hid for several minutes, peering into the bottom window and seeing nothing except a swarm of flies buzzing around the room as if something had died in there. The light was on and the curtains were only partially closed. A shadow figure crossed the room and the swarm rose again.

This gave Kelly extremely bad vibes.

She envisioned the woman lying dead in there, murdered by Jeremy's vicious hand. And it was in that moment she realised she had only one option.

When Jeremy got home that evening for dinner, which he did almost every night, she would sneak out and come and check for the woman herself.

Chapter 31

After having lunch with Angela and her parents and then joining the girl in her bedroom to see how she was holding up, Deborah left with promises to return again soon. Every time she left Angela, it was always with bittersweet feelings. On the one hand she was happy to see the girl coping as well as could be expected after her harrowing ordeal, but on the other hand, it made her sad to see this sweet little girl still bearing mental and physical scars no child should ever have to bear. All this time later, Angela still asked Deborah to promise her that her aunt and uncle were really dead. She was worried they might come back as zombies or monsters and hunt her down—Angela still suffered nightmares to that effect. Deborah swore they were dead and that eventually the nightmares would cease. Angela's therapist said the same thing which managed to reassure the girl in a small way. Deborah secretly feared that the nightmares would never truly go away, always lurking in the back of Angela's mind like a dark secret. And sometimes, Deborah could see the affects Angela's trauma had on her first-hand when she occasionally came to stay at Deborah's overnight. Angela would wake up next to Deborah, screaming and sobbing that her aunt and uncle were coming for her. Deborah would soothe the girl, point to the sleeping cat at the foot of the bed and reassure her that if anyone were to even think about hurting her, the cat would make sure it never happened—his fangs and claws were the biggest and sharpest in the whole world. This always got a little smile from her.

Deborah's sadness was heightened with the stark reality that her work would never be finished. There would always be another boy or girl out there somewhere being abused, crying out for help. But that help very rarely came. And often if it did, it was too late. Such a case occupied her mind now—that of the young teen who may be suffering abuse this very minute, but her boss refused to let her fully investigate on the grounds of lack of proof.

To Deborah, it defied belief. Some of the cases she had helped solve, had less evidence than in this case yet he still denied her the full authority she required. Contacting Social Services had gotten her nowhere, as she already predicted would happen. It seemed that the world preferred to pretend these things never occurred rather than take time and resources to investigate fully. Then, when the truth was eventually revealed, it became a political battle of who was more to blame instead of an investigation into the how's and why's to ensure it never happened again.

The case of Mandy Cogsworth and her family bore all the symptoms of heading in that very direction. And unless she did something about it on her own terms, she worried it might become yet another case of, 'why was nothing done until it was too late?'

Further phone calls to Mandy's husband and daughter had proven futile. Adrian and Jane seemed to have disappeared off the face of the planet.

"Fuck it," she muttered to herself after leaving Angela's home. It was a Sunday, and a rare day off work—which made her feel more guilty than anything else—so she decided to combat the feeling of uselessness by going to Mandy's unannounced. And she had no intentions of leaving until she saw all of Mandy's family.

It was early evening and the streets were relatively quiet, a steady drizzle dampening both hearts and spirits,

Loneliness is a Monster

except for those warm and dry at inside. As she climbed into her car, a roar came from a pub—some football team had scored a goal. If only happiness came to everyone so easily.

She reached Mandy's street and parked directly outside. A perfectly normal home, like all the others in the area, the only difference being it was a bungalow. A shiver ran down her spine as though she was staring at some notorious haunted house—a horror house as they were sometimes described by the press when it is uncovered that an atrocity has occurred inside. It seemed impossible such evil things could be going on behind a pleasant, yet unremarkable home.

Seeing no movement in the living room window, she climbed out of the car and decided to check around the back, perhaps she might stumble upon something that would give her reason to insist Mandy let her in. Quite what that may be, though, she had no idea. Once around back she discovered it was as unremarkable as the front. The weeds had grown tall in the garden and the grass was uncut, but for winter this was perfectly normal. Deborah was just as guilty for leaving her garden unattended when the weather got cold and wet.

There was a wooden shed in the corner, a padlock hanging open from the latch. This was slightly surprising—there could be all kinds of power tools and gardening equipment in there and if Adrian worked for a building company, it was likely he enjoyed a little DIY at home, too, so it would stand to reason he had plenty of tools stored inside.

Deborah opened the gate to the yard, which creaked ominously on its hinges, and stepped inside. She glanced first at the windows of the bungalow—no movement inside, nothing suspicious at first glance. That meant nothing, though. Her immediate concern was of the shed;

if they really were confined indoors with Covid, someone could have broken in, stolen their tools, and the family would be none the wiser. She tried the door to the shed. It, too, creaked open.

Deborah peered inside. It was pitch black, the only window grimy and covered in dust, and it was smeared with what looked like handprints. Her heart fluttered momentarily at the utter darkness inside, scolding herself for reacting to an old fear of hers; she should be over that by now, she told herself. The odour of mould and decay assaulted her nostrils. She fumbled for a light switch, found a hanging cord and pulled. A dim light bulb came on, equally grimy and smeared like the window, allowing little light to brighten the shed. She looked up and saw a beam going across the ceiling, a chain and pulley dangled from it, splattered with what looked like oil. But Deborah had seen enough to know it wasn't. The window and lightbulb were not stained with oil or grease but a dark red substance. It was splattered across the floor, too, smeared as though someone had attempted to mop it up. A schoolboy error.

Her heart began beating furiously and her stomach dropped, knowing full well the implications of what she was looking at and the potential repercussions if she was too late.

Deborah scrambled for her phone and cursed when she remembered she'd left it in the car. She ran back to the car and immediately dialled her boss to demand backup. She cursed again when he didn't pick it up the first time. Deborah remembered he often went fishing with his son on Sunday's and didn't always take his phone. Swearing loudly, she tried again. Finally, he picked it up.

Chapter 32

The evening set in and Kelly was as nervous. To the point she couldn't eat or think straight. Not that she was hungry anyway—her stomach was a nestled pit of venomous snakes, chewing on her intestines. She was almost sick at one point, taking deep breaths and trying to think of something different. But it was impossible. The only thing she could think of was possible outcomes and consequences. She had to do it, though. It was now or never. Kelly kept telling herself that poor woman could be in agony, or worse, right now. If she lost her courage and something terrible happened, it would be her fault.

As dinnertime approached and Jeremy failed to show up, her nervousness augmented. It seemed he wasn't going to come for lunch today, and she would have to go to school tomorrow and her chance would be gone until the following weekend. By which time it could be too late. Both for that woman and for her and her mother. At some point, Jeremy would be confronting her about sneaking into his room and the punishment would be something terrible. This was her chance, but where was he?

Finally, the door opened and Jeremy stepped in. Kelly, hiding in her bedroom, peered out the door and listened as he mumbled something to their mother while taking off his coat. She'd already told her mother she was going to a friend's house to play on video games and would eat there. Her mother had barely listened, only nodding, seemingly worried and nervous about something herself. Kelly's heart did a mad jig in her chest, the nest of vipers in her stomach on overdrive as she realised it was time. Within the next couple of hours, she could be either a heroine or in very serious trouble. Or worse.

But she had to do it.

She put her coat on, crept down the stairs as quietly as possible, straining to hear the clink of cutlery on plates, then headed outside. Without looking back, Kelly ran towards the bungalow, not stopping for anything or anybody. She reached the front gate then stopped to catch her breath. Inside nothing moved. She debated whether to go in the front door or head round the back and chose the latter, where the high brick walls surrounding the garden would make her less conspicuous should any neighbour look out and wonder who she was.

Kelly was on the verge of tears, such was her terror at being caught, but nothing could stop her now—things would be so much worse if she didn't. She needed to get in, find the woman, then get to the police. Not wanting to waste any time, she dashed down the garden path and tried the back door.

It was locked.

She gasped. The idea the doors might be locked had not even occurred to her. A sob escaped her. She felt foolish for not thinking things through properly. Of course the doors would be locked if he was holding someone against their will. She tried it again, maybe it was just a little stuck, but no, it wouldn't budge. Desperate, she looked around for a rock or something to break a window with. Before, the idea of breaking someone's window would have shocked her, but the threat of Jeremy and what he might do to her made it seem a minor problem to deal with. She looked around wildly, conscious her brother could return at any second, and saw a flowerpot next to the door. She picked it up, ready to throw it as hard as she could through the

Loneliness is a Monster

window when she saw the key underneath it.

For the first time in years, she thanked God, and then she tried the key. The door swung open.

An overpowering stench of rotting food, or something very similar, was the first thing to hit her, causing her eyes to water and for her to gag. As she stepped in, a swarm of flies rose from the kitchen sink to her left, the sink full of unwashed dishes. A large pot sat on the stove, flies crawling all over it. The floor was stained with globules and lumps of whatever had been cooked in the pot. It made her stomach squirm again, just looking at it, but she reminded herself she had a job to do and set about looking for the bedrooms.

She headed into the hallway. To her left was a room. The whole bungalow smelled foul as though it had been abandoned and was now used by homeless people as a makeshift toilet. Kelly covered her nose and mouth with her jacket and opened the door.

She gasped.

There, lying in a bed and handcuffed to the bedframe was the woman from the video. Flies crawled over her; her face was caked in some dry, brown substance that stank far worse than the stuff in the kitchen. She was naked, all bone and bruises, barely a patch of skin visible. Her mouth was horribly swollen, almost twice its usual size, hair clumped and caked in whatever the brown substance was. As Kelly tentatively entered the room, the woman turned slowly to face her, wincing, as if such a simple act required great strength and will power. Her eyes opened wide when she saw Kelly standing there and she began to writhe and try to sit up, apparently forgetting she was handcuffed.

""elp me," she managed. "'all the 'olithe."

She spoke as though she had a mouthful of food, but Kelly knew what she was saying. Feeling utter disgust at seeing the woman like this, the room smelling of urine, sweat, and faeces, tears ran down her cheeks. She felt disgust at her brother for committing such an atrocity. She was about to tell the woman not to worry, she was Jeremy's sister, but for some reason it didn't feel right to tell her. Maybe the woman would think she was in on it or something.

Kelly hurried over to her, but now she was here, her fears about what Jeremy had been doing confirmed, she was unsure what to do. Try to help the woman free from her restraints or rush outside and alert a neighbour to phone the police? Such was the state of the woman, she didn't even really want to touch her, which made her disgusted with herself too. But the pleading, terrified look in the woman's eyes decided for her. Breathing through her mouth, Kelly tugged at the handcuffs, the woman now frantic and making it hard for her. She tried to say something else but Kelly had no idea what it was, probably telling her to hurry. She focused on trying to free the woman rather than reply.

It was no use. They were proper handcuffs, not some cheaply manufactured set. As she pulled with both hands, the bed moved a couple of inches instead.

Then she had another idea.

"They won't break okay, so I'm gonna try something else. You need to be still."

Muffled moans were the woman's only reply. The bed looked older than it probably was, but the headrest where the handcuffs were fixed to wasn't very thick. It was just a metallic frame, similar to what Kelly had on her own bed and there had been times when she had accumulated so much anger towards Jeremy she would grip it with both hands and act as though it was his neck, strangling him with everything she had, and it had bent. It had probably only been a couple of minutes but it felt

Loneliness is a Monster

hours already. Kelly, convinced Jeremy was on his way back here already, kneeled on the bed and gripped the headrest with both hands then began to pull it towards her. Grunting and gritting her teeth, she pulled as hard as she could, her hands slipping down the pole as she struggled to maintain a grip. It only bent so far then refused to snap off, Kelly having to stop to get her breath and strength back, arms already tired.

The woman looked as desperate as Kelly felt, refusing to be still, constantly spitting out words that made no sense, drool running down her filthy face. Kelly was crying, utter terror threatening to overwhelm her, but she gripped the headrest again, grit her teeth and pulled as hard as she possibly could.

It started to bend.

Kelly stood up and used her foot to push down on it and when she thought she was going to have to give up again, a resonating cracking noise sounded and the bedrest snapped off from the bed.

She let out a loud gasp, not wasting a second, and pulled the handcuffs off the pole attaching them. The woman was free. Kelly expected her to jump up and run off with her, but it didn't happen. She was extremely agitated but could barely move and Kelly realised she was probably too weak to stand by herself—something else she hadn't taken into account. Tired herself from the exertion, Kelly had no choice but to help her, drag her out if necessary, so she grabbed the woman's arms and pulled her to her feet. Almost immediately, they both went crashing to the floor, the woman's legs betraying her, but Kelly maintained a firm grip and began to steer her towards the bedroom door.

"It's okay. We're gonna get help. You just need to try your best to walk a bit."

"Jane… 'aughter," she spluttered.

221

The woman had a daughter? There was someone else being held captive, too? Yet one more thing to add to the list of things not thought through.

"Your daughter is here as well? Where?!"

"'edroom."

"Shit."

Things were going from bad to worse. She thought she could manage to help this woman, who had to weigh less than she did, to safety, but two? Now she was in turmoil, not knowing what to do, but first she figured she should see in what condition and how old the daughter was. She dragged the woman out of the room who raised a shaking hand and pointed to the room next door. Kelly shuffled along and opened the door.

The woman holding onto Kelly's arms fell to the floor, yet Kelly was barely aware. She fell because Kelly, in her horror, had completely forgotten she was even there and her arms had lost all strength in them. Her first instinct was to turn and run, somehow she had stumbled right onto the set of some horror movie, but when her eye caught the woman crawling towards the emaciated figure on the bed, she understood what she was seeing.

The stench hit her then, a thousand times more potent than what she had encountered in the other bedroom. She gagged, clutched her stomach to try and prevent herself from throwing up and unconsciously took a step back, flight still a growing thought in her mind. As the flies settled once more on their feeding ground, Kelly saw more clearly the girl laying on the bed, barely breathing, body riddled with gaping holes, so many maggots on her it was almost impossible to tell if it was a human being lying there or not.

But if it was indeed the woman's daughter, she was still alive, albeit feeble, because there was the slightest of movements from her, a twitch of her arm, which sent more maggots tumbling down onto her bare stomach, some falling into the hole developing there. The only thing Kelly could think of right now was that her brother had done this, had allowed this to happen, and she wondered what her mother might say if she knew. What her father would say if he could see this. Jeremy was a monster. Not the type to live under the bed or come lurching out of wardrobes like in her childhood nightmares, but a living, breathing, human monster.

As the mother tried to push herself up onto the bed to reach her daughter, yet another thought occurred to her, even more terrifying; the thing on the bed could be her.

This broke her from her paralysis. Jeremy could be on his way here right now and if he caught them, after witnessing this, none of them would be leaving this place alive. The trouble was there was no way she could help get them both out of here. The mother could barely crawl, let alone carry her daughter. There was only one solution, run to the nearest neighbour and demand they phone the police before it was too late.

"What…what are you doing here? Oh my God, what the hell is this?"

Kelly screamed and turned around, her bladder almost betraying her at hearing the sudden voice. But when she turned to face the intruder, her surprise only slightly abated.

It was her own mother standing there, looking as shocked and horrified as Kelly.

Chapter 33

"I...I was, I just had to know. I couldn't sleep at night thinking my son might have done something terrible. I followed him, too. Oh my dear God, what has he done?"

Katherine surveyed the carnage in the room, ignoring the flies that buzzed around her head and landed on her face, only able to focus on the thing on the bed. For, a human being it surely couldn't be. It appeared to be some ancient mannequin that someone had brought home and dogs had either tried to eat or tear apart. The woman mumbling incoherencies and cradling the thing on the bed didn't fare much better—she resembled an escapee from a concentration camp.

"Mum! Are you listening? You have to phone the police! What if he comes back and catches us here? He'll kill us!" yelled Kelly.

Katherine turned to face her daughter, as if seeing her for the first time. She hadn't thought to question Kelly on why she was here but hearing her yelling brought her back to reality. It was all true, then. Katherine had been trying to deny it for so long, convincing herself that her boy was incapable of such atrocities, yet here she was, seeing it with her own eyes. Yes, he could be mean and vicious, especially towards his younger sister, but this? And she now had to accept the fact she was just as guilty for not listening to Kelly in the first place. She remembered once more Social Services failing to intervene the first time. Jeremy could have been stopped or received help, but the system had failed them and these two poor women as well, just as she now had. God would never forgive her. She could never forgive herself.

"Mum!"

As though slapped in the face, Katherine returned to

Loneliness is a Monster

the moment. "Yes, umm yes. We need to phone the police. I'll do it no—" But as she fumbled in her purse then her coat pockets, she realised she'd left her phone at home. She never had been a fan of the thing, much less since her husband died, so hadn't even thought to bring it with her.

"Shit, I left my phone at home. What do we do?"

"Go get the neighbour, Mum! Tell them to phone the police quickly and…Hang on, where is he, Mum? Where's Jeremy?"

"He said he was going to take a nap so that's why I decided to come now. What are you doing here anyway?"

"For God's sake, Mum! Get a grip. He could come back at any moment. Go find a neighbour, quick!"

"What? Oh, yes, right."

It was as if someone had taken over her mind. Things weren't being processed as they should. She should be listening to her daughter and running out of this damn house as fast as she could—they were all in grave danger—but the only thing that kept running through her head was, 'my son did this. I let him get away with this.' But her daughter's panicked yelling, the realisation that if he did return it was her and her daughter who might suffer serious consequences, brought her back to reality.

"But you're coming with me. I can't leave you alone here with…with them in case he does come back. We'll go together. Quick, c'mon."

"Well, what the fuck do we have here? All the women of my life come together in one spot. Aren't I the lucky guy?"

Screams, moans, and gasps reverberated around the room simultaneously. Jeremy walked in and slammed the door behind him, a hideous grin on his face that soon turned into a wicked sneer, eyes blazing with fire. His hands were curled into tight fists, the veins on his neck pulsing. It was as if time stopped for everyone except Jeremy, nobody knowing what to say or do.

"J...Jeremy, what is going on here? Why are these people in this condition?"

Katherine felt her daughter grip her from behind, like a toddler trying to hide from someone nasty. She was as conscious as ever now that her daughter's life may be in danger. The sneer on her son's face dropped.

"Well, here's the thing, Mother. You see, some people—women mostly, just don't seem to understand rules. It's really not that difficult when you think about it. I set the rules, you obey them. How is that so difficult? And well, my wife and our obnoxious little daughter apparently don't want to obey them and I've had to assert a little discipline and order.

"My little sister learned though, didn't you? Well, I thought she did but now you're all in my fucking home, snooping and spying like you were doing on my laptop. So obviously none of you have learned. Especially you, Mother. I can understand from a stupid little bitch girl, but you? Father would be ashamed, he really would. And what are we gonna do about that, huh?"

"Jeremy, listen to me. Listen, we can get you help. We should have done so all those years ago when you put Kelly in the hospital, but it's not too late. We'll call the police and an ambulance and then we—"

Katherine suddenly found herself on the floor. A punch to the mouth left her reeling, already tasting blood on her tongue. More screams filled the room.

"You don't tell me what to do anymore, Mother. Haven't you learnt your lesson or what? For fuck's sake. And you, little girl, oh you're in so much trouble."

Katherine tried to push herself to her feet to protect her daughter but was too late as Jeremy grabbed Kelly then threw her onto the sodden, filthy bed. Kelly's face collided with Jane's groin, a hoard of urine and faeces soaked maggots and dead flies sticking to her.

"Jeremy, leave her alone! I'm still your mother!"

But Jeremy ignored her. With Mandy still cradling Jane as though trying to protect her, Jeremy walked over to Kelly, and roughly wrapped a hand around her hair then pushed her face hard into the rotting, yellow-green flesh of Jane's groin.

"Eat it. Eat her pussy. I wanna see you eat it like the little slut you are. Like you all are. Do it, or I'll kick your teeth out just like I did to my wife over there."

Kelly's muffled screams broke Katherine's heart. There was a squelching sound as Jeremy pulled her head back then rammed it into Jane once more. Adrenaline and fear giving her more strength, Katherine pulled herself to her feet and tried to push her son off Kelly. But she was no match for him and another punch, this time in her eye caused her to fall again.

"Do it little girl. Chew on it."

Katherine's heart broke again as she saw the wet patch on Kelly's trousers, her bladder having let go, but she refused to do what her brother was telling her. Flies landed everywhere on Kelly, maggots running down her back. Katherine grunted as

Jeremy stepped down hard onto her face, preventing her from getting up again but not from seeing what Kelly was doing. No doubt terrified of what might happen if she didn't, Kelly was biting into Jane's rotting vagina, chewing on it, a thing that was covered in blisters, pus-leaking sores, blood and urine.

"That's it, see. She finally does as she's told. This is what you get for snooping in my room."

Jane's mother tried to swipe out at Kelly, push her away from her daughter, but she was far too weak to do anything. Jane herself was barely even aware, her life surely fading fast. A tearing sound came as Kelly managed to chew of a piece of the maggot-infested vagina and swallow it.

"See, you're all pieces of shit, dirty, stinking little maggoty pussies who won't learn."

He pulled Kelly away and threw the gagging, hysterical girl to the floor. Katherine felt a hand wrap around her neck and she was lifted up and soon found her own face pressed tightly against the freshly-bleeding groin.

"Your turn, Mother. Eat. Just like the vermin you are. Eat it. I wanna see you eat her clit. Bite it off. Refuse, you can watch me cut Kelly's out with a fuckin' knife."

"Jeremy, please stop!" she cried, barely able to breathe with her nose pressed firmly into the hole of the dying girl's vagina.

She grunted when she felt a knock to the back of her head, causing her to see stars. Maggots trickled down her throat. But knowing she had to try and stall her son for time, to allow Kelly to somehow escape, she did as she was told. It was like trying to tear off a rotting piece of meat that had been marinated for days in urine, blood and faeces. She couldn't do it. Jane started squirming and groaning, having found the strength from somewhere to complain about this new torture. Katherine managed to push herself up, despite the hand holding her down and turned to her son.

"Just let your sister go, Jeremy. She's just a little girl. You can take me instead. I'll look after you, I won't disobey you again, I promise."

As she spoke, she saw out of the corner of her eye how Kelly was crawling towards the door, ready to run and escape. She just had to keep his attention a few seconds longer. The taste and smell of that filthy concoction up her nostrils and on the back of her throat barely allowed her to speak, though.

"We'll...we'll all be good from now on, Jeremy. I promise. You're the man of this house, too, perhaps they just didn't understand like I do."

He shook his head and scowled. "You really do take me for an idiot, don't you? You think I don't know why you're here? You both went into my room and watched my private videos. For my viewing only. Then you followed me to see what was going on and if I hadn't come back when I did, the police would be here right now. You were going to betray your son. If father was here, it would be you tied to that bed and eating her dead husband for supper.

"Sorry, Mother, but I can't let you two come between me and my new family."

He pulled out a long knife from the back of his trousers. Katherine gasped. Kelly had almost reached the door and was standing up, tears streaming down her terrified face.

Go, Kelly. Run. Run as fast as you can. Go, she willed. She would give her life to see Kelly survive. It was the right thing to do after failing her son. It was the only thing. If she'd listened to her daughter the moment she mentioned the videos this wouldn't be happening right now. The two emaciated figures on the bed would be receiving treatment and therapy. If there was any way to pay for her sins, it was giving her life for theirs.

Kelly made to open the door and run when Jeremy turned around and threw the knife at her. The blade hit the back of her neck, penetrating skin but not hard enough to stick. Kelly howled.

"Run, Kelly! Go!" screamed Katherine.

But she wasn't fast enough. Jeremy grabbed her and threw her across the room. Then he dashed over to Kelly after grabbing the knife from the floor and pressed it tight against her throat, once more splitting skin, a dribble of blood running down the girl's chest.

Chapter 34

She had missed her chance. Her one opportunity to run and call for help, but she had been too late. She was always too late. Kelly could have told her teachers about the abuse years ago, the bruises and scabs on her body that Jeremy had inflicted upon her. They would have called the police and Jeremy would have been put in a prison for kids, never allowed to return home again. But she hadn't. She had been too scared, believing they wouldn't do anything about it anyway. Jeremy was the man of the house; he was allowed to do anything, right? No adult would listen to her, they'd say she deserved it for being a naughty girl and not showing him enough respect. Her dad would have said the same thing. Even her mother had said it. Her friend, who she told, agreed no one would believe her.

But even back then, she had always thought Jeremy would one day grow out of it, go off to university and leave her alone. Find someone else to shout and swear at and whip now and again. Someone as big as him might make him understand what he was doing was wrong. Maybe he would tell friends who would beat him up and make him realise what a horrible person he was. Lots of people got punched and kicked and spanked by horrible parents and family members, bullied by others, but eventually they got stopped either by the police or because someone found out what was going on and put a stop to it. Sooner or later it would have happened to Jeremy, too. She'd heard things at school, about parents abusing their children. She knew of one kid who always came to school in the same clothes, always hungry at lunchtime because his parents never gave him anything to eat. His hair was greasy and unwashed, he smelled.

Sometimes he'd have bruises on his arms or cheeks. Several kids at school suffered such a fate and to her it was almost a normal thing, to be expected now and again when one misbehaved. Despite her hatred towards him, she'd almost come to accept it as part of life.

So to discover the levels of depravity he had sunken to was something she could barely fathom. The brother who she had the vaguest memories of playing with when he was a child himself, taking her to the park sometimes, tickling her and making her squeal and giggle uncontrollably. This kid was now a monster who was allowing two people to starve to death, allowing maggots and flies to feast upon them as though they were roadkill. He was everything she had ever had nightmares about.

And now he was going to kill her.

Just ten more seconds and she would have made it out the door and could have run into the street screaming for help. Someone would have heard her and come to see what was going on. Instead, a sharp pain to the back of the neck caused her to crumble to the floor and now, here she was with a knife slowly pressing into her throat, blood tricking down her chest and Jeremy frothing at the mouth in rage, eyes burning with hate towards her and the others.

"Don't do it, Jeremy! She's just a girl. Your little sister. You'll go to prison for murder. But for this, you'll get help instead," wailed her mother.

"Shut up! She's old enough to know she shouldn't be going through my room and my private videos. Or to trespass in my new home. This ends here and now and then me and my family are moving away. Nothing but trouble since the stupid little brat was born. Should have fuckin' got rid of her a long time ago. Bitch,"

Her mother jumped up and ran at him, howling and screaming as though she was insane. She tried to go for his eyes, claw them out while yelling words at him Kelly didn't think she was capable of saying, but with his free hand, Jeremy punched her in the stomach. She doubled over, the air taken from her, then he brought back his foot and kicked her between the legs. The woman crumpled.

During the attack, while momentarily distracted, the knife had inadvertently sunken deeper into Kelly's throat. Her eyes widened in shock, she felt her bladder release its contents for the second time, a terrible throbbing pain in her neck. She looked up at Jeremy pleadingly, but he didn't appear to have even noticed, shouting obscenities at their mother. When she looked down, the front of her jacket was already wet with blood. She struggled to breathe, gasping for air and when Jeremy finally turned to look at her, instead of being horrified by what he had done, he grinned. The last thing Kelly was going to see before dying was that malicious, sick grin.

"How does that feel, huh? Does it hurt? I hope so, after everything you've done. I'm going to let you bleed to death then do the same to your mother. I'll probably feed you both to my wife and daughter. Dahmer would be proud. I think I'll eat your dirty little pussy, make a stew of it. It'll taste so good."

"Please, don't," sobbed Kelly, the knife still embedded in her throat.

Her mother tried to stand and fight him again, but then there came another noise. As though a gun had been fired, a loud bang that echoed throughout the bungalow. Her brother jumped, causing the blade to sink a little further in. There came the sound of yelling, screaming, people shouting out names, but before Jeremy could react or had time to do anything the bedroom door burst open, and a woman and two men came rushing in.

They stopped abruptly, eyes widening in shock when they saw what they were dealing with. First, it seemed they weren't quite sure what they were looking at. Flies buzzed around, a thick, black smog making it almost impossible to see, then they saw the two naked figures on the bed.

Then the woman saw Jeremy holding the knife to Kelly's throat.

"No," muttered Jeremy. "No, no, no. You can't come in here. This is private property. You're trespassing! Get out!"

"What the hell have you done? Get on your knees, you're under arrest for the kidnapping of Mandy and Jane Cogsworth," said the woman detective.

But he didn't seem to be listening. Instead, he looked at their mother, the women on the bed, and started sobbing, shaking his head in denial.

"I didn't kidnap them! How could I kidnap my own family?"

He raised his arm, pointing at his fantasy family, lying motionless on the bed as if demonstrating they were there of their own free will. But in doing so it seemed he'd also forgotten he was holding a knife to Kelly's throat.

"You need to step away from the girl. Right now. You're under arrest, you're not going anywhere, so don't do anything stupid."

One of the two men held what Kelly assumed to be a taser. She'd never seen one in real life before but knew they didn't carry guns in England. And it was the mention of his sister that made him spin around, groping for the knife that should have been in his hand.

But instead, it was in his groin.

Kelly had taken advantage of the distraction and pulled the knife out from her neck. Blood spurted from it like a leaky tap, which she ignored and she'd plunged the knife as far into her brother's testicles as she could manage.

"No!" yelled the female detective.

Jeremy hissed. He went pale instantly, glaring down at his sister while his hands went to the knife's handle. His knees buckled as the three detectives rushed over to him, but they were too late. He fell onto his stomach causing the blade to go even deeper into him, his head falling onto Kelly's lap as she lay there, glazed eyes looking up at her.

She was vaguely aware of one detective calling for an ambulance. The other rushed over to the two women on the bed, swatting away flies as he did so, while the female detective squatted beside Jeremy and Kelly, quickly pulling out a handkerchief to stop the bleeding from Kelly's neck. Jeremy groaned and gargled as he continued staring at her.

It was at that moment that all the rage, terror, panic and desperation she'd felt in the last few minutes overwhelmed her. Seeing his pathetic face on her lap, mumbling pleas for help. He disgusted her. He was a monster, a cockroach, an alien creature with no right to be in this world. As the detective pressed the handkerchief to Kelly's neck, saying things she was barely aware of, Kelly pulled out the knife with both hands and this time buried it as far as possible into his eyeball.

"No!"

But she didn't care. She didn't want her nightmares to be of a brother with pleading eyes begging for help. She wanted them to be of a sightless monster with terror on his face. That, she thought, she could live with.

Chapter 35

"Hi!"

"Hi!"

The two girls smiled at each other, one much taller than the other, but the look in their eyes hinted they might be sisters, sharing a dark secret, like twins finally reunited. There was a hesitation, like two strangers meeting, not knowing how to continue or what to say. Eventually, it was Kelly, the older of the two, who took a tentative step forward and embraced Angela. Only slightly reluctantly, Angela followed suit. Deborah smiled.

"How's it going?" asked Kelly, a typical question between strangers meeting for the first time, but in this case, Kelly guessed she knew the answer already. But she didn't know what else to say, anyway.

Angela shrugged as she let her arms fall and stepped backwards—Angela had grown to distrust most people and physical contact often made her shudder. Unless it was her mother or Deborah, of course.

"Better, I guess. How are you?"

"Better, I guess."

This caused a chuckle between them.

Since Angela was rescued, there had been the growing concern she may never overcome her ordeal. Child therapists had not been successful, continuously recommended, like they were going out of fashion. Deborah lost count of the number they tried, asking everyone she knew on the force who had professional interest in such things. But Angela was fearful of all of them. Every time she was asked gentle questions, trying to coax her into talking about the ordeal and the things that inspired her nightmares the most, she would clam up. Sitting on their comfy chairs, her arms wrapped around her little chest as though trying to protect herself against some approaching monster. As far as Angela was concerned, they were all monsters. This

Deborah could understand. The fact it had been close relatives who subjected her to the worst kind of abuse imaginable, Deborah thought she would have had a very hard time herself should it have been her instead of the little girl. The biggest fear, the therapists all agreed upon, was Angela might shrink into herself, never able to trust another human being again and become lost to her own dark thoughts. What went on in the minds of those who had been temporary guests in hell, they could only guess at. Until it was too late.

The cycle of abuse. Would Angela, years later, carry on where her uncle left off? Knowing only pain and suffering, believing it was the way things were and knowing nothing else. Like Claire Patterson, who killed at least three people in the area after suffering abuse for years.

But after a few months with Deborah by her side—at Angela's insistence—she had finally begun to open up. Her biggest question, as expected, was how a relative could do such a thing? If it was a complete stranger— Angela already knew monsters lived in the world—that was one thing, but a relative? Someone she had adored. If her own aunt and uncle could do such things, how could she ever trust anyone ever again? Her parents even? Had it been her fault? Had she done something to provoke them?

These were hard questions to answer but the recurring response by all therapists, including Deborah and Angela's parents, was that it was and never could be her fault. Sometimes people did bad things and were unable to stop themselves. She compared it to a child stealing a sweet, knowing full well it was wrong but unable to help themselves, needing it.

After a few months, the nightmares becoming less and less, she allowed herself to be hugged—albeit gently and briefly—by her desperate, distraught father. Her smile slowly returned like a rising sun, only occasionally thwarted by dark clouds. It seemed there was hope for a bright future with Angela, after all.

But then, it was time to start all over again with Kelly. The sun had been hidden once more, replaced by an all-encompassing darkness.

Spending twice-weekly sessions with a therapist Angela finally confided in, Kelly, being older, understood slightly more the horrors that often came disguised in human masks. She constantly asked about Jane and Mandy, which indicated she wasn't slowly drowning in her own despair but was seriously concerned about the welfare of the others in this despicable crime.

Of the two, Mandy was the one that suffered the least. It had taken hours or surgery before Jane's condition was not life-threatening anymore. She had to have both legs amputated but this was deemed less traumatic seeing as they were paralyzed anyway. Even so, Mandy spent a week in hospital, seriously malnourished and dehydrated with dangerous bedsores of her own to be attended to. Awaking in the night screaming, imagining Jeremy standing over her, a malicious, drooling grin on his face, come to finish the job.

These hallucinations eventually faded.

Jane spent weeks in hospital, in the same room as her mother, who spent the nights by her side when deemed sufficiently recovered, but Jane's condition was still touch and go. Her body was infected so badly, doctors and surgeons said it was a miracle she survived at all.

Loneliness is a Monster

For the first few days, the smell of rotting flesh permeated the hospital like a toxic cloud.

Katherine was treated for her injuries but the horrors that haunted her mind were more of a psychological nature, requiring an indefinite stay in Northgate Hospital for the Mentally Impaired. Guilt was a strong mental illness in many cases.

But as had eventually been the case with Angela, there was hope Kelly would pull through.

It had been Angela's idea to meet Kelly, after Deborah explained that another little girl had just been rescued similarly to how Angela had been saved. Both girls had another thing in common; both had saved themselves and their families by being the ones to inflict the fatal injury to their captor. Deborah immediately agreed to the idea, as did Kelly when asked. The three of them now sat at a restaurant eating hamburgers, a comfortable silence between them as they considered what to say to each other.

Deborah's phone rang. She stood up and headed outside to answer the call. It was another detective on the force. Apparently, a nurse had been arrested for torturing patients at Northgate Hospital for the Criminally Insane. It was believed she tortured them so she could record their screams to listen to them at night; It aroused her sexually, it was suspected. Deborah shook her head and hung up, looking at the two girls through the restaurant window. Men, women, sometimes youngsters, it didn't matter in which guise they came. The world was alive with them, and it seemed as though it would never end.

A world full of monsters.

The End

Afterword

Ming Sen Shiue was born in Taiwan. His mother was a math's teacher, his father a forestry researcher and was extremely successful. To the point when Ming was 7, his father was offered a job in Minnesota which he accepted.

Shortly after arriving his parents had two more children, two boys. Unfortunately, though, when Ming was 11 his father died, but on his deathbed he gave Ming some very important words. He was now the man of the house and it was his responsibility to take care of his family, something very common in his country. Something that Ming took a little too literally.

His two younger brothers, around 7 and 3, were now forced to wait on him like slaves. He would come home from school and they would have to be waiting for him, help him remove his coat, prepare snacks, take off his socks and shoes and massage his feet for him, anything and everything. If they failed to do so or did so in a way that wasn't to his standards, like heat his glass of milk too much, he would punish them.

He'd beat them with a belt, make them sit at the dinner table and go without eating while he ate. He'd lock them in a closet overnight, naked while it was freezing cold outside. One time he locked his youngest brother in the oven and kept turning it on and off. All with the compliance of the powerless mother.

At 13, he reached puberty and here things took on another level. He became a Peeping Tom, spying on women and girls in their homes. Then he started seeing his mother in a different light. He'd climb into her bed while she was asleep and pull down her pyjama bottoms to look at her. One night she woke up to see Ming under the covers with a flashlight and discovered he'd cut a

Loneliness is a Monster

hole in her pyjama bottoms and was inspecting her vagina. For a while she did nothing until a few months later, when he was 14, he became an arsonist, setting fire to nearby farmhouses until he was arrested and sent for a psychological evaluation. Upon this, his mother finally told psychologists what he'd been doing and it was recommended he be sent to a facility to be helped. Unfortunately, due to an administration issue, mistakes were made and he was released just a few days later.

When Ming Sen Shiue was 15 he developed a crush on his math's teacher who reminded him of his own mother. All he could think about was her. He developed fantasies where he was convinced she was in love with him too and for the next 15 years he would stalk her. He would have taken action much earlier but a few years after starting teaching at the school, she decided to move abroad as a missionary worker with her husband.

Ming was devastated, his whole life falling apart, but he never forgot about her. Some time later, he heard she may have returned and somehow managed to find out where she lived. He barged into the home only to be confronted by two elderly people living there whom he threatened believing they knew where she was. But finally, the teacher, Mary, returned with her husband and 7yo daughter, Beth, and 5yo son, Steve some 10 years later. Ming was ecstatic.

For the next few months he stalked her, memorising her routing until he put his plan into action. One afternoon, he grabbed Mary and Beth and bundled them into a van. Unfortunately, while doing so, two curious young boys witnessed this and one of them approached him to see what he was doing. Not wanting to be caught, Ming dragged the boy into nearby woods and strangled him.

Taking Beth and Mary to his home he kept them

locked in a closet, and Beth in a box for 8 hours while he went to work. He would rape Mary and film himself doing so every night, sometimes with Beth present, until one day Mary managed to remove a hinge from the wardrobe and call the police.

During the first trial, Ming was sentenced to 30 years in prison, but during a second trial, for the murder of the boy, while Mary was giving evidence he had somehow managed to sneak a knife in court with him, jumped onto her and cut her face, telling her that when released he would find and kill her. She needed 62 stitches to her face.

He is still in prison to this day…

As you can see then, a very disturbed individual and from the moment I watched the case on YouTube, I knew I wanted to write a story about it. I've taken certain liberties, of course—the abuse suffered to Jane is taken from another case where two parents left their disabled child to basically rot to death—but enough of the case is based on real events. I also wanted to add a scene where Child Services—CPS, in the US—once again failed to intervene in time or at all. Something so common in many cases I watch.

I'm already thinking about book 6 as I write this, although I don't have anything concrete decided yet, maybe the woman at Northgate at the end—her story sounds interesting! But as long as people keep enjoying this series, I will continue writing it!

As always, I'd like to thank everyone who helped bring this thing to reality. Ali Sweet my editor on this one—her first ever editing job and she did a great job too! Christy Aldridge who did the cover, and all my beta and ARC readers, too many to mention, but thank you as always! And a special mention goes to Em Wigglesworth, whose job as a police officer in England helping to rescue child victims of abuse was a massive help with the factual elements! Thank you so much! You're all awesome!

Now onto the next!

Also By J. Boote

They are all Monsters
Am I a Monster?
Born or Bred (Pigs and Monsters)
A Dark Web of Monsters
Loneliness is a Monster
Man's Best Friend—an extreme novella
Love You to Bits—an extreme novella
Buried—an extreme novella

Also by Justin Boote

Short Story Collections:

Love Wanes, Fear is Forever
Love Wanes, Fear is Forever: Volume 2
Love Wanes, Fear is Forever: Volume 3

Novels:

Serial
Combustion
Carnivore: Book 1 of The Ghosts of Northgate trilogy
The Ghosts of Northgate: Book 2 of The Ghosts of Northgate trilogy
A Mad World: Book 3 of The Ghosts of Northgate trilogy
Chasing Ghosts
Soul Searchers

The End of Things as He Knew Them (with Angel Van Atta)
In Grandma's Room (published by Wicked House Publications

The Undead Possession Series

Book 1: Infestation
Book 2: Resurrection
Book 3: Corruption
Book 4: Legion
Book 5: Resurgence

Printed in Great Britain
by Amazon